A Bo

Jennie Wood

Edited by: Kelly Ford and Michael Perkins
Cover Art and Design: Sarah Pruski
Content Consultant: Tate Fox

A Boy Like Me, first printing, 2014. Published by 215 Ink. No portion of this publication may be reproduced without written consent from 215 Ink. For all inquiries visit 215ink.com or email info@215ink.com.

ISBN 978-0692238066

For Natalie

Esse quam videri (To be, rather than to seem)
North Carolina state motto

Chapter 1

"Katharine, would you like to go next?" But Mrs. Blunt wasn't really asking.

The whole class watched me walk to the front of the room. A strange, stabbing pain from just below my stomach made it difficult to stand so I leaned against the podium. I cleared my throat because all the important people did this.

"This summer my family planned a trip to Myrtle Beach. It took Mom and Dad forever to get the car packed because they were arguing. Even in the car, driving down I-85, they yelled at each other. Mom turned up the radio because a Michael Jackson song was playing and to drown out Dad. She was happy because the radio *kept* playing Michael Jackson songs. I was happy because we were on our way."

Dad wasn't happy. He was never happy, but I didn't write that. A stupid assignment, summer essays were so third grade. I took a deep breath and finished reading.

"Wanna Be Startin' Somethin'" ended and so did our trip. A voice on the radio said the King of Pop was dead, causing Mom to howl like a dying wolf. I'd never seen her so upset. She didn't react like this after she and Dad fought, not even when Dad slammed his hand into the coffee table and needed eight stitches. Mom began breathing like Darth Vader and then she screamed until Dad turned around. We went home and stayed home. For five days, I read comics. Mom played Michael Jackson records and cried. Dad left and didn't come back. I hated Michael Jackson and my mother for taking away our summer vacation. The End."

The only sound was the paper shaking in my hands until Rebecca, my best friend, waved her hand wildly and asked, "May I go next? Please?"

Everyone knew what the subject of Rebecca's essay would be. She spent every summer in Israel, that's what made her different from everyone else in Wiley, North Carolina.

Mrs. Blunt stared at me and said, "Thank you for sharing, Katharine."

Some of my classmates snickered. Jason Webb, the principal's son, muttered "freak show" loud enough so everyone could hear. None of that mattered because I looked up to see Tara Parks smiling at me.

Walking back to my desk, the sharp pains got worse, shooting up my stomach. Not able to ignore the stabbing feeling any longer, I told Mrs. Blunt I felt sick and bolted out of there. I sat on the radiator in the handicapped stall of the eighth grade girls' bathroom – through two changes of class – even though it smelled like Corn Nuts and Clorox. I sat there thinking *what the fuck?* First Michael Jackson, then my parents, and now the new horror going on between my legs. I'd heard – knew – this was supposed to happen, but I never actually believed it would.

Normally, we melted in our seats all through September, but not this year. In the short dress my mother had forced me to wear – with stupid, girly shoes, no less – I might as well have been naked. Cool air traveled up my ridiculous skirt, coming from a hole in the wall behind the radiator. I wondered if the hole was big enough for a skinny person like me. I wanted so badly to squeeze behind that radiator and run, run away from my own body.

Every time the door opened and someone came in, I tensed, thinking a teacher had sent someone to find me, but it was always girls giggling about dumb stuff. They took forever unzipping purses and opening make-up cases. Their hairspray fumes made me dizzy, and I wanted them to go away.

"She wasn't just flirting with Jason, but all of his friends, too," one girl said.

"I saw her at his locker this morning. The way she leaned against the wall and watched him – it's like she was blowing him with her eyes," the other one said.

As they walked out, one of them sighed and said, "At least she's not a weirdo like Katharine. That essay she read today about Michael Jackson was mental."

The other one laughed and then the bathroom went quiet again.

A few minutes later, Rebecca stood outside the stall, tapping her foot. Her fruity perfume stank up the bathroom. "I know you're in there. What's wrong?"

"Nothing." I didn't want to tell anyone, not even my best friend.

"You've missed the last two classes. Of course something's wrong. What is it? Why are you hiding?"

My legs were so long that even sitting on the radiator, my shoes almost touched the floor. I slid off the radiator, and after looking under the stalls to make sure no one else was in the bathroom I said, "I'm bleeding."

"What?" Rebecca pounded.

I unlocked the door, and she pushed it open. Wearing a bright yellow sundress, she bounced into the stall like a brand new tennis ball.

"Where?" Rebecca examined my face, arms, and legs for blood.

I motioned toward the crotch area of my blue dress. "I shoved some toilet paper down there."

Rebecca glanced at the toilet paper roll and scrunched up her face. Bad enough my stomach felt like a drummer was wailing away inside, but Rebecca had to make me feel like an idiot, too.

"I don't have anything else to use." I didn't have change for the machine in the bathroom and asking the school nurse wasn't an option.

"Didn't your mom give you anything? Just in case?"

I shook my head. Like anything else she perceived as dirty, Mom didn't talk about being on the rag. When it came to girl stuff, Mom only wanted to discuss fairy-tale crap like wearing idiotic dresses and going to dances with boys.

Rebecca dumped the contents of her bright red purse onto the bathroom floor. I'd always wondered what she kept inside it, and now I knew – four Tootsie Roll pops, an iPhone, Chap Stick, Tic-Tacs, toothpaste, a toothbrush. And, two items wrapped in plastic – one a small square, the other tube-shaped.

"Now, I haven't started yet." Her big brown eyes widened to study my scraggy body. "I can't believe *you* started before me." Then, her eyes zeroed in on the top of my dress. "I mean, you don't even have anything yet." She motioned at the anthills forming on her own chest. Unlike Rebecca, I didn't want boobs. I didn't want to ride the crimson tide. Like the name my mother had given me, Katharine Anne, it didn't feel right.

"How long does it last?" I asked.

"Six days a month for most girls – and not just bleeding, but cramps, bloating, and mood swings." Rebecca scowled at me like Lucy scowled at Charlie

Brown. "According to my mom, you'll start crying for no reason and feel like you've gained fifty pounds."

I looked down at the two plastic-wrapped items. This couldn't, shouldn't be happening to me. This was worse than what happened over the summer – my parents fighting, Dad leaving. At least with Dad gone, the yelling at home had stopped, but this period crap was *not* going away.

"How can I make it stop?"

"You get really old." Rebecca held out the small tube. "Mom showed me how to use this, you just stick it up the hole. Doesn't your mom tell you anything?"

"Nothing is going in me!" No way. Because. It just wasn't.

"You can use this then, but it's kinda gross." She took the plastic off the square pad, which looked like a thin diaper. "You put it in your underwear, sticky side down."

The late bell rang, and Rebecca shoved everything back into her purse except for the pad, the lesser of two horrible options. I felt like both would kill me.

"Gotta run," she said and hurried out of the stall. "Drama class."

Seriously? The worst possible thing that could happen to me had happened, but my best friend dumped me for drama class. She left the bathroom, and I stuck the damn diaper inside my underwear.

I sat on the radiator all through history class, reading comics until lunchtime when two people hovered right outside. I heard deep breathing and kissing sounds like on Mom's soap operas. A tan backpack fell to the floor. Their bodies pressed against the door to the handicapped stall. My stall.

"It's stuck or something," the girl said.

"That's okay. Right here will do," the boy said in between kisses. He sounded like he was taking his last breath, drowning in deep water. "No one comes in here during lunch. They're all in the cafeteria."

I recognized his voice: It was that asshole Jason Webb. But who was the girl? I leaped onto the radiator to peek over the door, but unlike my favorite pair of Chucks, the dress shoes made a loud clacking noise. My right ankle twisted. I lost my balance and fell to the floor, landing on my wrist. My ankle and my wrist throbbed from the fall, but it didn't compare to what was going on down under. I stayed sprawled out on the floor, wondering how my day could suck any more.

"What the..." Jason said.

"Are you okay?" Peeking under the stall door were the bluest eyes I'd ever seen, Carolina blue. And they belonged to Tara Parks. All week, I'd been trying to work up the nerve to talk to her. She was the prettiest girl I'd ever seen. On the first day of school she'd worn a temporary tattoo of an electric guitar on her arm. Most girls would have picked a flower or butterfly. I wanted to tell her how amazing it was and tell her all about Uncle RB's music store, but so far I'd only held the door for her and said, "You're welcome" after she thanked me. Obviously, Jason Webb had gotten further.

I stood up and unlocked the stall. "I'm fine," I said.

She walked right in. She was almost as tall as me. Her hair was Barbie-doll blonde, and her round cheeks looked like they'd been pinched way too much when she was a baby.

Jason stood right outside the stall and smirked at

me. "Get lost, loser."

I didn't respond.

He stepped in and grabbed my arm. "Get out, Freak-en-stein."

I yanked my arm away and wondered if I could win a fight against Jason. I was at least three inches taller than him, but he was much wider. Tara moved between us.

Jason stepped back and waved his arms. "Oh, come on. Just having a little fun."

Tara crossed her arms. "You can't just go around grabbing people."

"You didn't seem to mind," he said to her chest.

"Leave or I'll scream, and you'll have to explain what you're doing in the girls' bathroom," Tara said.

She opened her mouth wide like a horror queen preparing to let out a curdling yell on cue. Jason stepped back out of the stall. I'd seen him get mad before, usually when a teacher accused him of throwing a spitball in class or tripping a student. He always gave the teacher a look of defiance, as if to say, "You're accusing me, the high school principal's son?" He was only going to get worse next year when we moved on to Wiley High School.

As soon as Jason left the bathroom, Tara examined my face, arms, and legs. Even though it made my insides bounce, I didn't want Tara to stop looking or touching.

"You gonna tell anyone?" she asked.

"No."

Her face turned blood red. She tried to hide it by bowing her head. "He offered to show me around since I'm new. Mom wants me to meet a nice boy at this school."

Show her around, that's what he was doing? I was the one who held the door open for her. Jason's not nice. I'm nice. Certainly nicer than Jason.

"I can show you around." I leaned against the wall, trying to act all cool.

"Thanks, but you're not a—" I figured she was going to say you're not a *boy*, but she stopped herself.

I glanced down at my body, the dress. The cramps came back full throttle, and my wrist ached. What she was about to say, "But you're not a boy," made me want to cry like a stupid girl. But I couldn't admit that. Not to her, not to anyone.

"What's wrong?" she asked. Her eyes studied my face like a math equation she was on the verge of solving.

"Nothing." No way was I telling her. I couldn't believe I had my fucking period in front of a hot girl. Did she know? Could she see the diaper through the dress? I pulled at the dress. Bad enough I had on girly clothes. Embarrassed, I turned away and kicked off my shoes.

Tara picked them up and ran her fingers over the ribbons at the toes.

My stomach cramped. My dress itched. How did girls get through one day like this?

After examining my shoes, she looked me over. "If you're fine, why aren't you in the cafeteria?"

"My lunch money's in the back pocket of the jeans I planned to wear to today." Of course, that wasn't the only reason. The whole being on the rag business had killed my appetite.

"Why didn't you wear them?"

"Mom made me wear this." I tugged at the short hem. "I wanted to wear my Tar Heels sweatshirt."

"It's pretty."

"I hate dresses. They don't feel like me." I hadn't expected to say this much to her. I didn't tell her how Mom had cried that morning and begged me to wear it, saying it would take away some of the pain of Dad leaving.

Tara glanced at the main bathroom door and waved me back into the stall. She followed and locked it.

"Take it off," she said.

"What?" She couldn't mean take off the dress.

"Let's trade." She did mean take off the dress.

"Here? No way." There were tiny anthills forming on my chest. Rebecca didn't know. No one did, thankfully, and I didn't want Tara to see them.

"You're miserable, and you'll probably break a leg or something if you walk around in those shoes for the rest of the day."

She didn't wait for me to come around. "This is my older brother Manny's," she said while unbuttoning her shirt. "It'll look good on you."

My arms shook while taking off the dress and throwing on her shirt. I worried she would see the pad bulging through the front of my underwear. But watching her slip off her jeans, I couldn't turn away. The worst morning of my life quickly turned into the best lunch period ever. She had on a brown bra with white polka dots. Three moles rested between her bra and belly button, one big one and two smaller ones. If connected, they'd form a semi-circle.

My body looked like a stick figure. Hers was fascinating, curvy. Her skin looked smooth, soft. Mine was rough. Just the thought of feeling her smooth skin creating friction against mine caused a different kind of ache underneath the horrible cramps. This ache felt good - so good it was probably wrong.

She took the dress and handed over the jeans. Manny's name was written in black ink on the inside.

"Mom refuses to buy me new clothes and dresses until I lose weight. That's why I'm always in my brother's hand-me-downs. Mom says I'm so tall that boys will never like me if I'm fat, too."

"You don't need to lose weight," I said and wondered why her mom couldn't see that Tara was beautiful.

The jeans hung off my hips and needed a belt. I tried tucking in the shirt to hold the jeans up, but she stopped me.

"They're boy jeans. They're supposed to hang right here," she said, putting her hands on my hips.

I hurried with buttoning up the shirt, not wanting her to see my chest. Tara pulled my dress over her bra. A little snug, it ended right below her knees, good enough for school. I probably looked at her too long because she asked, "Does it look bad on me?"

She looked so good my insides were beating to get out, but I couldn't say that. The dress made Tara's eyes even brighter, but I didn't know how to compliment girls the way my Uncle did. He always knew exactly what to say to a woman to get her to smile.

"No. It looks good on you."

She leaned on me to slip her feet into my shoes. A few strands of her soft blonde hair fell against my face. I caught the smell of vanilla and lavender, but then she pulled away. Dressed completely in my clothes now, she looked at me and laughed.

"Here." She reached over and unbuttoned my shirt. I'd missed a hole. With her so close and leaning over, I saw half of a polka dot on her bra. It's like the polka dot was winking at me. My stomach grew tight, and I ached even more between my legs where the jeans were hanging. I tried hard not to grin at the thought that I'd gotten to see more of Tara than Jason did. But the desire to grin faded when I realized the ache wasn't going away. It only grew stronger the longer I looked at her. My hands got sweaty. I was thirsty all of a sudden and nervous. I never got an ache like that around Rebecca.

"Better?" she asked.

I nodded, but she looked me over like something was missing.

"Your name should be Peyton. Spelled P-e-y-t-o-n." she said.

"Peyton?"

She played with her necklace, pulling the cross back and forth along the chain. "Where we lived in New York, there was this great street musician named Peyton. He would play the drums and sing. You look like him."

"It's cool, I guess." Truth was, I'd thought a lot about having a different name. Mom had always dreamed of being a famous actress and named me after her favorite, Katharine Hepburn. But Katharine never sounded right for me.

Tara stared at me, so I scrunched my face and said in my best tough guy voice, "What you looking at?"

She laughed, warm and thick. It vibrated off the walls like John Bonham's kick drum, which was my favorite sound in the world until I heard Tara's laugh.

She sat on the radiator and crossed her legs like a lady. "Do you mind if I eat my lunch in here?" she asked.

"No, but why are you eating alone?"

She shrugged. "I don't get what the big deal is about eating alone. Mom always wants to know who I sit with at lunch. Sometimes I make up names so she won't worry. In New York, my made-up friend was Sarah. She and I had a lot in common. Our names rhymed and we both hated Sundays because it meant the weekend was almost over."

When I didn't say anything, she turned her attention to the contents in her lunch.

"I saw the guitar tattoo on your arm," I said, hoping to tell her about Uncle RB's music shop.

She glanced up at me. I winked at her the way Uncle RB winked at women, but she didn't smile. She had this serious look on her face. Oh God. I needed to practice in a mirror or with Rebecca. We'd been best friends since first grade and she always told me the truth whether I'd like hearing it or not, like if I had a creepy wink.

"You really shouldn't skip lunch." Tara pulled out a sandwich and insisted that I take half. She must not have found me too creepy if she was willing to share her sandwich.

"Thanks," I said, between bites of the sandwich. Not only did it have turkey, but bacon, tomato, mayonnaise, and mustard. Mom only made peanut butter sandwiches without jelly.

I asked questions between bites, not wanting to miss my chance to learn things about her. I hoped she didn't prefer talking to Jason or some made-up friend.

"Why'd you move here?" I asked.

"Dad's in the military. We move around a lot."

"How long do you stay in one place?"

"Usually two years."

Two years wasn't that long. I needed to get her to like me, and fast. When we'd finished the sandwich, I looked through my backpack for something to give her in return.

"You can have *Superman*."

She closed her lunch bag and yawned. "No, thanks."

"But you shared your sandwich. I want to give you something. You can have any of my comics except *Thor*." *Thor* was my favorite and Uncle RB had bought it at a store in Atlanta.

"I don't really like comics." She grabbed her backpack and left the stall. "Let's meet here after the last class to change back."

The thought of seeing her undress again after school almost made the idea of having to wear that dumb dress again bearable. Watching her walk through the main bathroom door, I couldn't believe what a moron I'd been, offering her comics and talking to her about *Superman* and *Thor*. She wanted a boy to like her. That's what brought her into the bathroom in the first place. I'd blown it.

Just as the door was about to close, all my hope lost, she glanced over her shoulder and smiled the most amazing smile I'd ever seen.

When the door closed completely, I looked in the mirror. I stepped closer and tried to imagine what Tara saw when she looked at me. My honey-brown eyes looked sad, droopy even. And my hair annoyed me because it wasn't straight or curly. It was wavy and black as tar. The jeans and shirt felt so much better than the dress. It was easier to stand up straight, and I liked how I looked. Everything just matched better, even my square jaw. Mom was always saying how she wished I'd had her jaw instead of Dad's, but I liked it.

And I liked Tara Parks.

Thinking about those old movies Uncle RB always watched on weekends, I narrowed my eyes, clenched my jaw and gave the mirror my best Dirty Harry. "I'm gonna make that girl like me."

At the end of the school day, Tara and I returned to the bathroom to swap clothes. Afterwards, we walked out of school together toward the parking lot.

"What are you doing this weekend?" I asked.

"Why?"

I didn't have a response. I wanted her to ask what my plans were so I could talk about helping Uncle RB out at his store. Someone needed to pay for things in my house. Dad never sent any money, and Mom said she couldn't get a job because of bad circulation and very close veins – the way she always pronounced it.

But Tara didn't ask. She stood close, forcing me to stand up straight. If I slouched, we were the same height. I wanted to be taller, bigger, big enough to wrap my arms around her because girls liked that stuff, according to Mom and those soaps she watched.

She chewed her gum for a while before speaking. "Mom is taking me to Charlotte for an ice skating class."

"Ice Skating?" I laughed. My mom sometimes watched ice skating on TV. It looked ridiculous with all the feathers, shiny dresses, and men wearing their pants too tight.

"Shut up, jerk. Don't make fun of it. I'll have you know it takes someone super strong to be a good skater, especially a boy who can lift me up and twirl me around," she said. "My mother thinks I can be a champion figure skater."

She was so close I smelled her grape bubble gum. "I came in first last week during the fast skate at the roller rink," I said.

She blew a bubble, unimpressed.

"Can I take the class with you?"

A Mercedes-Benz SUV pulled up. The driver, a blonde woman with aviator sunglasses, didn't smile or wave as Tara walked toward the car. "Sure, I'll tell Mom you're coming with me next Friday. You can sleep over."

Spend Friday night? With her? Ice skating was my new favorite thing.

As her mother's SUV drove away, Tara leaned out the passenger side. "Bye, Peyton."

I tried not to get too excited, but she had to like me a little bit. She wouldn't have invited me to ice skating class with her if she didn't.

Like every other day after school, I found Mom on the couch at home, blanket draped around her, watching *General Hospital*. She didn't allow talking during her soaps so she never asked me about school, which I was especially thankful for today. I paused in the hall and peeked in at her. She lifted a hand in a half-wave, but her eyes never left the TV. She'd been upset lately because some of her shows were being cancelled. She even wrote letters to the networks begging them to reconsider, even though she said all her letter writing was pointless. No one cared what she thought.

She wore a flower print dress she'd gotten on sale at Kmart when Dad was still around. She thought it was pretty and fashionable, but a two-year old with finger-paint could've designed a better print. The crazy thing was, even though she rarely left the house now that Dad was gone, she still curled her hair and put on a face full of make-up every day.

I went into the bathroom and found Mom's stash of those diaper-like pads in the bottom cabinet. I grabbed a few and went up to my room.

Friday night meant going to Uncle RB's lake house for the weekend – without Mom. I tossed the dress under my bed and put on what I'd wanted to wear to school that day, my Carolina Tar Heels sweatshirt and a pair of Levi's.

I'd grown over the summer, and the Levi's were almost too short. I pushed up a sleeve and flexed my bicep. I'd been doing fifty push-ups every night before bed and even using Uncle RB's weights when I stayed with him, but so far I didn't have muscles like him. Girls always came into Wiley Music and stared at him. I wanted Tara to notice me the way those girls noticed him. Mom said the women liked Uncle RB for his pouty lips and brooding brown eyes. I wondered what Tara thought of my lips. They were like Uncle RB's.

My height wasn't the only thing that had changed over the summer. Those damn anthills had shown up on my chest. I hoped that lifting weights would turn them into muscles instead. Thankfully, they weren't showing through my clothes yet, but it didn't matter. I knew they were there. I tried to press them in with my hands.

The door to my room swung open. I jumped. As usual, Mom marched in and inspected my room like it was a crime scene. Her eyes stopped on the small stack of mini-diapers.

She picked them up. "This mean what I think it does? Did my little girl become a woman today?"

Gross. Just the words – my little girl, woman – all

gross.

Tears filled her eyes. Hoping she wouldn't cry, I let her hug me for what felt like forever. Her bony shoulders cut into my chest. Adding to the discomfort, her hands smelled like onions, making my eyes tear up. I hadn't cried earlier that day. And I wasn't about to cry because of a damn onion.

"Mom," I said, finally pulling away. "Remember, we need to have dinner early. I'm going over to Uncle RB's."

"Meatloaf's in the oven." She sat on my bed and waited for me to say something. When I didn't, she asked, "How do you feel?"

"My stomach ached this morning, but it's fine now."

"No, I mean – I remember when I started. I realized things were suddenly different. It's a big life change. You can have babies now."

"Mom!" Nothing was going in me and nothing was coming out. Period. "That's gross."

"Katharine Anne Honeycutt, it is not gross."

Peyton Honeycutt. Not Katie, not Katharine, not Katharine Anne.

"Babies and love and boys – it's all beautiful. Oh, I can't wait 'til you have your first boyfriend and go to your first dance."

"I have homework to do." I pulled a North Carolina state history book out of my backpack.

"But it's Friday."

Ignoring her, I flipped open the book to the chapter about Sir Walter Raleigh and the Lost Colony. "My name is Peyton now."

She set the stack of pads back down on my

dresser and left my room as quickly as she'd entered it. She slammed my door and stomped down the stairs, but I didn't care. I had a new name.

Mom was worse than Rebecca and most other girls at school, always wanting to talk about clothes and make-up and silly TV shows. Not wanting to look at the stupid diapers, I stuffed them into the bottom of my backpack and collected my things to spend the night at Uncle RB's.

Later that evening at the lake house, Uncle RB and I used the last bit of daylight to practice shooting with the BB gun. He had a make-shift firing range, a row of tree stumps, between his house and the lake. I loved the crinkling of the leaves under my shoes and the smell of the wood-burning fireplace from the house down the road. I raised the gun and yanked the trigger, thinking about the ice skating lessons and the girl I'd be missing time at the lake for.

"Peyton, you've got to be patient." Uncle RB took the BB gun away from me. "You can't just lift the gun up and shoot."

Unlike my mother, Uncle RB had no problem calling me Peyton. He did have a problem with the way I shot a gun. Demonstrating one more time, he put the gun against his shoulder. His eyes focused for a long time on the Cheerwine can on top of the tree stump several yards away. The sun was setting in front of us, over the lake, forcing him to squint. He chewed a toothpick, moving it from one side of his mouth to the other. He stood completely still for what seemed like a full minute before shooting the can right off the stump.

He handed the gun back to me and walked over to pick up the can. I put the gun against my shoulder just like he taught me.

He held up both hands. "Wait 'til I'm out of the way."

I lowered the gun. "Sorry."

I enjoyed shooting guns with Uncle RB, the weight and feel of the gun in my hands. He said we'd go hunting as soon as I learned how to shoot properly. I needed to focus, pretend the can was something I wanted to shoot, like Dad for leaving.

Uncle RB walked back over to me, pushing up the sleeves of his UNC Tar Heels sweatshirt. He'd gotten us both one last year when we went to a basketball game.

"You can do it. You just have to hold the gun steady and aim before you fire. Like anything, it takes practice."

He kept saying that, but Uncle RB made everything look easy: playing drums, shooting a gun, talking to women who came into the store.

He waited for me to try again. My eyes drifted from the can back to the lake house behind us. Might as well get it over with.

"I can't come over next Friday night because I'll be spending it with Tara – the new girl at school."

"Okay." Uncle RB put his hands in his pockets. He didn't seem disappointed or even surprised.

"I'm taking an ice skating class with her. But I can still help out at the store on Saturday," I said. At the mention of ice skating he did seem surprised. He probably thought it was stupid.

He shifted his weight from one leg to another. "Ice skating, huh?"

"Tara needs a partner, to lift her and stuff."

Uncle RB ran his hand through his hair slowly.

His eyes took in my scrawny frame.

"You don't think I can lift her?" I asked, accidentally waving the gun.

He dodged the gun and rubbed the back of his neck. His face had a worried look. "I think you can do anything. But will they let you skate with her in this class?"

I shrugged, careful to keep the gun pointed at the ground. "Why wouldn't they?"

Uncle RB massaged the left side of his forehead. He did this a lot in his shop when he was trying to figure out the best way to repair a broken amp or electric guitar. More than once, Mom had caught me massaging my left temple while working on math homework. She'd always swat at me to stop, but I did it anyway.

Uncle RB got quiet. He glanced over at the sun disappearing behind the lake.

"I could come here with you after work on Saturday. We could go hunting on Sunday morning," I said.

He nodded and watched as I raised the gun slowly. Like he'd instructed, I took a deep breath, steadied my hands, aimed, and pulled the trigger. The BB hit the Cheerwine can, knocking it off the stump. But Uncle RB still had a worried look on his face.

Chapter 2

Tara skated backward and forward in front of the bench while I took forever lacing up my skates. The rink smelled like popcorn.

"You need help?" she asked.

I smiled, worrying about skating on ice for the first time. Of course, she was great at it. "Show off," I said.

I sat there with my skates on, waiting for the teacher to show up. The level one ice skating class had fifteen students total, mostly girls. Tara being new to the area, she had to start in a beginner class even though she wasn't one. She skated out on the ice backward and briefly lifted up one leg before spinning around six times. I counted.

She stopped in front of me and stood perfectly still, not even losing her balance a little. She held out her hands. "Come on, I'll show you."

"I don't need help," I said.

"Thought you said you'd never skated on ice before?"

I pushed off the wall with my hands. My feet went one way, the rest of my body another. I got control of one foot, but the other one slid away. Finally, my body found the wall along the rink. I slammed into it and fell onto the cold ice.

The girls in our class tried not to laugh. They weren't much better. No one had hit the wall, but several had wiped out. One kept rubbing her butt.

Tara didn't laugh. She helped me up. Even when I found my balance, she didn't let go of my hands.

"Bend your knees a little," she said. "And suck your stomach in, like you do when you're trying to make yourself taller than me."

She'd noticed that? Shit. "I *am* taller than you."

She laughed, which almost made us both fall. Then, she skated backward slowly, pulling me forward. We circled the rink like that not once, but twice, and stuck together for the whole class.

Mrs. Parks drove us to Tara's house after ice skating class. Soon as we got there, Tara and I hurried into the house and up the stairs, but a man's voice called her name. We turned to see her parents standing at the bottom of the stairs, looking up at us. Col. Parks smiled. Mrs. Parks eyed my suitcase in her daughter's hand. Tara had warned me about her mother, saying she didn't care for most people. I'd vowed to make her parents like me so Tara and I could spend a ton of time together. The way Mrs. Parks studied the suitcase, winning her over wasn't going to be easy. She'd barely said two words to me on the whole drive to Charlotte and back.

My main worry was saying something stupid. Once when I was four, Uncle RB brought a date over for dinner. Afterward, I walked them to the door. In front of Mom and Dad, I waved to Uncle RB and his date and yelled, "Good riddance." I thought it was a fancy way to say goodbye. Ever since, I'd been nervous about saying something stupid.

"Pumpkin, you going to introduce me to your friend?" Col. Parks asked.

Tara left the suitcase at the top of the stairs and moped back down. I followed and shoved my hands into the front pocket of my UNC Tar Heels sweatshirt. We stood next to each other in the living room, our shoulders almost touching.

Tara's parents stood far apart. Mrs. Parks had on a black dress, heels, and make-up. Her wavy blonde hair was perfectly styled. Unlike Mom, Mrs. Parks wore a fashionable dress, just one solid color. She didn't overdo the make-up. Mrs. Parks belonged in *Cosmopolitan* magazine, not Wiley, North Carolina.

Col. Parks was barefoot. He wore faded jeans ripped at the knees and a t-shirt with the arms cut off. An Army green duffle bag sat on the floor between him and the couch. His uniforms spilled out of it.

"Dad, this is Peyton."

Col. Parks shook my hand. "Nice to meet you, Peyton."

"Nice to meet you, sir."

Uncle RB had told me all about using sir and ma'am, especially with military folk.

Col. Parks eyed my sweatshirt and grinned. "You like basketball?"

"Sometimes I play with my uncle," I said, glad I wore the sweatshirt. At least Col. Parks seemed to like me.

"Tara's great at basketball. Isn't that right, pumpkin?" He winked at Tara.

"I'm okay."

"Okay? Don't let her fool you, Peyton. She was the high scorer two years in a row on the girls' youth team in New York," he said. "Not sure who she gets it from. I played in school, but spent most of my time on the bench."

"Maybe she got it from me," Mrs. Parks said. "I was captain of my cheerleading squad in high school. We were known for our athletic routines, even won awards for it."

Laughing, Col. Parks turned and faced his wife. "Cheerleading is not a sport."

"You're hardly an authority on sports." She cut her eyes at him.

He laughed harder. His laugh was almost as full and warm as Tara's.

"We're already late for the party," Mrs. Parks said to him. She grabbed his duffle bag and left the room.

Col. Parks followed her. "Come on, Barbie. You have to admit, it's funny – thinking Tara got her athleticism from you."

Tara dug her elbow into my side, nodding toward the stairs. She entered her room after me and locked the door. On her dresser, next to the cherry candle she lit, was a half-eaten chocolate cupcake.

"It's for you," she said. "Mom made cupcakes for a bake sale at church. She could only spare one."

While I ate, Tara put my suitcase on her bed. The stuffed suitcase popped open as soon as she unhooked the metal latches. She examined each item of clothing I'd brought: the blue dress she'd traded me for in the bathroom stall, three other dresses, the fuchsia skirt, a yellow blouse, and a similar white one. She squealed when she got to the bright red corduroys. I hadn't mentioned those. She kicked off her Converse and Manny's hand-me-down jeans. The corduroys fit, showing off her long legs.

"Your mom buys you all this stuff?" she asked.

"Nah, with Dad gone, she asks Uncle RB to buy it for me."

"Sorry about your dad."

I didn't respond.

"Are you sure you want to give me all of it?"

I nodded. She'd look better in the clothes than me. I wanted to tell her that, but I didn't.

Tara handed me Manny's jeans and motioned to the bottom drawer of her dresser. Her part of the bargain.

Filled with hand-me-downs from her brother, I picked out a flannel shirt to wear and put the other flannels, long-john tops, t-shirts, and jeans in my suitcase.

It had been her idea to trade clothes. She'd said Mom couldn't make me wear clothes if I'd "loaned" them to her. Both our moms would have a fit when we wore each other's clothes to school, but we agreed it was worth it.

Tara tied a white blouse at the waist, exposing her belly button and the lowest mole on her stomach. She caught me staring so I shifted my eyes and pretended to look around her room.

Tara sucked in her stomach and studied it in the mirror. She barely had a belly, not even an inch to pinch. I fought the urge to reach over and try.

While she took her time folding each piece of clothing I gave her before placing them in the dresser, I walked over to the antique globe. It took up a whole corner of the room. In the other corner was a Fender Stratocaster. A telescope stood in front of the only window. Two Led Zeppelin posters hung on the wall next to her bed.

She had more stuff in her room than I had ever owned. She had a huge iMac on her desk. A television set with a Wii hooked up to it sat at the foot of her bed. Who cared about fancy clothes, I thought—I'd rather have a Wii. She told me her grandfather had sent both her and Manny one for Christmas. He'd always assumed she'd want the same thing as her brother. I thought of

Uncle RB. That would be the kind of thing he'd do.

She disappeared into her closet. I turned both the TV and Wii on, thinking maybe I could get Mom and Uncle RB to get me more dresses to trade for the Wii.

Tara walked out of her closet and tossed a green hat to me. The hat had a leprechaun spinning a basketball on the front and worn edges. The words Boston Celtics circled a leprechaun. Something had been scribbled on the back in black marker.

"Sam Jones," she said. "He's from North Carolina. Dad said Jones was super fast and always made game-winning shots. That's how he got the nickname Mr. Clutch."

The hat fit my head perfectly. I didn't even have to adjust it, but I couldn't stop touching it and wondered why she'd given it to me. "Thanks."

She motioned for me to scoot over. She hopped onto the bed and grabbed the Wiimote. "Now I'm going to kick your ass," she said.

While Tara fired up the game, I relaxed for the first time since I'd arrived at her house. With her parents gone to a party and her brother away at Appalachian State, we had the house to ourselves which was more than fine with me. My sleepover with Tara Parks was the most exciting night of my life so far.

In early January we walked down my street together for the first time. She'd pestered me constantly to sleep over at my place, saying it was only fair since I spent every Friday night with her. That weekend, we didn't have ice skating class so I had no excuse.

Tara tried to guess which house was mine. She pointed with her index finger sticking out of a smoker's glove, which kept her hands warm, but her fingers free. She used her hands a lot, always pointing. I liked it when she got all serious about things like music and pointed her index finger right at me.

Each house she pointed to was bigger and nicer than the one I lived in, making me more anxious about having her spend the night. When we got to the modest, white two-story with green paint peeling off the front porch, I motioned toward it, waiting for disappointment to show on her face.

She said, "It's cute" and took off for the porch.

"Wait. I forgot to tell you – don't interrupt Mom and her show."

Tara had already gone in, the screen door slammed behind her. Mom didn't like visitors because she claimed she didn't have money to keep up the house. But when Uncle RB offered to do stuff like paint, she said not to bother. I ripped off a piece of cracked paint that hung by the door and tossed it over the porch railing. I should have bothered. From now on, I would.

I grabbed the mail and went in, expecting Mom to tell us to be quiet and go up to my room. Instead, she and Tara were sitting together on the couch, watching the last few minutes of *General Hospital*. Mom wore her favorite green dress from JCPenney.

"Got the mail."

Both Tara and Mom said, "Sh."

I put the bills, including a couple of overdue notices, on Mom's piano - the piano she loved, but never played. She made me play it instead. Before Dad left, I took lessons from a woman down the street. At least now I didn't have to go to lessons. Thanks, Dad.

On TV, a shirtless guy kissed a blonde girl. They

made sounds like Tara and Jason had in the girls' bathroom. The thought made me burn, and I was glad when the show went to commercial.

"You watch *General Hospital*?" Mom asked Tara.

"Sometimes I watch with Mom before I do my homework. It's her favorite show."

All the characters did on the show was talk and kiss and hang out at a hospital or a restaurant. Sometimes they kissed at the hospital. All that kissing made me think of Tara and Jason again, and I punched the couch pillow.

"You want a Cheerwine?" I darted down the hall to the kitchen before Tara could even respond. Thinking about her and kissing made me restless.

Mom had actual plates out on the counter, not paper ones. Thank God she could return to the land of the living while Tara was there. From the living room, I could hear them laughing. Mom had given me a lot of grief for letting Tara "borrow" all my dresses. Maybe she'd stop harassing me now.

After *General Hospital*, Mom put on a Michael Jackson record and we all made meatloaf together. With Tara next to me in the kitchen, listening to him wasn't as bad. I broke up the ground beef with my hands. Tara stood next to me to cut the onion and her arm kept bumping into mine. Every time her skin touched mine, I almost dropped the ground beef.

Finally, after dinner, we went up to my room to watch *Iron Man* on the old big box TV Uncle RB had given me. Tara had watched Mom's show, but instead of watching my favorite movie, which she'd never seen, she looked around my room. Probably because *Iron Man* didn't have as much kissing.

"This is way better than *General Hospital*," I said.

"I don't see how Mom can stand that show." Or Tara.

She walked over to my bookshelf. "Dad says Mom watches her shows every day for companionship because we move so much. She always has to say goodbye to people, but the characters on her shows are always there, every day." She looked up. "Maybe that's why your mom watches? Since your dad's gone?"

I didn't know what to say. Yeah, she was repeating what her dad had told her, but she had a different way of seeing things. She was smart, probably the smartest in our class, definitely smarter than me.

She ran a finger along my books, touching each one. She stopped, noticing some magazines hidden behind the books. I didn't panic because the first few on top were hunting magazines. Like Mom, I figured she wouldn't be interested. Mom didn't go near my books and had zero interest in the magazines, but Tara pulled issue after issue off the stack.

"Those are really old," I said and jumped up. But it was too late.

By the time I got to her she'd found the *Playboy* I'd swiped from Uncle RB. I waited for her to ask why I had a magazine of naked girls, but instead she flipped through it. I locked the door to my room before sitting back on the floor.

"I've looked at stuff online, but I've never actually seen one of these," she said.

"Your dad probably has some."

"No," she said. "Manny and I looked all over for them."

Tara sat right next to me and took her time looking at all the pictures before she turned the pages. I tried to focus on the TV.

She pushed the magazine over to me. "Which one's your favorite?" she asked.

I turned to page twenty-four, a dirty blonde in the act of pulling her shirt off.

The model held the bunched-up shirt in her mouth, her arms covering most of her breasts. Other photos showed way more nudity, but I liked how the model on page twenty-four stared into the camera. The look in her eyes said it was okay to look at her, to want her. She also had a mole above her belly button like Tara. The photo cut off right at her hips. I liked imagining the rest of the model, the parts I couldn't see.

"She's beautiful," Tara said.

Not sure what to say, I went back to the TV. Iron Man and Iron Monger were fighting, the best part of the whole movie.

"I can do that pose." Tara stood and pulled up her shirt. Her pink bra fell to the floor, right by my knee. She wrapped her shirt up in her hands, bringing it up to her mouth like she was about to pull it over her head. Her chest was exposed until she got her arms into position. My insides wanted to get out. She stared at me like the girl in the photo and I couldn't stop myself from looking back.

"What are you doing?" I bolted to the curtains to close them. "Cover up."

She pulled her shirt back down.

"You don't think I'm sexy?" She flopped on my bed, face down.

"You're beautiful." I sat on the bed, a hand-me-down from Uncle RB.

"Beautiful isn't the same as sexy." Irritated, she inched away from me as much as the dip in the old bed would allow.

I glanced over at the dictionary. Beautiful was a bigger compliment than sexy, I was sure. Something told me looking up both words and reading them aloud to her wasn't the right thing to do in that moment.

"You're beautiful *and* sexy," I said.

"Too late."

"You shouldn't go around throwing your shirt off for just anyone." Or just kissing anyone. Like Jason.

"I thought you'd like seeing the real thing. I know I don't have as much as that model – yet." She rolled over on her back and looked at me in a way that made me nervous. "I see you, Peyton."

She stopped talking and stared. I was more nervous than I'd ever been around anyone and too afraid to ask what she meant. She could've meant she gets that I like her. Or she could've meant something more.

I turned off the TV. Without the TV, the only light in my room was from the fake glow-in-the-dark stars. Tara's eyes bounced around the ceiling, studying every star. I put my head down on a pillow, not too far from hers, but no part of my body rested. Electricity shot through my body.

"I put the Big Dipper in the wrong place," I said.

"I like it. It's Peyton's night sky." We stopped moving, and I listened to the slow rhythm of her breathing.

After a few minutes, Tara propped her head up with one arm. "Your mom sure loves that you're learning to ice skate," she said.

"She's surprised I'm even interested."

"Why are you?" Tara asked.

She made me uncomfortable being so close. I glanced back up at my Big Dipper to distract me from those big, searching eyes. How could I get the Big Dipper wrong? Never mind the detailed instructions that came with the fake stars. Uncle RB always pointed out the Big Dipper in the night sky at the lake house.

"Are you doing it just to please your mother? Because if you are, then—"

"Why would you think that?" I asked.

"You wear the clothes she wants even though you hate them."

I sat up and leaned against the wall. Her eyes were relentless, studying me, as if I was in the wrong place like the fake Big Dipper.

"I'm not ice skating for Mom," I said.

She sat up and leaned her head right next to mine. Her face, lips were close, too close.

I stood up on the bed and ripped off the stars that formed the Big Dipper. I couldn't stand them in the wrong spot any longer.

After completing levels one and two, Tara and I enrolled in the pairs skating class during the spring. We were excited to finally get to skate as a pair.

Even Mrs. Parks was excited. The class was at a mall in Charlotte. Above all things, Barbie Parks loved to shop.

On our first day, the instructor, Mrs. Tyree, came a few minutes late. She wore bright red lipstick which matched her hair. With an orange tan and fake nails, she was what Uncle RB called "artificially pretty." Back in December, he'd argued with Mom about artificial Christmas trees. He'd gotten us a real one; Mom wanted a fake. Real ones, she'd said, were too much work – not that she had to do any of the work. The only time she made an effort was when Tara came over.

Mrs. Tyree asked us to form two lines, one for boys and one for girls. I skated to the other line, opposite Tara. Mrs. Tyree skated in-between the two lines. She blocked Tara from my view, but not for long. Tara scooted slightly to the right.

"I need you to get in the correct line," Mrs. Tyree said.

Surely Mrs. Tyree could see I belonged with the boys. I was taller than most of them and just as built. I tried smiling at her, but she didn't smile back. She wouldn't look me in the eye. My voice quivered when I said, "I'm in the correct line, ma'am."

Uncle RB always said to be polite. And respectful, especially to women – even when the other person's wrong.

"You need to get in the other line. This is pair skating – boys skate with girls."

"I'm here to skate with her. She's my partner." I motioned to Tara. Mrs. Tyree turned to look at Tara and the whole class giggled, except Tara. Her teeth and fists were clinched.

"Quiet everyone." Mrs. Tyree turned back to me. "A girl can't skate with another girl. It's against the rules."

"I'm here to skate with her," I said, refusing to move.

Tara left her line and skated up to Mrs. Tyree.

"Why can't we skate with whomever we choose? It's a free country, right?" Tara asked. "You're contradicting what we learn at school."

"This is pairs skating, not a history lesson. You can either respect the rules or leave this class."

All Tara and her mom ever talked about was how

she'd be a great figure skater one day. She'd shown me a timeline for when she'd make state, then nationals, then the Olympics. Last month, she'd added my name to the timeline. We're a team, she'd told me, and not even broken bones or blindness would keep us off the ice. She'd made me pinky swear. If I walked out of class, she'd follow me.

The class and Mrs. Tyree were staring at Tara now, too. They were looking at both of us like something was wrong.

I skated to the end of the girls' line, away from Tara, opposite the boys. She tried to get my attention, but I kept my head down. She'd thank me later.

Mrs. Tyree began class by having us partner up. A boy, thicker and shorter than me, motioned for us to skate together. He was an okay skater, not that I paid much attention. My eyes rarely left Tara and the broad-shouldered guy she skated with. He wasn't able to lift her. He didn't even try. Would he do not one, but two hundred push-ups every night before bed for the sole purpose of one day being able to lift her like I had? Doubtful.

As soon as class was over, Tara went to a bench and removed her skates. Mrs. Parks would be a while. Dillard's was having a huge spring sale. We'd heard all about it on the way to the rink.

"What are you doing?" I said. "It's our time to practice."

She threw her skates across the floor and yelled, "So you want to skate with me now that everyone is gone?"

She was mad at me? But I went to the other line for her.

"Why didn't you skate with me in class?" she

asked. "I thought you liked skating with me."

"I do." I sat next to her on the bench. "She wasn't gonna let us." Tara should be mad at the teacher, not me. "You need to practice." With a boy, I thought. A tiny ball of anger worked its way around my gut. "So you can become a champion figure skater. That's what you want."

"No. That's what my mother wants. She wanted to be a figure skater – not me. Her knees were too bad, so lucky me. Last week, I overheard her praying that I wouldn't grow any taller or gain more weight. She won't even let me order the hot fudge cake at Shoney's. That's my favorite dessert, Peyton! The only thing I enjoy about coming here is skating with you."

I stood up and skated onto the ice, thinking about what she'd just said. The ice felt shaky beneath me. I had to bend over and put my hands on my legs to steady them.

"Get your skates back on," I said and held out my hand. "I'll show you how much better I am than that guy you were with in class."

Tara didn't move for several seconds. She stared out at the ice like she wanted to melt it.

Finally, she shoved her feet in the skates and laced them. She held onto my hand and let me pull her up from the bench. "I already know you're better. He breathes funny."

I wondered if she noticed his breathing only because whenever we skated together, I was so afraid of disappointing her that I held my breath.

The next day, while I packed to spend the night at Uncle RB's, the phone rang. I was still in a good mood from the night before. On the ride back from skating in Charlotte, Tara and I had played punch buggy, although Tara called it slug bug. I'd never tell her, but for a girl, she hit real hard. My arm was a little sore, but I didn't mind. The ache reminded me of her.

Two minutes later, Mom's feet pounded up the stairs. She appeared in the doorway of my room, giving me the look of death.

At first, I thought her glare was over the Celtics hat on my head or Uncle RB's old work boots on my feet. The boots were a little big, but my feet were growing into them and they were perfect for hunting. Her stare of death was most likely due to the Marilyn Manson t-shirt.

"Tara gave it to me." I pulled at the shirt so she could take in the whole thing, hoping she'd change her mind because it used to belong to Tara. Some days, it felt like Mom liked Tara more than me.

"That was Mrs. Tyree. She said that you," she had trouble even saying it. "You insisted on lining up with the boys."

I grabbed some socks from the bottom drawer and tossed them into my backpack. Thank God Uncle RB would be there soon to pick me up.

"Do you mind telling me why my daughter wants to be in line with all the boys?" Mom asked.

Her daughter. Her Katharine Anne.

While searching through a drawer for pajamas, I glanced in the mirror. Was something wrong with my eyes? To me, I looked way more like the boys in line than the girls. Did I just see myself differently?

Mom sat on the bed and sighed. "Please tell me that it's because you have a crush on someone in the class, and you wanted to be closer to him."

Him? I balled up the pajamas and shoved them in

my backpack. Yes, Mom, I wanted to be closer to someone. A girl. Her. Tara.

"Boys don't like it when girls are too aggressive. You need to stand in line with the other girls. Let the boy make the first move."

I zipped up the backpack and headed downstairs to wait. Mom followed.

"Tara is such a sweet girl, and Mrs. Parks is so nice to drive you to Charlotte every week," she said. "What do they think of you standing in the boys' line?"

I pressed my forehead against the screen door. Please Uncle RB, please drive up soon.

"Why can't you be more like Tara?" Mom asked.

Bad enough every thought in my head was about Tara. Now I had to listen to Mom talk about her nonstop, too.

When Uncle RB drove up, I ran out to the car without even waving goodbye.

Chapter 3

That summer, I spent the afternoons helping Uncle RB. Wiley Music was the only store in three counties that sold and repaired musical instruments, so we were pretty busy most of the time. But in late July, the afternoons dragged. A lot of people were on vacation, including Tara.

She'd been gone for most of the summer. First, Mrs. Parks took Tara to stay with her grandparents in Jacksonville. After three weeks there, the whole family went to Orlando.

Uncle RB rigged the front door of Wiley Music so that every time it opened Martha & the Vandellas's "Dancing in the Street" played. The week Tara was due back, I jumped every time I heard the song. When I picked up the Windex, the color reminded me of her eyes. I'd set the bottle down quickly and focus on giving the front windows a good clean, attempting to remove every speck of dust, every fingerprint, every uncomfortable thought of Tara. Throughout eighth grade we'd grown closer, but it hadn't happened without a nervousness also growing in my stomach. It was kind of like watching a scary movie. Things were going too well. Something bad had to happen.

After washing the windows, I shined every harmonica in the counter display. With nothing left in the front part of the store to clean, I sat on an amp in the guitar section and played the riff to "Eruption" over and over. Two college kids from Duke who heard me play it in the store had said it was almost as good as Eddie. They had to know what they were talking about – they attended *Duke*.

Finally, "music, sweet music" brought Tara

through the door, although I pretended not to notice. I looked down at the floor – not at her and not at the guitar. I wanted her to notice how my guitar playing had become so advanced I didn't have to look at my hands. She listened until my version of "Eruption" was finished.

I finally looked up. She had on cut-offs and an Orange Crush t-shirt. Her usual pale skin was pink in some spots, red in others. She held a small wrapped box.

"That solo is just Eddie showing off," she said. "Dad calls it artistic masturbation."

I put the guitar down and turned off the amp. Great, she thought I was a show-off, too.

"I got you a present." She grinned, waving the box.

Uncle RB had given me two tickets to the Rolling Stones, for helping him with yard work at the lake house. I hadn't even thought to wrap it for her. Why did Tara get me a present? What if it was better than the one I had for her?

She tossed the present to me, perfectly wrapped. It blew me away how girls always knew how to wrap gifts.

Inside the box was a metal key chain in the shape of a small license plate. On the very top it said Florida and in the middle, in big letters: Peyton.

"It's even spelled right. Can you believe it?" she asked.

I put my house key on it. "I've got something for you, too."

Tara slipped her hands in her pockets and glanced around the empty store. Uncle RB was in the back re-fretting an electric guitar. I went up to the front counter, wishing I'd at least thought to put her ticket in a box. I pulled both concert tickets out from my copy of *Y: The Last Man*.

"One's for you," I said.

She picked up one of the tickets and studied it. "I've never been to a rock concert."

I sat on the stool behind the cash register because my legs wobbled when I flashed to Tara sitting right next to me at the concert. She'd have to lean over because some creepy, burly dude would be directly in front of her. I'd move a little to share the armrest with her. We'd sit like that all night, our arms touching, listening to the Rolling Stones.

"Tell your mom that Uncle RB's gonna take us. He's bringing a friend, too, and we'll be with them the whole time."

"Okay." She put the ticket back down on the counter.

She was supposed to jump up and down, run around the counter and hug me or something. It was the Stones. Maybe she really had changed in the time she'd been gone that summer.

"So you'll go?" I asked.

"Yes. Of course. Why wouldn't I?"

Uncle RB walked out from the back of the store carrying a '72 Telecaster and held the fret board up to the light. "It's like that son of a bitch let his dog play fetch with it." He grabbed the guitar's case from behind the register and slid it inside. He noticed Tara standing nearby. "Hey Moxie, what's up? How was Florida?"

The first time she'd been in the store, she told him she didn't care if Jimmy Page had sometimes played sloppy because he played with passion, and *passion* was all that mattered. After she left, Uncle RB had said to me, "Now, that's the kinda friend you wanna have around.

She's got moxie."

Tara gave Uncle RB a review of Disney World until a long honk interrupted her. Tara hurried out without even looking back at us.

Uncle RB saw both concert tickets on the counter. "She not coming?" he asked.

"She's coming."

Still, I couldn't help wondering why she left the ticket behind.

Rebecca and Tara and pretty much everyone else in my class were looking forward to high school, everyone except me. I'd just gotten most of the teachers and staff at the middle school to call me Peyton. Dealing with new teachers wasn't going to be fun.

The only thing I looked forward to was that every student got to pick a music elective: band, orchestra, or choir. The choice seemed obvious: choir was for girls, and violins were for geeks.

The approaching Rolling Stones concert was the main thing on my mind when I picked up my schedule and met my new teachers during orientation. It'd been a month since Tara had left her ticket on the counter. She hadn't even bothered to mention the concert.

Auditions for band were at the end of the day and held in the music building. They were held in alphabetical order so I was way ahead of Tara in line. She wasn't even in the music building yet when the band teacher called my name.

"Peyton Honeycutt."

Ms. Matteo was the first and only teacher who got my name right from the beginning. I wondered how she knew. She sat perched on a stool and checked my name off a clipboard she had grabbed from the music stand. She wore an AC/DC t-shirt, faded jeans, and cowboy boots. No one else in Wiley wore cowboy boots in August. Most people wore annoying flip-flops. I hated the squishy noise of flip-flops, the worst sound in the universe. Tara didn't wear them either. She wore sexy, black slip-on sandals with a strap for support.

Ms. Matteo motioned for me to sit down in the chair across from her. The room looked like a zoo of instruments: keyboards, drums, horns, saxophones, and one guitar.

She was younger than my mother, probably Uncle RB's age. She had a wide smile to match her oval eyes. Cue an AC/DC riff, cranking in my head like a motorcycle engine.

"It's nice to finally meet you, Peyton. My band sometimes shares a bill with your Uncle's at Shadows in Charlotte. Though, here at school I try to keep the fact that my band plays in bars a secret." She lifted her index finger to her lips. She wore cotton candy blue nail polish that looked like it could dissolve in my mouth like real cotton candy.

She looked back down at her clipboard while I wondered if Uncle RB had slept with her. "Why do you want to play piano?"

"Because I'm good at it."

I leaned back in the chair and crossed my arms, trying to decide if Ms. Matteo was pretty or not. She wasn't pretty like Tara. Yet there was something about her, dirty blonde hair pulled up, but not neatly. The few free strands were wild and wavy. Like Tara, she chewed gum, something frowned upon in school. Chewing it quickly, she stopped now and then to blow a small, firm bubble, never losing control of it.

"Why don't you show me." She motioned to a piano that leaned slightly, like it was drunk, wood chipped around the edges. The fresh flowers on top made the piano look even older. The yellow keys reminded me of the fake teeth I wore one Halloween for my Hobo costume.

I sat at the bench and launched into Scott Joplin's "Entertainer," the piece I always played at home because it was Mom's favorite. I closed my eyes and played it perfectly, not missing a note.

"Slow," she said.

I stopped and opened my eyes. Ms. Matteo was leaning on the piano, arms folded, biting her lip. Mom would have freaked out. No one leaned on any part of her piano.

"Ragtime should never be played that fast," she said. "Slow it down."

She tapped a slower tempo against the piano. I felt the vibrations, closed my eyes and started from the beginning. I slowed to her rhythm, and a totally different piece emerged. The song was no longer something just to play over and over to keep Mom happy.

I finished and kept my eyes on the yellow keys. Fighting the urge to glance at Ms. Matteo took a lot of effort. No longer able to stand it, I looked up. Her head rested on her arms. With Ms. Matteo so close, I realized Tara wasn't the only girl I found attractive.

"What instrument do you really want to play?"

I leaned back on the piano bench and smiled.

"Drums, but Mom doesn't like them as much. She makes me play up in my room with muffs on them and the door closed. Uncle RB got me a vintage Ludwig kit like John Bonham played."

At the mention of Uncle RB, Ms. Matteo's smile grew. "It's important to pick the right instrument, one you feel passion for. Otherwise you'll lose interest."

That damn word again, passion.

Ms. Matteo walked back to her music stand. I followed, noticing a Washburn acoustic in its case. Washburn guitars had the warmest sound, according to Uncle RB.

"Do you like jazz?" she asked.

I nodded even though I'd never played those records in Uncle RB's collection: Miles Davis, John Coltrane, Nina Simone.

Ms. Matteo asked me to play something on the drum kit in the back of the room. I did a few seconds of my best impersonation of Bonham's famous "Moby Dick" drum solo - all moves Uncle RB had shown me.

Ms. Matteo laughed. She had a husky laugh, even lower than her speaking voice.

"Not jazz," I said. "But one fine piece of music."

"I think you'd be a nice fit on drums in Jazz Band. How does that sound?"

"Like music, sweet music," I said, imitating Uncle RB.

"That reminds me - will you please convince your uncle to take out that crazy doorbell at the store? I love that song and want to keep it that way."

While she signed my orientation form, I wondered why I'd never seen her in the store. I'd worked every afternoon over the summer - unless she came by later, closer to closing time.

She handed me the form. "See you Friday, then."

"You mean Monday."

"No, I'm going with you to the Stones." She turned back to the music stand and scribbled on a notepad, like it was no big deal that I would be going on a double date with my new band teacher.

After my audition, I found Tara and Rebecca outside. They were huddled together near the picnic tables, whispering. My thoughts still bounced from Jazz Band to drums, from Ms. Matteo to the Rolling Stones. From a supervised concert with Uncle RB to a date.

"He's not the type of guy I'm supposed to like," Rebecca said. She fanned herself with her freshman orientation folder.

"What type are you *supposed* to like?" Tara asked.

Rebecca hesitated, looking around. It's like she didn't see me standing there. Neither one of them did. Tara touched Rebecca's arm and said, "All that matters is that you like him."

I looked around, trying to find the object of their attention, but the only thing around was a mosquito trying to get at me. Thankfully, summer was almost over. No more bugs, no more heat, no more several days in a row without seeing Tara.

"If I tell you, you have to swear not to tell anyone," Rebecca said. "Not even your diary."

Tara nodded. Rebecca finally looked at me.

"I swear," I said.

"Sammy Evans," Rebecca said, more to the ground than us.

"Oh, he's cute," Tara said.

I grunted. When she called me that summer all she talked about was cute fingernail polish she'd found at the mall, cute sandals her mom wouldn't buy her, cute handbags she couldn't afford. Cute was a stupid word. If Tara insisted on using it, I wanted her to be talking about me.

Tara shot me a look. "He *is*."

Rebecca sat on top of a picnic table. "He plays basketball every day in the park near my house. He's so good."

"I bet he makes varsity this year as a freshman," Tara said.

"I hate sports," Rebecca said. "I just like watching him, the muscles on his arms."

I reached my arms above my head to call attention to them. All summer I'd lifted weights and done push-ups in the hopes that we'd go back to ice skating classes in the fall. Tara and Rebecca both stared at my biceps. They didn't comment, but Tara kept looking long after Rebecca lost interest. Forget cute. What really caught Tara's eye were muscles. My muscles.

A red Jeep zipped into the school parking lot. Tara's eyes widened when Col. Parks got out.

She ran to him and squealed. "Dad!" She looked at him like he was famous or a superhero.

"Were you able to move up your band audition?" he asked.

"Yeah. The band instructor's cool. She wants me to play guitar in Jazz Band."

I didn't know much about jazz, but there seemed to be a lot of guitar solos. That meant Tara would have at least one solo in every song and all eyes would be focused on her.

"That's great, pumpkin."

"I'm playing drums in Jazz Band," I said.

"How 'bout that," Col. Parks said. "You two will be playing together."

I liked the idea of being in the same band as Tara, but why did she have to play guitar? Why couldn't she play French horn? Guys would notice her less if she were stuck behind some large instrument that never had any solos.

Watching her father walk toward me with his shoulders back and chest out, I tried to do the same. Col. Parks gave my hand a firm shake.

"Still enjoying the Celtics hat?"

I nodded. "Yes, sir."

Col. Parks said hello to Rebecca before he and Tara headed for the jeep.

They drove off with "When the Music's Over" blasting. I couldn't help but think that maybe the music really was over. Tara was different, and it irritated me that she didn't seem to care about the concert at all.

The day before the Rolling Stones, the door to Wiley Music opened. Martha & the Vandellas blared, and there was Tara. She had on a black tank top and my old, bright red corduroys – in late August. Even Mother Nature couldn't tell Tara Parks what to do. I didn't complain. The corduroys fit her nice and snug.

For the first time, Mrs. Parks came into the store. She stood at the door, shopping bags in hand, while Tara approached me at the counter. Mrs. Parks didn't take her eyes off us the whole time.

Tara came so close I smelled her passion fruit lip-gloss. I fought the urge to lick my lips. Her face was redder than the day after she got back from Orlando.

"Hey," she said, like the word weighed fifty pounds. She clicked the counter with her "cute polish" nails from the mall. She glanced back at her mom, who stood stone-faced. "I can't go with you to the concert."

I pressed my hands down on the counter. "Wha –

why not?"

"Dad wants to take us to Hilton Head for the weekend." She kept her eyes on the floor. She didn't bother to look up at me when she said it. She couldn't even give me that. "I'm sorry."

My whole body threatened to collapse. For the first time ever the smell of her lip-gloss made me so nauseous that I stepped back and dropped the packs of guitar strings I'd been restocking behind the counter.

"It's not too late to find someone else." She finally glanced up and smiled a fake smile. "You should ask Rebecca. She'll totally get into Mick Jagger's dance moves."

I didn't care about Mick Jagger's dance moves or experiencing "Satisfaction" live or seeing anything without Tara. I didn't want Rebecca leaning in close, sharing the armrest with me. I wanted Tara.

"Peyton," she said and reached out like she might touch my arm, but stopped herself.

"I need to finish restocking."

"Come on, Tara," Mrs. Parks said. "Let's go."

"In a minute," Tara said to her mother.

They exchanged a look. I couldn't tell if they had planned this together, if Mrs. Parks was in on it, if maybe Tara was using her mom as an excuse because she really didn't want to go. The only thing I knew was that the one thing I cared about wasn't going to happen. That, and I wanted Tara Parks to leave.

Instead, she pulled a slip of paper out of her pocket and slid it across the counter. "This is the name of those pink guitar picks I wanted."

Pink guitar picks? The nerve of this girl.

"Please," she said. She pushed the paper across the counter. The corner scratched my arm.

"Just leave it." I turned back to the box, restocking, moving fast so she couldn't see the strings shake in my hands.

"Make sure you get the order in, today if possible."

I slammed a pack of guitar strings down on the counter. "I'll do it. Unlike you, I do what I say."

Martha & the Vandellas played. The next time I glanced up, Tara and Mrs. Parks were gone and Uncle RB stood at the counter.

"You okay?" he asked.

I wanted to yell and cry and tell him what had me so upset. Instead, I nodded.

Uncle RB picked up the note on the counter and unfolded it.

"The princess wants special pink guitar picks," I said. "Medium size with a built-in grip." I wanted to walk back to the acoustic room and take the most expensive Martin guitar, the one Tara liked to strum, and smash it into a billion pieces.

Uncle RB didn't react. He read the note, put it back on the counter and pushed it toward me. "Try not to be too disappointed. Parents get all wrapped up in protecting their kids and sometimes they make the wrong call on things. We'll bring her back a T-shirt."

I threw a stack of guitar strings back in the box. What was Mrs. Parks protecting Tara from? Early onset hearing loss? Uncle RB had earplugs. All she had to do was ask! "A T-shirt?"

"Read the note," Uncle RB said.

He went back to the repair room and I looked down at the note left unfolded on the counter. Written in black magic marker on the top was "Pick Boy medium pink." On the bottom of the note, written in pencil:

Peyton,

Mom won't let me go. She says I'm too young even with a chaperone. Dad tried to reason with her. I begged her. I'm so sorry. I wanted to go.

Please don't hate me

– Tara

I re-read the note twenty times. It didn't make sense.

I didn't hate her. I couldn't hate her. If she wanted to go with me to the concert, nothing would have stopped her. The girl wore corduroys in August.

Her mother was just an excuse.

I picked up the phone and ordered the stupid pink guitar picks.

Chapter 4

In October, two months after *not* going with me to the Rolling Stones, Tara Parks sat in Jazz Band, playing the guitar all wrong. First, she held her new pink pick upside down, strumming the strings with the fat end. Her dad said it would give the guitar a thicker sound – and it did. She always drowned out everyone else, even my kick drum. Once, Ms. Matteo asked her to turn down her amp.

Tara had saved her allowance to buy an expensive Marshall amp, the kind heavy metal guys used. I pounded the drums hard, wanting to be louder than her. No matter how much time had passed, I still didn't understand why the girl who wore corduroys in August wouldn't defy her mother and go to the concert. Deep down, I believed she just didn't want to go with me.

Even the way she played chords was annoying. Her fingers were long, but pencil thin. So instead of playing bar chords, she played chords in strange places down the neck, not where the beginner's book told her to play them. Ms. Matteo never corrected her. She actually praised Tara for playing chord variations. It was like because they were both girls and musicians, they'd formed some secret society or knew something I didn't, which pissed me off.

The thing that got me the most was when she played the wrong notes, like the day she had to play the Charlie Christian solo. No one noticed that Tara played the wrong notes. Ms. Matteo tapped along with that girl conspiracy smile even though Tara's solo sounded like shit.

"Great solo, Tara," Ms. Matteo said when it was

over.

You've got to be kidding me. "*How* is it a great solo? She didn't even play the right notes."

Ms. Matteo stared at me. "She's playing in the same key. It's called improvisation. We haven't gotten to it in our lessons yet, but it's an important component of jazz."

"But the notes weren't right," I said.

"It's not a matter of right or wrong. It's about key and mood."

Ms. Matteo's response sure put me in one. Tara glanced over, but I wasn't giving her the satisfaction of acknowledgment. Not after she ditched the concert.

I tore out of the room when the bell rang, thankful it was the last class of the day.

Tara ran to catch up. "What's your problem?" she asked. "It's not wrong just because I play it a different way. There's more than one way to play the notes."

I kept walking and tried to outpace her.

Rebecca cleared her throat from behind us to get our attention. Tara and I both stopped and turned around, but refused to look at each other.

Mrs. Parks honked impatiently from the cul-de-sac where the parents who couldn't be bothered with the school parking lot picked up their kids. Tara said goodbye and sprinted off.

Go, go, go Tara Parks, with your wrong notes and your bouncy blonde hair and your autumn sweater that made me crave caramel apples and your red corduroy jeans that were getting too tight for your curves. If I noticed, other guys had probably noticed, too. I didn't exhale until her mom's SUV was out of sight.

"What are you doing right now?" Rebecca asked.

"Nothing," I said and headed the six blocks

toward home.

Rebecca followed at my heels. She whistled or tried to, but it sounded more like a dying cricket. Thankfully, after a couple minutes, she stopped. "Want to come with me to watch Sammy play?" she asked.

I removed my hands from my pockets and walked faster.

Rebecca almost had to run to keep up. "I was hoping you'd find out if it's true that he kissed Yolonda Livingston at the recreation center's Fourth of July party."

"Who cares?" All I wanted to do was go home and figure out how to improvise on drums.

Rebecca grabbed my arm and yanked me around. Her eyes were watery. I could never tell if she was really upset or producing tears to get what she wanted.

"I care. Yolonda's a junior. She's probably kissed lots of boys. If they kissed, I need to know. I'll have to practice so I'm better than her."

Rebecca's competitive nature made me laugh. She grinned and magically her tears disappeared.

"Help me with Sammy, and I'll help you fix things with Tara," she said.

At the mention of her name, all that anger shot up again. "Who says things need to be fixed?"

"She thinks you're still mad about the concert."

I was still mad about the concert. More than anything, it bothered me how much I'd wanted her to go, how much I wanted to sit close to her. Now when would I have the chance?

Rebecca took a deep breath in and an even slower one out, her nostrils doubling in size. She stood so close that whatever perfume she was wearing made my nose itch.

I kicked at a rock, but it ended up being attached to some bigger iceberg rock under the dirt. My big toe throbbed and took away some of the anger at Tara. I wanted to fix things with her, but I didn't know how. Every time I saw her, that abandoned ticket on the counter flashed through my mind. "How would you go about fixing things, anyway?"

Rebecca grinned. "Just ask your mom if you can spend Saturday night at my house."

"How's that gonna fix things?"

Rebecca sighed. "I'll invite her, too, you moron."

I hadn't spent the night with Tara since we'd quit ice skating last spring. She claimed weekends were the only time her whole family got to be together, but like the concert, I wondered if it was just another lie.

"Fine," I said and tried to act nonchalant. But the idea of a slumber party with Tara was irresistible to me and Rebecca knew it.

True to my word, I went with Rebecca to watch Sammy play basketball. When I saw him, I got why Rebecca had been nervous about saying anything. Sammy was black. A lot of people at our school and in Wiley would have a problem with a white girl liking him. But I got what Rebecca and Tara had been going on about. Sammy had muscles and one of those chiseled faces you'd find on statues at museums.

Not one to just sit around and watch, I ended up playing with him and even went back the following afternoon without Rebecca. She elected not to go, sending me alone on her fact-finding mission.

Sammy and I practiced layups on the city park's basketball court. He made nearly every one. I made one out of three, but that was better than the day before.

The ball hit the rim and bounced away from the basket. A rare miss for Sammy. He sprinted after it.

I didn't want to like Sammy because Rebecca and Tara did, but there was something about him. I didn't like him the way Rebecca did. I wanted to *be* him. I wanted his muscles and broad shoulders and hoped that practicing basketball with him would give me round biceps like his.

After about forty minutes of layups, we took a break and hit the vending machine. The cold Cheerwine and shady bench felt good after working up a sweat. I was happy just to sit there with him in silence, but remembered why I was there. What was the big deal about a silly kiss? It's not like they went all the way or something.

"Why the sudden interest in basketball?" he asked.

"I thought maybe I'd try out."

"No shit?"

I nodded, thinking about Tara and Rebecca up in the bleachers watching Sammy and me at the games.

"You keep coming here, and we'll get you ready. Bet you make girls' varsity," he said.

My last sip of Cheerwine nearly came out through my nose. Girls' team. That's where they'd make me play, just like with ice skating.

Why did I feel so different from how other people saw me?

Sammy scrunched up his Cheerwine can, interrupting my thoughts. He tossed it into the trash and stood up. Tara probably saw me, like Sammy did, as someone for girls' varsity. Bet she never thought about kissing me the way Rebecca wanted to kiss Sammy.

"Have you ever kissed a girl?" I asked.

Sammy sat back down and smiled. "I thought there was another reason you were coming here."

He worked fast, his hands on my arms, pulling me to him. His grip was strong, lips tight on mine. He smelled like metal and sweat. For a few seconds, I thought maybe this was what kissing felt like, a tongue thrusting and thrashing around in my mouth like a goldfish out of its bowl, flopping around, sucking in its last breath. I didn't feel anything except tongue. My heart didn't speed up and there was no ache like when Tara undressed that day she and I first met in the bathroom.

My throat closed up. I couldn't breathe. Finally I did feel something: my sandwich from lunch pushing its way up my throat. I pushed him off, pretending to be annoyed that he'd knocked over my Cheerwine. I'd never be able to drink the stuff again without being reminded of Sammy's tongue in my mouth, tasting of cherries and sugar.

"I'll get you another one." He held his hands out to apologize.

"I'm not thirsty anymore." Part of me felt bad, but another part was disturbed by it all.

He sat still on the bench, like he wasn't sure what to do next.

Wanting to get the hell out of there, I asked, "Did you and Yolonda Livingston kiss last summer?"

"Yeah, but it was nothing. Honestly, most girls get on my damn nerves," he said. "Not you, though."

I tossed my empty can into the trash, grabbed my backpack and made some lame-ass excuse about needing to get home to help Mom peel potatoes. I didn't look at him. I didn't want to think about him. All I wanted was out.

That night, I told Rebecca he'd said kissing Yolonda was no big deal. I didn't tell her about Sammy kissing me. I wanted to forget about the whole stupid thing.

On Saturday, per instructions, I showed up at Rebecca's house thirty minutes after she'd sent a text saying that Tara had arrived. Rebecca said Tara would be anxious to see me.

I wanted to know why, but didn't ask. I didn't want Rebecca going back and telling Tara that I cared. Tara hadn't talked to me all week, not even in Jazz Band when Ms. Matteo made us partner up and work out a new song together.

Both Tara and Rebecca were always making lists of things to do, books to read, movies to see. I made a mental list of things I did not understand about girls:

1. Why do girls make lists?
2. Why do they keep diaries?
3. Why does it matter when a person shows up?

Still, I showed up when Rebecca told me to and found them huddled around the kitchen table. The Uno cards were still in the box so they'd been talking, probably about me, which made me nervous. After I walked in, Tara shuffled the cards and Rebecca grabbed the pizza out of the oven. Tara didn't glance over at me once through two rounds of Uno. She won both times.

After Mrs. David went to bed, Rebecca, Tara and I took turns brushing our teeth. When we passed in the hallway, Tara practically slid against the wall to keep from touching me. What had her panties all in a wad?

Everything in Rebecca's room was Pepto-pink, including a lacy bedspread that made my legs itch. Even her bookshelf was pink.

Rebecca locked the door. "Now we can practice."

"Okay," Tara said. "But Peyton's the boy."

My eyes shot over to Tara. Was she serious or making fun of me? I buried my hands inside my back pockets so Rebecca and Tara wouldn't see them shaking.

Rebecca applied hot pink lipstick and fluffed her curly, brown hair.

"A kiss is nothing. You don't need to practice," I said. Tara was probably a great kisser. It would be one more thing she was better at, like ice skating and improv.

But they both acted like I'd just told them the earth didn't really exist.

Tara flipped her hair back over her shoulder. "Fine. I'll be the boy."

If we'd been in a cartoon, my eyes would've popped out of my head.

Tara squared her shoulders and attempted to walk all macho over to Rebecca. "Hey Rebecca," she said in a low voice. "What's going on?"

"Oh Sammy." Rebecca put her arms up around Tara's neck. "You're so handsome. I just can't stand it."

Tara tilted her head one way, and Rebecca tilted the other way. They closed their eyes and kissed.

My stomach got tight the way it had when Tara undressed in the bathroom stall. I took my sweaty palms out of the pockets of my jeans and crossed my arms.

They kept on going. Jesus, did Tara treat everything like an Olympic sport?

Finally, Tara pulled away. When she opened her eyes they were on me, like they were asking, "Truth or dare?" – like it was all some game.

"Wow," Rebecca's eyes popped open. "I didn't realize all the things you could do with your tongue. Where'd you learn that?"

Done, I grabbed my backpack and left Rebecca's room. I hurried out the front door as quietly as possible. A crisp October day had turned into a windy, bitter night. I'd left my jacket inside, but wasn't going back. After being in Rebecca's stuffy room, the cold air cooled my anger.

Rebecca's house was on the other side of town from mine, but it didn't matter. I could walk and cut through the park where Sammy had kissed me. Everything seemed so unfair. I didn't want to kiss Sammy.

I wanted to kiss Tara.

A hand tugged my arm. "Peyton."

I didn't want to stop, but my legs wouldn't listen to my brain. They halted to her touch. "I can't stay here with you and —"

"Do you really hate me that much?" Tara's cheeks and forehead were all mashed up. Tears flooded her eyes.

"How can you kiss Rebecca like that?"

"You just said kissing was no big deal." Her eyes stayed on me while she fought to hold in the tears. The wind blew her blonde hair across her face, and she moved it out of the way. One stubborn strand stuck to her lips. It took Tara three times to get the rebel hair to stay back behind her ear. I was jealous of that strand of hair, of Rebecca.

"You like kissing her?" I asked.

A dog barked from one of the neighbor's

backyards. Birds went flying and a trash can tipped over. It sounded like we'd woken every animal in the neighborhood.

Tara wouldn't answer, clearly into torturing me.

"Do you pose like magazine models for her, too?" She shook her head, but still said nothing.

I had to ask again. "Do you like kissing Rebecca?"

"It's *pretend*," she said.

"Like the day in Wiley Music when you pretended for your mother?" I folded my arms across my chest and not because it was cold.

"I knew it! This is still about the Rolling Stones. What is the big deal with that concert? It's not like they're your favorite band. You're acting like I missed Led Zeppelin with Bonham back from the dead."

She remembered that Led Zeppelin was my favorite band. That was something, but I was still pissed. "You could've demanded to go, stood up to her."

"Like you stand up to your mother when she asks you to wear make-up and clothes you hate?"

She was right. I'd always given in to my mother when she cried or threatened to take something away, like spending the night at Uncle RB's. Before Dad left, when I didn't give in at first and take piano lessons like she wanted, she'd blamed him and his Led Zeppelin records, yelling at him that he was a bad influence on me.

Had Mrs. Parks done the same? What did she threaten to take away from Tara?

I put my arms around her and she fell into me, soaking my t-shirt with her tears. All the nervousness I had felt about being close to her washed away when I held her in my arms. Holding her felt right, good – too good.

Spending more time with her felt right, too. The following Monday Tara showed up at the park with Rebecca after school to play basketball with Sammy and me. We played for two hours, before Sammy had to leave early for his sister's piano recital. Rebecca said she needed to get home, too.

Tara threw the ball right at my chest. "Guess that means one on one."

I dribbled and tried to suppress a grin. Tara swiped the ball, running around me for a lay-up.

"You're serious," I said.

"Always."

We played hard, slamming into each other while the sun set through the trees. The crickets chirped, the sprinklers hissed and the scent from a wood-burning stove mingled with the crisp fall air.

Dinnertime had passed and I was hungry, but I wasn't stopping until Tara did. We were playing more physically than we had with Sammy. When Tara had the ball, she kept digging her shoulder into my chest. When I had the ball, she kept both arms raised and her chest out. Every time I tried to dribble around her, she'd move and my body would slam into her chest. The contact should've hurt, but each jab awakened that ache.

Tara insisted on keeping score. I'd pulled within two points of her lead. Determined to stay ahead, she planted her feet in front of me. I backed up, dribbled a couple times, and tried to run past her. She jumped in my path, refusing to move. We both went down, Tara on the cement, me on top of her.

"You okay?" I asked.

"Yeah."

At least she didn't hit head-first, but I held up three fingers just to make sure. "How many?"

"Three. I'm fine."

Almost every inch of my body pressed into hers, her hipbones on mine, her breasts against my chest. She didn't make any effort to push me off.

"You're sure?" I asked.

"Yes."

Even through my sweatshirt, I felt the heat of her hands on my lower back. I also felt heat in another area, the same place as that day in the bathroom. Her heartbeat hammered in the center of my chest, and I smelled the sweetness of Cheerwine on her breath, erasing any thought of Sammy when it came to that soft drink.

My head jerked up at the sound of a car. I pressed my hands on the court, on either side of her and pushed myself up.

"It's just a car," she said.

"I know." I held out my hands to help her up, but she wouldn't take them.

She stood slowly. "You jumped up like someone was shooting at us."

The too-good ache from being on top of her spread to my whole body. My fingers and legs twitched. I didn't know it was possible for something to feel this good.

Tara stood there like she was waiting for me to do something, so I grabbed the basketball for some more one on one.

She glanced at her cell phone. "I should get home." Her voice sounded tight – in a way I'd never heard. I didn't know why she was pissed and was too afraid to ask.

"Want me to walk you?"

"No, thanks." She walked off the court without a glance back.

I followed, annoyed that she'd said no, and stayed a good three blocks behind her as she walked home. I told myself that I wanted to make sure she got there okay, even though Wiley wasn't exactly a crime hotspot. The truth? I didn't like watching her walk away from me.

The following week, I caught Tara crying at her locker. She tried to hide it, but when I demanded to know why she was upset she told me we needed to go somewhere private. I suggested the bathroom. She shook her head and whispered to meet her in the band storage room during lunch.

The music building was completely empty. When I got to the cramped storage room she stood there crying, surrounded by a bunch of dusty music stands and broken, abandoned instruments.

She put her arms around my neck. "Dad's being transferred. We're moving to Germany."

"What? When? How soon?" Even though I knew it was always a possibility I hadn't thought about her moving. Like death, it was too big, too scary to consider.

"Next month." Tears poured out the corners of her eyes. "I don't want to go."

She didn't move when I touched her face so I took a step closer and she leaned into me. Her soft hair rested against my face. What would school, Jazz Band, my life be without Tara Parks? My goal when I'd met her had been simple: get her to like me. But she meant so much more to me now. Instead of a goal in my life, she'd become my life.

She lifted her head from my shoulder. I fought the impulse to step back, to push her away. More than that, more than anything, I wanted to kiss her. But I was afraid. Not just afraid of screwing up, afraid of what it would mean, afraid of what it would look like in the eyes of other people, the same people who'd be disgusted by Rebecca liking Sammy.

Her eyes waited. How much time did I have? This was it. I had to make my move. I ran my thumb along her soft cheek and her body relaxed into mine.

The kiss was a little rough at first with our teeth smacking into each other. But after a few seconds, we worked together. Our tongues danced in a circle around each other. She tasted minty fresh, like her current favorite gum, Wrigley's Doublemint.

Leaning into her, my whole body shook until I thought it was going to explode into hers. After a while, we stumbled back a bit and knocked over a music stand. Tara jumped when the stand hit the floor. Seconds later came that booming laugh of hers. Thankfully, no one else was in the music building.

She smiled and rubbed her thumb under my lip. "Still think a kiss is nothing?"

I responded by kissing her again.

Chapter 5

The next day, Tara sent another text asking me to meet her in the band storage room. By the following week, no text was needed, and I'd bought a family-sized pack of Doublemint.

The only thing I remember clearly about those two weeks in November were the kisses we shared in the storage room. Every other moment got in the way. I lived two lives. One drab: classes, meals, sleep. The other wild: Tara and I sharing a symphony of kisses, some harsh, some soft, surrounded by music stands and instruments. Before the room became our meeting place, the broken instruments and empty cases seemed sad to me. Now, the round edges of the cases seemed to smile. They welcomed us, new friends who wouldn't judge why we were there.

I was careful not to move my hands too much. It's not that I didn't want to explore the regions of Tara, like those three moles on her belly, but I was terrified she'd want to do the same with me. I hated the little nubs on my chest and was convinced Tara would hate them, too.

One afternoon, while kissing a favorite spot at the base of her neck, I noticed goose bumps on her arms and ran my hand over her skin.

"Want my jacket?" I asked.

She shook her head and blushed. "I'm not cold."

"Oh."

She took my hand and for the first time pulled me down to the floor. We had always kissed standing up. I went to kiss her again, but she moved her head. I kissed her cheek, her neck, wondering if something was wrong.

"I'm moving in less than two weeks," she said.

"All the more reason." I worked my way down her neck. I didn't want to think about it. And the only time I didn't think about it was when we kissed.

"It's like you don't care that soon I'm not going to be here."

I pulled away. "That's not true. That's not true at all." I didn't have a fucking clue how to explain to her how I felt. My body was in a state of emergency; a natural disaster swirled inside, an earthquake, tornado, and tsunami all in one. "You're all I think about."

Her face softened, and in a rare moment of shyness, she glanced away. A soft, half-smile escaped when she looked at me again.

"You'll just move on to someone else … like Sammy."

"What?"

She laughed. "He keeps emailing me about you and asking if you like anyone. He thinks he scared you off when he kissed you in the park."

I sat back on my hands and wondered if she got jealous or even cared that someone else liked me. "Please don't tell Rebecca."

She made a zipping motion across her lips and laughed again. Clearly, she needed it so I laughed along, okay with being the butt of her joke.

"What do you say when he asks if I like anyone?"

"That you and I don't talk about that kinda stuff." Her face tensed again, "which was true until now."

This time while we kissed, I couldn't shake a creeping nervousness. It felt like the instruments and cases were watching, shaking their heads, warning: It's a good thing she's moving because it would never be enough. I would never be enough.

The next day, walking to the band room during lunch, I tried pushing away all thoughts of never being enough.

"Hey, Peyton." Ms. Matteo lifted her head from her desk.

Salad, fruit, and juice were spread out on her desk. It took several seconds before I said hello back because it was strange to see her there at that time of day. She usually ate lunch in the teachers' lounge. I couldn't ask what she was doing in the music building considering that's where she had all her classes. The door to the band storage room, behind her desk, was closed.

"Class isn't for a couple of hours. What brings you here?"

Before I could answer, we both turned at the sound of footsteps.

All the color vanished from Tara's apple cheeks when she saw Ms. Matteo. She didn't even look over at me.

"Peyton and I needed a place to study for our algebra exam." It knocked me out how fast Tara came up with an excuse.

Ms. Matteo's eyes moved like a metronome back and forth from Tara to me. She was no fool. Thankfully, she didn't call us out on it.

"You're welcome to work here. I'm just grading tests for marching band, but you two shouldn't skip lunch. It's not healthy."

Tara and I walked down the empty hall to the cafeteria in silence. Our footsteps echoed off the walls like there were two pairs of us walking. It made me think about how we had this secret, double life. Maybe Tara was thinking the same thing. She reached over to hold my hand.

Even though no one was around, I worried about all the names our classmates would call Tara and me if they found out about the storage room. She looked like I'd slapped her when I slipped my hand in my pocket, then she sped up to walk ahead of me.

"Tara. Wait."

"No. Forget it."

"It's just – if someone sees," I said and grabbed at her arm.

She dodged my hand and walked faster. "Who gives a fuck?"

She ignored me the whole time we stood in the lunch line. Across the lunchroom, Rebecca sat with Sammy and his friends, entertaining them with one of her stories. Some kids had begun to call Rebecca ugly names because she and Sammy were friends. She pretended not to care, but when we were alone one night at her house, she'd cried real tears – there was no mistaking that – and confessed that it bothered her. But here she was, still sitting with him. I was amazed she could withstand it. I looked over at Tara, not sure I could.

Our presence gave Rebecca an even bigger audience, which made her happy. Sammy insisted I sit next to him. Thankfully, he knew about Rebecca's crush on him so he never talked to her about his crush on me. He looked at Tara then back at me.

"Where have you two been?" Sammy asked.

"They've been skipping lunch to work on an extra credit project for Jazz Band, writing a song together," Rebecca answered for us.

"I'd love to hear it." Sammy looked right at me when he said it.

Thankfully, Rebecca went on with some story about seeing some famous actor while in Charlotte with her mom.

Tara sat right across from Sammy and smirked. She reveled in how uncomfortable Sammy's crush made me.

I tried not to look at her. She didn't make it easy. Eating her chicken noodle soup slowly, she held the spoon just below her lips, blowing on it. I tried not to think about those lips, what they'd be doing if Ms. Matteo didn't have grading to do.

She nodded her head toward Rebecca. "Look at Rebecca, not me," the nod said, but I wanted to look at her. I wanted to hold her hand in the hall. That's when the thought I kept pushing away came back again: It was a good thing she would move soon. What we were doing in the storage room, always confined to one room, wasn't enough for me either.

I pushed the thought away again. As scared as I was of what would happen if she stayed, of the kissing leading to other things, I was even more terrified of a life without Tara Parks.

The next day the storage room was locked, probably by no fool Ms. Matteo, so Tara and I met in the bathroom during lunch. She sat on the floor making a list. I closed the handicapped stall door and sat next to her. The list had some of her clothing items on it, some books. I got the feeling there would be no kissing today.

"What's the list for?"

"I'm running away on Friday, and I want you to

come with me."

My first thought was if we ran away together we could kiss all the time. There was no second thought.

"Uncle RB's lake house. We could go there. I know where he keeps the spare key."

Uncle RB also had a small apartment above the music store. Lately, he'd been spending all his time there because Ms. Matteo preferred it to the lake house.

Tara bombarded me with questions. How long were we going to stay at the cabin? Won't Uncle RB look there first? Where would we go next? Girls. Always asking about the future, always wanting to know what was next. I told her not to worry. I'd come up with a plan. First, we had to get to the lake house.

Tara paused from making her list. "Okay. Tell your mom you're spending Friday night with me. Put all the clothes and snacks you can fit into your backpack. How much money do you have?"

After paying for electric, heat, phone, and groceries, I'd still managed to save some from working at the music store. "About ninety bucks."

Tara tossed her hair back out of her face and grinned. "Great. I have a hundred and fifty."

How did she have more than me? She didn't even have a job. But she also didn't have to use her money for bills and groceries. Col. Parks took care of all that, like a dad, an adult should. Like I would if I were a dad.

She went back to her list. I was okay with not kissing that afternoon, thinking about how much time we'd have alone together at the lake house. But with all that time, she'd want to do more than kiss. I glanced down at my body. How could she want this? There was nothing to want. Soon, she'd realize I had nothing to give her. Scary as the thought of disappointing her was, of not being enough, the idea of not being with her became more frightening. The fear of losing her outweighed all my other fears.

Tara and I passed the "Thank you for Visiting Wiley NC Come Back Soon" sign.

Every time Mrs. Parks had driven us to ice skating classes in Charlotte, she'd commented on how awful the sign was.

Tara mocked her mother as we walked by it. "What idiot puts up a sign with no punctuation? What example does that set for kids? It makes Wiley look like a town of hicks."

The sidewalk ended and fewer cars came by. The cars that did pass us drove much faster because it was that kind of road. Uncle RB said the road reminded him of a sexy woman. He wanted to rename it something like Curvaceous Way. We sped up, too, as we walked past Dunn's Mountain, site of devil worshipping as some people claimed. I didn't exactly believe the rumor, but it was kind of creepy the way the leafless trees formed a circle around the hill.

Tara and I didn't say much. She just walked, eyes straight ahead with a determined look on her face: She was not going to Germany. We'd be free, like the von Trapp family fleeing over the mountains.

My backpack grew heavy. Still, I offered to carry hers, too, but she insisted on carrying her own. We needed to get to the lake house.

"You know where you're going, right?" she asked.

God, she thought I was an idiot who couldn't

even find my way to a lake house I'd been to a thousand times. "Yeah. Wink's fish camp is coming up on the left. We can get dinner there."

Uncle RB had lots of canned goods at the lake house, but not much else. He'd taught me how to catch, clean, and cook fish, which would be perfect while we stayed there.

Even from half a mile away we could smell the fried fish and hushpuppies, the first whiff of which made me drool. Wink's Fish Camp used to be a hot spot for people itching for something to do on a Friday night. With the live band and square dancing, it was the closest thing we had to a nightclub. Of course, Mom didn't like it because the music was loud and the service was slow. Dad had loved it, and insisted we go about once a week. They always argued through the whole meal, usually about whether we could afford to be there or not. Dad would always say it was pointless to worry too much about money.

I'd heard that some people had stopped going to Wink's because a guy from New York City had opened a bar across the street. Apparently, the good people of Wiley did not appreciate its proximity to a family establishment. People liked to claim that there wasn't a bar within the city limits, even though beer was served at the pool hall on Fisher Street and wine was available at most church functions.

As we walked closer, I studied the bar. There was a Budweiser logo over the door, but no sign with the bar's name. I'd worked on some music store ads for *The Wiley Post* with Uncle RB. That seemed like poor advertising to me.

A truck blasting Lady Gaga pulled into the bar's half-full parking lot. Three well-dressed guys jumped out of the back and headed for the bar. One of them had on a black leather jacket.

A car approached, so we waited to cross the street from the bar parking lot to Wink's.

"Son of a bitch," Tara said.

A red Jeep – Col. Parks's red Jeep – pulled into the fish camp.

He parked next to a minivan, dodging the family exiting it and jumped out, looking right at us. Busted.

"How did he find us?" I asked.

Tara dragged her feet over to him. I followed, not knowing what to expect. What if she was grounded? Would he pull her out of school, not let her finish the last week? What if this was the last time I saw her before she moved? Our chance, my chance to be alone with her at the lake house was gone.

"I thought you were staying on base until tomorrow."

"I finished early," Col. Parks said. "Thought I'd pick up some dinner and surprise your mom."

He wore a dark orange v-neck sweater, jeans, and a baseball hat, which he had pulled down low over his forehead. Something about him seemed off. At first, I thought it was just that I hadn't seen him in a while. But he'd lost weight – a lot of it – and his skin was whiter than the margins of notebook paper.

I waited for him to yell at us for being out in the middle of nowhere or ask what was in the backpacks, but he glanced up and down the street.

"What brings you two out here?" he asked.

"We're getting dinner," I said.

Col. Parks studied our backpacks. He smiled, and I exhaled. Maybe he wouldn't even tell Mom or Mrs.

Parks.

"This got anything to do with Germany?" Col. Parks asked.

Tara kicked at the gravel and grumbled. "I don't want to go. Can't you talk to Mom? Convince her to let me stay. I can live with Manny in Boone."

"Your brother's still in the dorms."

"So?" Tara asked.

"You can't live in the dorm with him."

Tara bowed her head, defeated. Col. Parks glanced across the road at the bar. They both looked sadder than I'd ever seen them. Even worse, families were coming in and out of Wink's, laughing and having a great time together.

"I like it here, too, but you'll make friends in Germany," he said. "We both will."

Tara grabbed my hand. "But Peyton won't be there."

Col. Parks pulled forty bucks out of his wallet. He handed the money to Tara and motioned toward Wink's. "Get enough for everyone, including Peyton."

"I want to get our dinner," I said and reached in my pocket. That was the least I could do if he decided not to rat us out, and the least I could do if he hadn't yet decided.

"I got this one," he said.

Tara let go of my hand and took her father's money. When she opened the door of the fish camp, I heard the clanging of dishes, the screeching of silverware and the roar of excited chatter. I liked Col. Parks, but damn him for leaving work early, surprising Barbie Parks who didn't deserve it, and ruining my plans. Tara didn't want to go to Germany, and I didn't want her to go without me.

"Col. Parks, sir — "

"Call me Joe."

"I have almost a hundred dollars saved. I have a job helping Uncle RB at his music shop. Tara could stay here with me."

Col. Parks got this weird expression on his face like he recognized me from somewhere else. "We need her with us in Germany, especially her mother. It can get lonely in a foreign country."

Funny how mothers always needed us when it should be the other way around. For example, I knew I could get on just fine without my mom, but who'd mow her lawn, go to the store, and help pay the bills if I wasn't around?

The door to the bar across the street flew open. Some guy in a western style shirt, jeans, and cowboy boots walked toward us. He approached Col. Parks like they were old friends.

"Can I help you?" Col. Parks's voice had an edge to it.

The guy's eyes darted from me back to Col. Parks. "Sorry." His voice and smile dropped. "Thought you were someone else," he said and hurried back across the street.

Col. Parks watched him until he disappeared into the bar. His face looked exactly like how I felt about Tara leaving.

I got the sense that I didn't need to worry about Col. Parks telling anyone about Tara and me.

Mrs. Parks was not happy to see us. She was making her way through a bottle of red wine and some cheesy romance novel when we arrived. Tara brushed by her and set out to make a mock fish camp in the dining room, complete with country and western music. Mrs. Parks yanked Col. Parks's arm and led him out of the room.

While washing up in the bathroom, I heard Tara's parents arguing down the hall. I knew better, but I couldn't help myself. Call it habit, whenever my parents would fight I had to listen and be prepared to step in if things got too violent. I stepped near their closed bedroom door to listen.

"So you reward them by bringing *her* back here?" Mrs. Parks yelled. "They should both be grounded."

She didn't even attempt to lower her voice. At least Col. Parks tried to whisper.

"The separation is traumatic enough—"

"They're too close. There's something not right about that girl."

What? Tara was the closest thing to perfect I'd ever seen.

"She dresses like a boy, always in ball caps and those boots," Mrs. Parks said.

I glanced down at my old, beat-up work boots. Shit.

"It's a good thing we're moving. Otherwise, we'd have to send Tara to that Christian school," she said. "I won't have my daughter corrupted by a freak."

I leaned my head back. I hadn't eaten since Tara and I'd left school, but bile inched its way up my throat.

Tara's parents were fighting about me like when my parents used to fight. Except my parents argued about everything, not just me. They argued about bills and how Dad spent too much time and money down at the pool hall. Mom went on and on until Dad finally left.

"She's just a kid. They both are. Christ."

"Don't you dare take the Lord's name —"

I ran back to the bathroom and turned on the sink right before Col. Parks marched by on his way to the kitchen. A few seconds later a door slammed.

Mrs. Parks's words rattled through my head: *Corrupted by a freak. It's a good thing we're moving. There's something not right about that girl.*

How was I corrupting her daughter? No one knew what Tara and I had been up to in the band storage room. Unless Ms. Matteo figured it out and said something. People were going to find out about us. About me.

Mrs. Parks had confirmed what I'd felt all along – not right, different, something bad. A freak.

Maybe Mrs. Parks was right. Maybe I was a freak. Maybe Tara would be better off without me. Dad certainly was. He never came back. He never even called.

Before heading into the kitchen, I splashed water on my face. That's what people always did in movies to make themselves feel better. It didn't help.

Tara and Col. Parks leaned over their plates of fish and hush puppies at the dining room table. They had waited for me before eating. They shouldn't have. Thankfully, Mrs. Parks had stayed in the bedroom down the hall where the door was shut and the lights were off.

"Do you know where hush puppies got their name?" Col. Parks asked.

Tara shook her head. As soon as I sat down, she bit into one.

"Before the Civil War, runaway slaves would put acid in them and feed 'em to the guard dogs so they could escape. Hush the puppies."

I took a bite of one and stared at the rest while chewing. People had to do desperate things sometimes, things they'd never normally do, like poison dogs. They did it to save themselves or the people they loved. I could barely choke down my food.

After we loaded the dishwasher, Col. Parks offered to drive me home because I said I wasn't feeling well.

While her dad was in the bathroom, Tara followed me to the door.

"I know you're not sick. I know you're upset because we got caught. I am, too."

I couldn't look at her.

I walked out to wait by the Jeep. She didn't follow, but I could feel her eyes on me. I needed to do something, something I never imagined doing: Leave her alone.

The following Monday was Tara's last day at Wiley High School. I ignored her texts and went to lunch instead of the band storage room. I couldn't deal with it being her last day or knowing that if she stayed in Wiley her mother would send her to another school. All of it sucked. The worst part was feeling so helpless. Since I couldn't do anything about it, the best thing to do was avoid her.

Jazz Band was the hardest because we sat close to each other. I got there right at the bell. Everyone else was already seated. Ms. Matteo waited for me to get settled.

I found a note folded up on my seat: *You're avoiding me.*

I glanced over at her and lied. "No, I'm not."

Tara stared me down like a hunter and whispered, "Bullshit."

During our music composition test, I noticed small spots of water on Tara's paper. She was crying, and it had nothing to do with the test. No, she was crying because of me, and that made me want to die a painful, slow death – a hush-puppies-made-with-acid death.

After finishing the test, I pulled out a blank sheet of paper. My hand twitched, the pen slipped, my handwriting was terrible.

Thankfully, I knew what to write. I'd stayed up all night thinking about it. But I couldn't remember anything being as hard as writing those words to her. Tara liked lists, so I used that format:

1. What's been going on in the storage room is wrong.
2. It's a bad idea for you to be around me.
3. I think it's probably a good thing you're moving.

I folded the paper and considered throwing it away. But Tara would be better off without me in her life. I handed her the note.

When she read it, her eyes looked like they would burn a hole through the paper. Ten seconds later, her hand shot up.

"Ms. Matteo, I'm not feeling well, can I go to the nurse?"

Ms. Matteo nodded. And ten seconds later, Tara Parks left the building and never returned.

Chapter 6

I spent my sophomore year forgetting Tara Parks. I chucked Col. Parks's Celtics cap under my bed and replaced it with the UNC Tar Heels. I shoved my hair up in it and pulled the bill low on my forehead. I'd outgrown Uncle RB's work boots so he got me a new pair. I wore baggier shirts to hide my slightly bigger anthills, and hung jeans on my hips the way Tara had shown me.

About a month before I turned sixteen, during the early days of January, Uncle RB, Ms. Matteo and I installed a recording studio in the basement at Wiley Music. Ms. Matteo came up with the idea; she had a way of making Uncle RB see things differently, like how the broken pinball machine, wobbly pool table, and empty boxes in the basement were wasting space. With a recording studio, he wouldn't have to pay some novice in Charlotte to record his band, and they could record other bands there. Uncle RB liked the idea of expanding his business. I liked the idea because it was another distraction from Tara. Plus, it meant I'd make more money to help Mom with bills, and have even less time to spend at home.

First, we had to soundproof the basement. We lined the floor and walls with foam. Ms. Matteo said we could do it cheaper by using egg cartons, but the foam would give the studio better acoustics. She'd helped build a recording studio in Chicago while she attended a music conservatory there. Uncle RB didn't like hearing all the details because she'd built the studio with her ex-husband, but I wanted to know everything. She told me the fading sound you hear in a studio after the band hits the last note of a song was called "room decay." I decided right then that's what I'd call my band if I ever had one.

One Saturday evening while Uncle RB and Ms. Matteo installed the glass wall surrounding the vocal booth, I ran out to get us food at this new diner, Know Good, the only place in historic downtown Wiley serving up more than just BBQ or ice cream sodas.

I waited by the door while someone else picked up their order. Every table was full. The place was small, just a square room, and warm. A fireplace on one side of the dining room and a brick oven in the kitchen pumped heat from both directions. I'd heard that the owners, Shelby and LouAnn, had moved to Wiley from somewhere in Georgia. People around Wiley tended not to like outsiders. But if you could cook like Shelby and LouAnn – they made comfort food, *good* comfort food – they'd make an exception. They always gave me extra truffle fries. I didn't know what a truffle was, but it made the fries taste so good.

Still, not everyone liked them. One of the nicer nicknames older people gave them was Ellen and Portia. LouAnn resembled Ellen with super short hair and Shelby sort of favored Portia with longer, blonde hair. If they knew all the stuff people called them – Butch and Sundance, carpet munchers – they didn't seem to care.

I didn't want to be called those things, and it almost made me glad Tara was gone.

LouAnn waved from the kitchen and said my order would be up in two minutes. While waiting and checking my phone, I caught a glimpse of a blonde walking by outside. She wore a thick coat and a hat, but several strands of golden blonde hair had escaped. She was the right height, too.

I ran out of Know Good and raced up to her. "Tara?"

A much older, confused woman turned around. Not Tara.

"Oh," I said and pulled my ball cap down even lower. "Thought you were someone else."

Why was it starting up again? Right after she'd moved, every time I saw a hint of blonde, my stomach flipped. She never came back to class after I gave her the list. Now, over a year later, she lived a thousand miles away in Germany. I'd been by her old house a couple times. Different cars in the garage, blinds drawn, tacky lawn decorations. Someone else lived there now.

Knowing she was in Germany hadn't stopped me from darting out of Wiley Music every time I caught a glimpse of light blonde hair beneath a hood. Never Tara, the girl was always too short or too old or not blonde enough. The walk was never quite right. The deliberate saunter, the way her hips swayed as if to say "we rush for no one" was missing.

All I saw was Not Tara. It hadn't just happened at Wiley Music, but in the grocery store, CVS, the movie theater, the car wash, the laundromat. Every woman was not her. Right after she moved, cold weather brought thick coats, scarves, and hats shielding faces so that even a few guys and tall children were Not Taras. Everyone in Wiley became a disappointment - a bitter, wintry mix of no dimpled chin, no porcelain skin and no apple cheeks. By the end of the season, I'd managed to stop chasing down every hint of blonde, but now it had started up again. I swore, on more than one occasion, she'd walked by the window of Wiley Music. Or maybe I was finally going full-on crazy.

"Peyton? You forget something?"

I turned to see Shelby holding the door and my order, a bag full of three grilled cheeses and fries.

"I was coming back," I said and walked back to the door, where she stood.

She handed the bag to me. "You okay?"

I nodded, but I wasn't okay. I never was after seeing Not Tara. Every time, I felt more depleted than before.

"Too hot in here?"

"No. It's warm and cozy," I said. "Like a home should be."

She smiled. I gave her twenty bucks and told her to keep the change.

As soon as she headed inside, I heard someone snicker. Walking toward me with his usual strut was Jason Webb.

"Of course, *you* eat here," he said. "Takes one to know one – or two, in this case."

My appetite disappeared the second I saw Jason. If Uncle RB and Ms. Matteo weren't starving, I'd have hurled the bag of food at his face.

"Hear the food's not bad. But two women *should* be able to cook something good. What I don't get is what else they do together? I mean, how?" Jason stuck his tongue between his index and middle finger.

I wanted to yank his tongue out of his mouth. No one was ever going to make that gesture about me. I wasn't like Shelby and LouAnn.

Jason grunted and shoved my shoulder with his as he passed.

I looked through the window at Shelby and LouAnn helping a customer select one of their homemade pies. Was that why they were always giving me extra food? Did they think the same thing about me that Jason did?

Ms. Matteo and Uncle RB had mounted the door to the vocal booth by the time I returned. I put the bag on a black and red table they'd found at a yard sale the weekend before that matched the color palette they'd chosen for the recording studio. Black and red was how I envisioned Jason's face after punching it a couple times. No matter what else I focused on, the image of Jason's tongue wouldn't go away.

"Maybe we should start ordering from somewhere else," I said and wrapped my fingers around the back of a chair. I didn't want to go into Know Good and have people think of me like they did Shelby and LouAnn.

Uncle RB pulled all of the food out of the bag. "You find a hair in the fries or something?"

"There's nothing wrong with the food," I said. "It's Shelby and LouAnn. They're not right."

Uncle RB and Ms. Matteo exchanged a look before distributing napkins and packets of ketchup. They sat down and started eating. The smell of the truffle fries filled my nose and my stomach rumbled, but I didn't move. I stood and leaned against the chair. I felt wrong, like a record played backward or a guitar out of tune. Everything I had said felt wrong.

Uncle RB motioned for me to sit like I was a dog who'd misbehaved. He took a bite of his grilled cheese and chewed slowly while his eyes narrowed at me.

"Look, I don't know what kinda crap you've been listening to, but there's nothing wrong with two people – whoever they are – loving each other. Probably why the food tastes so good," he said. "It's made with love."

He exchanged another look with Ms. Matteo. I sat

down, embarrassed, confused, and starving. I took a huge bite of my grilled cheese and almost choked on it. Of course I didn't think there was anything wrong with LouAnn and Shelby, but it felt like there was something wrong with me. Before I'd even swallowed my first bite, the tears came. There's nothing worse than crying while eating. My throat closed up. My tongue grew heavy, not wanting to move, not wanting to taste. Ms. Matteo reached over and put her hand on my arm, making me cry harder.

Uncle RB leaned over and draped his arm around my shoulder. I grabbed a napkin and wiped the tears away.

Uncle RB and Ms. Matteo exchanged yet another look. I started to feel like they'd already had this discussion without me. Ms. Matteo kept her hand on my arm. Uncle RB kept his arm across my shoulder. They both turned their heads down toward the table, like they were praying for me. And I hoped they were – praying for the Lord to save me, to make me normal.

"Peyton, is there something you want to tell us?" Uncle RB asked.

I pulled back from his arm and Ms. Matteo's hand, saying nothing.

"Whatever it is, it's okay," he said.

That's when I knew for certain they had talked and thought the same thing about me as Jason. Uncle RB and Ms. Matteo knew how upset I'd been when Tara couldn't go to the Rolling Stones. They'd seen me try not to cry on the way to Rebecca's house to pick her up for the concert. Ms. Matteo was there when Tara ran out of Jazz Band after reading my list.

Were they right? Something felt off, different.

Was that it? I was attracted to Tara and even Ms. Matteo, but I didn't *feel* like Shelby or LouAnn. I didn't see myself in them. I chewed a little more, but was too upset to taste anything. Not the butter on the grilled cheese or the truffles in the fries.

After a couple minutes of quiet, Uncle RB spoke. "I'm not trying to make you uncomfortable. I just want you to know I love you and if you ever want to talk to me about anything, whatever it is, I'm here and I'm always gonna love you, no matter what. That's never gonna change."

I cried even harder and reached for another napkin. I knew what they wanted me to say – I was like LouAnn and Shelby. At that moment I didn't know exactly why I couldn't, except it didn't feel right.

We were done eating before I could talk. Even when I did, it came out shaky. "I'm sorry for what I said about LouAnn and Shelby. I didn't mean it."

"I know," Uncle RB said.

Before we went back to work, Uncle RB cleaned off the table and Ms. Matteo put John Lennon's *Walls and Bridges* LP on, skipping straight to "Whatever Gets You Thru The Night."

As they sang along and danced, I watched and thought about how most people in Wiley wouldn't agree with them or that song.

For my sixteenth birthday Uncle RB closed Wiley Music early so we could get my license from the DMV. Bad at keeping secrets, Uncle RB let it slip earlier in the week that we were going to Granite Quarry afterwards. His Army buddy's car dealership was the only thing Granite Quarry had that Wiley didn't, save for a public pool – and that was closed for winter.

They'd served in the Gulf War together and greeted each other with a big, burly guy hug, Jeb almost lifting Uncle RB off the ground. Then he motioned for us to follow him out to the lot. Before he put on his coat, I noticed he had the same skull tattoo on his arm as Uncle RB. The tattoo looked better on Uncle RB because of his muscles.

"You're in luck, Peyton. I've got lots of cars that are popular with teenage girls. Over here's a brand-new Honda Civic." Jeb pointed to a white vehicle that looked like every other car on the road.

Uncle RB laughed when I grimaced.

Jeb pretended not to notice and walked over to a car that looked like a giant shoe. "This here Scion xB is a very popular car right now. What do ya say, girl? Want to take her for a spin?" He waved the car key like he expected me to roll over and do tricks for it. When I didn't, he looked to Uncle RB for help.

"See something you like?" Uncle RB asked.

I walked farther on down the lot, past a couple looking at minivans. The wife was pregnant. They looked familiar to me, but so did most people in the county. Beyond the vans were Jeeps, far more appealing than what Jeb had shown me. On the other side of those, something even better caught my eye, the one for me: a dark cherry Ford Mustang Fastback.

I went right to it. Uncle RB and Jeb followed.

"Looks like the one I had before I got my Camaro," Uncle RB said.

"This here's a 1970," Jeb said. "Thought a girl like you'd want something newer, easier."

I shook my head, but couldn't say anything. Each time he said the word "girl," my teeth clamped down harder on my tongue.

Uncle RB grinned and opened the driver's side. The interior was black leather. The car smelled new. The leather felt cool under my fingers.

"It has updated features, a new stereo," Jeb said.

Uncle RB inspected the seats and popped the hood. He tugged on wires and hoses, looked underneath things. I wanted to know this car like he did and learn how to fix her if she broke down. I'd keep every curve clean and polished.

"Want to try her out?" Uncle RB asked.

"Yeah." I already knew she was the one, but I wasn't about to turn down the opportunity to get behind the wheel.

Because they were old friends, Jeb let Uncle RB take the car out with me alone while he tried to sell the couple a brand new minivan. Once we got on I-85, I accelerated to seventy-five miles per hour. I thought Uncle RB might complain, but he had a smile on his face. We got off the highway and pulled into a Food Lion parking lot. We tried out the brakes, windshield wipers, high beams, and A/C. Thankfully, everything worked. I didn't want to leave Granite Quarry without her.

Uncle RB didn't even have to ask. We headed to Jeb's office to sign the forms.

A calendar next to Jeb's desk featured a girl in a bikini reclining on a motorcycle. Spread across the wall behind his desk was the Confederate Flag. There was really nowhere safe to look in that office except down at the worn, shit-colored carpet.

Jeb scribbled some numbers out on a notepad. "So which payment plan would you —"

"No payment plan." Uncle RB pulled out his checkbook and grabbed a pen from the desk.

"I can do monthly payments. I make enough at the store."

"Nope. You need to save up for college. This is it, though. Next few birthdays, it's dinner at Shoney's." He winked at me and handed the check over to Jeb.

The way Jeb held the check, I could tell that few people opted out of a payment plan. He kept looking at all the zeros in the amount box. For a second, I thought I saw drool in the corner of his mouth.

I had to sign some forms because the car was in my name. My handwriting was shaky and not just from the excitement of getting my own car. Jeb stared at my chest while I sat across from him. I glanced down at my Led Zeppelin shirt, jeans, and boots. I tugged at my hat and thought about how all my hair was stuffed up into it. Then it hit me. Jeb kept calling me girl as a dig.

"You still go hunting?" Jeb asked Uncle RB.

"Yeah. Peyton and I go every weekend."

"Really?" Jeb glanced at my chest again. It's like he was looking for something and wondering why it wasn't there.

"We should get a drink some time, catch up," he said to Uncle RB while his eyes were still on me.

Uncle RB stood up behind my chair and didn't respond.

The couple looking at minivans stepped into Jeb's office. Jeb said he'd be with them in a minute and asked them to wait in the lobby. Then, he turned his attention back to Uncle RB.

"'Course we'd have to go to Charlotte." Jeb grunted. "Unless you want to go to that fag bar across from Wink's."

Uncle RB stood still. "I don't like that word." His

voice was calm.

I scribbled my signature on the last form.

Jeb shrugged. "They're taking over Wiley. Two dykes have a diner near your store. I say we go over there and..." Jeb made a pounding motion with his fist.

"Enough." Uncle RB tapped my shoulders. "Let's go."

Jeb motioned toward me. "Oh, come on. She's not a child."

Close enough to hear, the couple glanced in at us. I wanted to tell them not to buy a car from such an asshole, but instead, I grabbed the keys, *my* car keys, off Jeb's desk and walked out with Uncle RB.

In my new Mustang, I followed Uncle RB to Shoney's. My hands gripped the steering wheel while Jeb's words replayed in my head.

We pulled into the parking lot and waited for Ms. Matteo to arrive. Mom had been invited, but she'd said she wasn't feeling well. I was glad she hadn't come, not after what happened. Mom would get upset if Uncle RB mentioned the exchange with Jeb. Sweat from my hands stained the steering wheel. My new car was already dirty.

I stepped outside the car and leaned against it. Uncle RB ran his hand along the side and stared at his reflection in the shiny red paint.

"Sorry you had to hear that back there with Jeb," he said.

"Nothing I haven't already heard." I licked my finger to rub out a spot of dirt on the hood and tried to pretend like the thing with Jeb was no big deal.

Uncle RB leaned next to me. "Well that's the last time we get a car from him."

"But he's your friend." Once again, like with Tara

and her parents, my presence had stirred up trouble. "We served together. We kinda had to be friends." He parted his hair with his hand. "If that couple hadn't been there, I would've really put him in his place. That kind of talk's not right."

I bowed my head.

He cracked his knuckles. "Maybe I should've. But, there's a right time for these things, and that wasn't it."

He waited for me to say something, but I wasn't sure what.

"I feel like I let you down," he said.

No Uncle RB, I let you down. Not just you but Tara, and Mom. Because I can't explain how I'm feeling. Even if I could explain it, this wasn't the right moment. I motioned to my new car. "No way. You just bought me this."

We both stood and stared in awe. Under the parking lot lights at Shoney's, my new dark cherry Mustang shined.

The night before the big game against New Life, I walked into the kitchen and found Mom at the table in a pink bathrobe. She had a stack of Soap Opera Digests, some older than me. The pages had yellowed with age. She was cutting out photos and articles featuring her favorite actors and putting them in a scrapbook. It would've been funny if there wasn't something so sad about it.

"It's the last game of the regular season tomorrow. We play New Life," I said.

After she placed one more picture in the scrapbook, she looked up at me. "You're going to lose."

"Wow. Thanks." I already regretted my decision to invite her.

"New Life is a Christian school so God's on their side. Your team doesn't have a chance."

She went back to cutting another photo of some aging actor still on one of her shows. She focused so intently, careful to cut each side straight.

"If we win, we're in the playoffs. Just thought you might want to come. Uncle RB's going."

At the mention of Uncle RB, the scissors in her hands slipped and she cut into the actor's ear. "Damn it."

I refrained from pointing out that God wouldn't like her swearing.

She slammed down the scissors. "Of course your Uncle's going. He's the one who got you playing basketball."

"I play basketball because I like it."

"I hate basketball. Why would I want to go?"

My heartbeat sped up and jaw tensed. It didn't matter to her at all that the game was important to me, that I'd want her there. Maybe I was an idiot for even asking. I'd been spending more time playing basketball and at the music store because being around her was miserable. The more time I spent away, the angrier she got, especially at Uncle RB. But I couldn't stand it at home with her always in her bathrobe, always in her misery.

I fought the urge to say something hurtful back, something like "No wonder Dad left," but I didn't. Instead, I went back to my room and avoided her for the rest of the night.

My last basketball game of the regular season promised to be a doozy. We were tied in our division with New

Life Christian School. The winner had a chance at State. New Life had been to State before, winning just two years earlier. Our varsity team had never been close to making the playoffs. The Wiley Coyotes – yep, our name – were the underdogs.

Everyone said we were doing so well this year because of me – because I played like a boy. Everyone loved me when I was on the court. Everyone wanted to go to the playoffs. But after the buzzer sounded, it was back to normal. Parents glanced at me and then looked away. Jason and his friends continued to laugh and call me Freakenstein, like it was the funniest thing ever, even though it wasn't all that original.

My teammates weren't much different. It didn't matter if we were in the locker room or on the bus, where the girls braided each other's hair and talked about boys. Everything reminded me that I didn't belong.

It'd been over a month since Uncle RB had asked me if there was anything I wanted to talk about while we ate grilled cheese sandwiches. He hadn't brought it up again. Despite what Jason called me and my teammates not really talking to me off the court, Uncle RB was always there. Every now and then, I'd look up to see him sitting there with Ms. Matteo in his usual spot, three rows up from our bench. When Uncle RB waved, none of the other stuff mattered.

Warming up with my team, I swore I saw Tara on the other end of the court. I turned away, proud that I hadn't thought about her for a while. Besides, it couldn't be her. She was in Germany and not coming back. I'd probably never see her again. The blonde girl warming up with her New Life Crusader teammates was just another Not Tara. Still, I glanced across the court again, just to be sure, like all the others I'd chased over the past year.

New Life's coach motioned for them to form a huddle. Not Tara stood in the circle, her back to me. While in the huddle, she passed around a bag of Skittles until the coach scolded her.

Not Tara. She didn't eat Skittles. Tara Parks ate Jawbreakers.

Our coach called us into a huddle. I kneeled down, my back to the New Lifers. Focus, Honeycutt, I thought. It's been over a year, get over her. It's not right.

While Coach Turner gave each of my teammates individual notes, I glanced up at the stands. Sammy was there with Rebecca. He and I still practiced together every chance we got. Even though he still had a thing for me, I always felt more comfortable on the court with him than guarding girls. Coach always wanted us to be aggressive, even in practice, but it felt wrong, getting right up on a girl. I had no problem charging into, over, and around Sammy.

The buzzer signaled the start of the game. The crowd came alive. People yelled and pounded their feet against the stands.

I walked onto the court with my teammates. My feet were headed to the middle circle, preparing for the jump ball when my heart stopped. Skittles girl was headed toward the middle circle, too. Not Tara, I told myself. Focus. Except I knew that walk, the walk of New Life's center. She deliberately sauntered right to the middle of the floor.

She had her eyes glued to the ball as the ref came over with it. Rule number one was to never, ever take your eyes off the ball. The whistle blew, the ball went up.

My eyes and arms followed, but so did New Life's center, jumping in front of me.

The vanilla lavender smell of her hair rattled me next. My eyes lost the ball, gravitating to the girl with the dimpled chin and apple cheeks at the basket, making the first two points of the game.

There was something even worse than Tara Parks in another country, a thousand miles away and out of my life: Tara Parks in Wiley, on the opposing team, close enough to touch yet completely out of my life.

My teammates brought the ball back up the court, passing me where I stood frozen.

"Wake up, Honeycutt," Coach Turner yelled from the bench.

I barely caught a pass from a teammate.

Tara planted her feet to block me. I smelled Doublemint gum, sending my mind back to the band storage room. The ache that had started with her in the eighth grade bathroom returned. She kept her eyes on the ball, waiting for the chance to steal it.

"You're supposed to be in Germany," I said.

"We're going to kick your team's ass." She reached for the ball, but missed, hitting my arm instead. Her touch made my insides bounce. "Then you won't have to see me until we do it again next year."

I tried to dribble around her, but she kept jumping in front, always a half step ahead of me. To get by her, she wanted me to go through her. The idea of my body slamming up against hers was too much. I dribbled the ball back a step.

"Come on, Honeycutt," Coach Turner yelled.

Coach never had to yell at me, but I'd never played in a game against Tara Parks. We'd fooled around on Wiley Park's court, but that was for fun. I'd always imagined her up in the stands at games, cheering me on. Not playing against me.

Not able to bring myself to charge through her, I passed the ball to a teammate. The teammate passed it right back. Tara came at me again.

"Don't you dare go easy on me because I won't go easy on you," Tara said.

At Wiley, our height had brought us closer, a couple of giraffes stuck in a herd of sheep. Now, it pitted us against each other. I wanted to shrink.

I responded to her comment by faking a pass and sending a jump shot over her head for a basket. I was still a bit taller than Tara – when I stood up straight – and stronger.

"So you can jump. What else can you do?" She dribbled right up to me after I got into position at the other end. "Oh right – I forgot – you can also be a total asshole," she said and bounced the ball right off my chest. The crowd, her team, even my own teammates laughed.

I didn't say anything. What could I say? She had every reason to be furious about the list I'd given her. I was furious at myself for it. At the time, it felt like the hardest thing I'd ever done. Since then, it felt like the stupidest thing I'd ever done.

"Honeycutt! You're better than this!" Coach Turner was now off the bench, standing, hands on her hips.

Tara tried to pass the ball to a teammate, but I swiped it as soon as it left her hands. The ball dropped through the basket before she and her Bible-thumping teammates knew what happened.

"That's it, Honeycutt." Coach Turner clapped her

hands.

"Way to go, Peyton," I heard Ms. Matteo yell over the rest of the crowd.

The New Life Crusaders clearly didn't achieve their winning record on just muscle. Except for Tara, they were mostly muffy girls with big bangs and rich parents. They were obviously undefeated due to three things: Tara, brains, and prayer. Like Mom had said, if God was rooting for a team in our game, it would be the good Christian girls.

At halftime, Tara pointed in my direction, plotting with her teammates. I saw it on her face and in her pointing – she wanted to beat me. Not my team, me. For her, it was personal.

Coach Turner reviewed our game plan, which wasn't that different from the first half since we were up 28-16. She discussed minor adjustments for each player. Her only one for me was that I needed to guard their center more closely.

Tara's snarling comments stung. I'd started out practicing basketball with Sammy, as a way to help Rebecca, but also to impress Tara. Now Sammy liked me instead of Rebecca and Tara was my opponent. How had things become such a mess?

I'd spent the first half showing off in front of Tara, running around her on the court. Every time she'd gotten close to me, I smelled her damn shampoo. I also smelled something new, over her sweat, a sweet scent, a girl's antiperspirant. The smells distracted me. I knew if I stood still she'd take the ball right out of my hands.

During the second half I listened to Coach and guarded Tara close, but every time she brushed up against me, my knees gave and she pushed right past.

Her body had changed since she'd pressed it against mine in the band storage room. Her curves were more defined. And her chest was larger, moving in unison with the rhythm of her dribbling. I kept telling my eyes to stay on the ball, but my eyes kept being pulled to the mole right below her left ear. At Wiley, she'd always worn her hair down so the only time I got a glimpse was in the band storage room. Now, with her hair in a ponytail, the mole was on display for the whole gym to see.

She breezed right around me for an uncontested jumper. Coach Turner called a time out. Our 12-point half time lead was gone. We huddled around Coach.

"Honeycutt, what is wrong with you?" Coach Turner asked.

That's a good question, I wanted to say. Coach reminded us the game was always more physical at the end. She said we needed to push back.

The buzzer called us back to the court. The crowd grew rowdy again. They clapped and stomped. New Life fans yelling "Keep it up!" while Wiley supporters screamed "Come on!" Tara met me on the court.

"I told you not to go easy on me," she said.

Ms. Matteo had always talked about how in music, a silent pause was usually the most powerful part of the whole composition. I'd learned the same thing was true for playing ball. Most players, Tara Parks apparently included, liked to trash-talk. It drove them crazy when you didn't bite back.

I dribbled the ball around my back, through my legs. She stayed with me.

"Enough of the Globetrotter crap," she said. "All that matters is if you score."

I made my way to the front of the basket, near the

free throw line. My team needed this. It would tie the game, but Tara Parks had her hands up, blocking me on both sides. She was trying to make me knock her down. I just couldn't do it.

I took a step back and bounced the ball through her legs, meeting it on the other side and slamming it into the basket. Every person in the gym jumped to their feet, even New Lifers. Guys whistled. Women yelled. Everyone cheered the only slam-dunk of the night. I pounded my chest, but the king of the world feeling disappeared when I saw Tara's face.

The papers would later report that it was the first dunk on record by a girl in North Carolina. But the dunk and the attention didn't matter to me. All that mattered was the hurt look on Tara's red and crumbling face. My teammates pointed at the space between her legs and laughed at my stunt. I wanted to rewind and take it back.

My basket tied the game. Tara waved her hands for the ball as God's team took its last possession. The crowd still cheered as Tara dribbled the ball down the court.

"Get on her," Coach Turner yelled to me.

Coach's order would've been funny if it didn't hurt so much.

Tara's wide eyes narrowed, like the ball was her bone and she wasn't about to let me near it. She pivoted one way, I was there. She went the other way, there was my hand. She backed up and held the ball for the last shot. If she made it, New Life would win and she'd be the team hero.

She took another step back. Three feet behind the foul line was a low-percentage shot, even for someone as tall as Tara. She would need to charge the basket, but she didn't plan to. I could see what she was going to do in her eyes, even though it was a high-risk shot. I should've put my hands up in her face, but I thought letting her take the shot would make things better. Make me less of an asshole. So instead, my arms went out wide to keep her from charging by me.

She jumped up, released the ball over my head, and it dropped right through the basket.

Coach Turner yelled my name, not in a good way, while everyone else in the gym cheered. It was prettier than my dunk and even more unbelievable.

Crusader fans chanted "New Life, New Life." Their cameras flashed. They made their way on the court to congratulate the winning team. The gym filled with sounds, the different shoes squeaking across the floor. High fives. Shouting.

Meanwhile, Wiley Coyote fans dispersed. Uncle RB and Ms. Matteo motioned that they'd meet me outside.

Tara's coach and teammates charged her, hugging and picking her up on their shoulders. I looked in the stands for her mother or Col. Parks. Not even Tara's brother was there.

No one on my team spoke to me and Coach Turner sat on the bench, head in her hands. After everyone shook the other players' hands and everyone else on my team congratulated Tara, I walked over to her.

"Nice shot," I said.

She took my hand and squeezed it hard like she wanted to break my fingers. She waited for me to react, but I didn't even though a jolt of pain shot up my arm. She finally let go.

"You didn't answer me before," I said. "What happened to Germany?"

"Why do you care?"

I opened my mouth, but didn't even know how to start. My eyes got blurry. I was closer to tears than words. My chest started to throb and split apart, an earthquake going on inside.

"We didn't go," she said. "The house had been sold already so we moved and I changed schools."

My heart threatened to bust through my chest. She'd been around here the whole time, but hadn't contacted me. No emails, no texts.

Even worse, Mrs. Parks had gotten her way and sent Tara to the Christian school. My mind leapt to Rebecca. No way could Rebecca have known and not told me. People couldn't live in a small town and not be noticed – unless they didn't want to be noticed, unless something else was going on.

"Why didn't you go?" I asked.

Tara's teammates called her back over. They wanted to take pictures and celebrate together. She turned and motioned that she'd be a minute. Her eyes came back to mine, and an avalanche of emotion hit me.

"Next time, don't just let me have the shot," she said and pointed her magic wand index finger, sending a familiar electric charge through my body. "I want to earn it." She turned and headed toward her teammates.

Was there hope that we could still be friends? She and her teammates snapped photos with their iPhones and shared Skittles. I needed to find the right time and way to apologize for the list, but in that moment I could only form one thought, one sentence, one fact in my mind: I loved Tara Parks.

Chapter 7

The next evening, Uncle RB let me off work early so I could get to Rebecca's house before sundown and have her call Tara. But, when I got there she wasn't home yet.

I kept checking my watch. All that waiting made me antsy so I headed to the kitchen to hang with Mrs. David. She wasn't crazy about Rebecca not being home yet either.

Mrs. David looked like an older, less dramatic version of her daughter. She didn't have Rebecca's teasing grin, but the curly, milk chocolate-colored hair, petite build, and show-stopping brown eyes were there.

First, I lit all the candles in the kitchen. Then I turned on the burner underneath the teakettle. I opened the cabinet and pulled out the box of chamomile from the assortment of teas. Mrs. David smiled. She always had Earl Grey in the morning and chamomile at night.

Lately, I stayed over on Friday nights, another way to get away from Mom. Mrs. David never said so, but I suspected she liked someone around to light the candles and make her evening and morning tea. She was so different from my mother, who said she liked hot tea one week, but the following week looked at me like I was crazy for suggesting it. Also, Mom was always rearranging things in the kitchen. At Rebecca's, I knew where to find stuff, and Mrs. David never asked about boys and if any of them liked me.

"I know Rebecca will want some hot chocolate. Make yourself some or whatever you like," Mrs. David said.

As soon as I opened up the cabinet to grab a mug, I heard a door slam. Rebecca breezed into the room.

I turned around and blurted out, "Tara's here.

She never moved."

Rebecca tossed her purse and backpack down on the counter. "I know."

"You know? How long have you known?"

Rebecca crossed her arms. "She made me promise not to tell you."

"You've known the whole time?" I grabbed my hair and yanked at it.

"You told her it was a good thing she was moving, asshole!"

"Rebecca – language," Mrs. David said.

"Do you have any idea how much that upset her?" Rebecca asked.

"Let's calm down," Mrs. David said while gently pulling Rebecca toward the kitchen table. "Peyton is making tea and hot chocolate."

"We're gonna need a whole lot more than tea and hot chocolate," Rebecca said.

She sat down with her mother at the table. I stayed by the stove.

Rebecca didn't move for the next couple of minutes. In all the time I'd known her, she'd never been that silent and still. Her stillness made me antsy. I grabbed the bag of marshmallows from the cabinet.

"Tara's dad is sick. Cancer," Rebecca said. "That's why they didn't move."

I shook my head. Rebecca was joking. Or it was a stupid dream. I'd wake up and Tara would be in Germany, her dad healthy.

"What kind?" Mrs. David asked.

"The dying kind. Tara said the doctors give him maybe a few months." Tears streamed down Rebecca's cheeks.

The kettle whistled and gave me time to consider what I'd just heard. Even though I poured the hot water slowly over the teabag, a little water spilled on the counter. My hands shook as I delivered the hot mugs. Col. Parks? Cancer?

I sat at the table, not wanting anything except for the news about Col. Parks to be wrong. Tara loved her father more than she loved Jimmy Page or guitar or anything.

Rebecca wiped her tears and poked the marshmallows I'd put into her hot chocolate. "She asked me about when Dad died, but I don't remember."

Mrs. David stared at her mug of hot tea. Mr. David had died when Rebecca was four. Mrs. David motioned toward the fridge. "There's some cookie dough. Make the whole thing. Brownies, too. Tomorrow you and Rebecca can take some to Tara."

The news, just the words – *Col. Parks had cancer* – were so much bigger than anything else my mind had ever processed. It's one thing to hear about people I'd never met, but the father of the girl I loved?

After Mrs. David had gone to bed, Rebecca and I sat at the kitchen table and watched the cookies rise in the oven. The sweet smell of chocolate chip cookies took over the room, but did nothing to help Rebecca's mood. She was upset about Tara's dad. She was also angry with me for the note. She scooped up the last of the raw cookie dough from the wrapper and ate it. She licked the spoon and wiped imaginary crumbs off the table. She kept busy doing everything except looking at me, almost like she was challenging me to speak first. Maybe if I could make Rebecca understand why I wrote it, she could help me find a way to explain it to Tara.

Finally, when the last batch had one minute to

go, I blurted out, "Mrs. Parks doesn't want me around Tara. I heard her threaten to send Tara to another school if they stayed here. And she did. That's why Tara's at New Life."

Rebecca kept her eyes on the spoon even though we were out of cookie dough. There was no point, not with her, not with Tara. Everyone thought I was an asshole. Maybe I was.

"That's why I wrote the note."

Rebecca got up, put the spoon in the sink, and motioned for me to pull out the last batch of cookies.

I put the last batch on top of the oven to cool. The smell of fresh baked cookies didn't make me feel any better. I wanted to go home, be alone in my room, away from everyone else.

"It's kinda like Romeo and Juliet."

My fingertips hovered on the edge of the oven, ready to push me up and out. But I was desperate to fix things between everyone. "What do you mean?"

"Their families didn't want them near each other. That's why they had to die."

So the only way Tara and I could be together was to die? Sometimes, Rebecca got a little carried away with the drama.

She walked back over to the table and sat down. "You need to tell Tara what you just told me."

I shook my head. "I don't want to cause any more problems with her mom."

Rebecca grabbed both my hands. "You have to tell her."

I didn't want to make things worse, especially with her dad so sick, but this was my chance. Tara was a car ride away. I nodded.

"Problem is, she doesn't want to speak to you." Rebecca got up out of her chair and looked around the kitchen as if the answer might come to her from the toaster or blender. "Okay, let me get some sleep and tomorrow, I'll help you come up with a plan."

The following night, several hours after sundown, I stood beneath a half-moon and the second-story window of Tara's room, holding a full bag of Skittles. Earlier that day, Rebecca and I had stopped by Tara's new house to deliver the cookies and brownies. Tara had answered the door, eyes red and swollen. She gave us a quick tour, but had to get ready to go visit her dad in the hospital. Rebecca made a note of where Tara's room was located.

Mrs. David had told us that some families needed their privacy in these situations. Tara's was probably one of those families. I thought about writing a letter, but worried I'd write something stupid again. Mrs. David said the best thing to do was wait until Tara reached out to me, but would she? I decided to go with Rebecca's Romeo and Juliet-inspired plan instead.

I launched a Skittle at Tara's window. Ping.

I imagined her in bed, reading or trying to sleep, hearing tiny balls hitting the glass. Would she think it was a hailstorm or the end of the world? To her, it probably already felt like the end of the world.

I waited at least 30 seconds between each throw, careful to keep my arm steady, hitting her window almost every time. Ping. Ping.

After several Skittles, I thought maybe she wasn't home. Maybe she was still at the hospital with her dad.

Ten minutes later, just as I was about to surrender to the voice in my head saying give it up, the back door opened. My heart leapfrogged into my throat.

Tara squinted at me with tired eyes. She closed the screen door behind her and walked over to me. Her hands were in the front pocket of her sweatshirt. Her shoulders slouched forward. Even her hair seemed to be missing its bounce. She shivered, reminding me that it was still March and still chilly, even though I didn't feel cold at all.

I handed her the bag of Skittles. She shook them to feel their weight.

"You wasted half of them," she said.

"Got you out here, didn't it?"

She looked up and down her driveway. "Where's your bike?"

"At home."

"You walked here?"

I shook my head and motioned toward my Mustang parked at the end of the block. Both her eyebrows went up.

"When did you—" she stopped, remembering. "You turned sixteen last month." She tugged at my ball cap. I'd found the Celtics one her dad had given me.

She walked over to the car and hopped in the passenger side. I followed.

It was weird sitting next to her. The Mustang had been the one place where she'd never been, unlike my room or Wiley Music. I could drive around and pretend Tara Parks didn't exist.

She opened the glove compartment and laughed when several *X-Men* comics spilled out. She gathered them from the floorboard and placed them back into the glove compartment. She ran her hands along the seats and dashboard. "I'm so jealous. Mom won't let me have a car."

"Wanna go somewhere?" I asked.

She put her hands back in the front pocket of her sweatshirt. "No."

Disappointed, I placed my hands at ten and two on the steering wheel. Everything was closed, but it didn't matter. It would've been cool to drive around with her.

I fired up the engine and turned on the heat. From her coat pocket, she pulled out a square pack of cigarettes. The box was wider than other cigarettes, and red, with the word DUNHILL across it.

"You mind?" she asked.

"No, but when did you —"

"The day I found out Dad had cancer."

She pressed the lighter button on my car. I'd never used it.

She shivered. I took off my coat. She leaned forward and I put it around her shoulders. She put her arms through it, shoving the Skittles into a pocket.

She kept her eyes on the street in front of us. I tried to do the same.

"How is he?"

"Mom's convinced he's getting better —"

"That's great, right?"

"Except he isn't."

I wanted to put my arm around her or do something to make it better, but that was the problem. Nothing would make things – him – better.

"Do you believe in miracles?" she asked.

I thought of Mom's favorite Christmas movie, *Miracle on 34th Street*, and little Natalie Wood's line, "I believe, I believe, it's silly, but I believe." I wanted to believe, but Mom's second all-time favorite actress, Natalie Wood had been dead for over thirty years. Still, if hope was what Tara Parks needed, I wanted to give it to her. "Yes."

We were silent for a while. Tara put her cigarette out in the passenger door ashtray and reached for the handle.

"I'm sorry about my stupid list," I said.

She didn't move, but I needed to say more before she got out. I ran my fingers over the steering wheel and searched for the right words. Rebecca was easier to talk to about this, but Rebecca didn't make my insides ache.

Before losing my nerve, I blurted out, "I heard your mother tell your dad she didn't like you hanging out with me, that she'd send you to another school if you weren't moving."

Tara continued to sit still. "But we were moving. You didn't have to write it."

Why did I? Because of what Mrs. Parks had said. *Corrupted by a freak. It's a good thing we're moving. There's something not right about that girl.*

I couldn't tell her that part.

"You're right. It was shitty. I'm sorry."

She took this in, still not moving, except to look over at me. Now it was too hot in the car. I turned down the heat.

"Is there anything I can do? For you? For your dad?"

She went back to looking through the windshield. "They had to move him to Charlotte General. It's almost an hour away. I'd love to spend some time with Dad without Mom there."

Wiley Music was closed on Sundays. "I can drive you tomorrow, if you want."

She tilted her head back toward me. "That's perfect. Mom's going to visit some friends after church."

We made plans for me to pick her up when she got home from church. She reached for the door handle.

I glanced at her house. I tried not to think about Mrs. Parks, but it had to be hard on her, too. "How's your mom doing?"

"Not good. She's never been alone. I mean, he's been her whole life, since high school."

Since high school, since Mrs. Parks was my age. I could imagine loving someone since high school. I certainly knew what it was like to love someone in high school. It felt like ten thousand bricks strapped around my chest.

Tara reached over and took my hand, squeezing it almost as hard as she had after the game, but not in a mean way this time.

"Thanks for the Skittles serenade," she said. "But if you ever write a list like that again, it's over Honeycutt."

She moved out of the car and into the house so fast, I didn't get the chance to ask what would be over. Did it mean something was on? My knees quivered at the possibility.

She'd slipped my coat off and left it in the passenger seat. The Skittles were no longer in the pocket and it smelled like cigarette smoke.

I'd told her about the note. Tomorrow I was driving her to see her dad. And something wasn't over. This was all really happening. Now if only Col. Parks would get better.

Nothing could have prepared me for seeing Col. Parks. If it wasn't for those bright eyes he shared with his daughter – sunken in, but still impossible to miss – I would've thought Tara had the wrong room. His eyes were the only thing left of the man I knew. I wanted to dive into his face and pull them out. They were too blue, too beautiful; a sunken treasure surrounded by ruin.

His flesh clung to his bones and had a pasty quality, like flour. His skin looked bone-pale except for purple and brown lesions on his face, neck and hands – every part of his body I could see.

Tara had been quiet on the car ride, smoking and blasting Led Zeppelin the whole way. But with Col. Parks, she put on her game face, telling him about her week, about an article she'd written for New Life's student paper. "The school district said that due to budget cuts, there'd be no more music classes after the next school year," she told him. "New Life won't be affected because it's private, but Ms. Matteo will be out of a job, which sucks."

I pulled up the sleeves on my sweatshirt and leaned forward in the chair next to hers. "I told Uncle RB he should set up a music school as an addition to the store, but he thinks it'll be way too much work."

Tara stared at me. I couldn't tell if she thought the music school was a good idea or not.

She turned back to her father and grabbed a book from the stack that had been placed on a small bedside table: *The Adventures of Huckleberry Finn, The Great Gatsby, Franny and Zooey, The Old Man and the Sea.* That afternoon she read *The Call of the Wild.*

Around four, she left to hit up the vending machines for snacks. I offered to go with her, but she said no. I didn't press, sensing she needed a few minutes alone. With her out of the room, Col. Parks turned his attention to me.

"Come closer," he said, in what sounded like a

two-hundred-year-old voice.

I took a step closer. I'd never seen anyone *really* sick. Mom occasionally got the flu, but nothing like this. I tugged at the Celtics hat, hoping he'd notice.

Tara had told him I was there, but it was like what she said didn't register at all.

"Closer. My eyesight's not so good these days."

One step closer and the smell overwhelmed me, like he was decaying right there in the bed. Bleach and Mr. Clean couldn't cover it up.

On the drive there, Tara had talked about how she spent hours reading to him and playing his favorite music. How did she stand the smell? The sunken eyes?

He waved for me to come even closer. He reached out to touch my face, so I held my breath and bent forward.

He ran his hand over my cheek. It was colder than Lake Norman in February. A tear dripped down his face and fell onto the pillow. Eyes that blue weren't meant to cry. Not his, not Tara's.

I took a step back and inhaled. "I don't mean to upset you, sir."

"I knew a beautiful boy like you once," he said.

That's when I remembered Wink's fish camp and the hurt look on the cowboy's face when Col. Parks didn't acknowledge him.

No wonder Mrs. Parks didn't want Tara around me. *Corrupted by a freak. It's a good thing we're moving. There's something not right about that girl.*

And that's why Col. Parks defended me. Barbie and Col. Parks believed I was like him.

My throat closed up, and the room spun. I was losing someone, too, someone important.

I wanted to run out of the room. What could I say

to him? He was so out of it that saying something heartfelt wouldn't mean anything to him, but it would to his daughter.

I took a deep breath and leaned in toward him.

"Col. Parks, I've always thought – well, if I grow up to be anything close to who you are—" Not able to finish, I cried from some place deep in my throat.

He reached up and put his hand on my shoulder. The chill of his hand cut right through my thick sweatshirt.

"It's gonna be okay." It took all his energy to smile. It took most of mine to smile back.

Unbelievable. He was comforting me. And I let him.

The smell became too much, but I held out until Col. Parks fell asleep. Then I rushed to the nearest restroom, getting there just in time. At least it was the kind of bathroom without stalls so no one heard me lose the three Krispy Kremes and the orange juice I'd inhaled on the drive. I sat on the bathroom floor, empty and scared. Who would stand up to Mrs. Parks for me now?

I knocked the back of my head against the wall out of guilt for thinking about myself at a time like that.

Walking back to his room, I found Tara in the hall, arguing with Mrs. Parks. Tara's back was to me, but I could tell she was upset by how her shoulders were up around her ears.

Mrs. Parks maneuvered around Tara and came right at me. She wore her Sunday best, armed with the Bible.

I was already sweating and twitching from having thrown up. She made it worse. "I'm sorry about Col. Parks."

She shook her finger at me. "Don't pretend you're here for my husband."

"I wanna help," I said.

"We don't need your help."

"Mom." Tara grabbed her mother's arm.

"I'm not here to cause trouble," I said.

Mrs. Parks shook Tara's arm off and said, "You're grounded for the next two months for taking off without me and not telling me where you were." The words came out of her mouth like gunfire.

"That's not fair," Tara said. Her eyes were like a dam about to burst.

Two nurses walked by and Mrs. Parks exchanged hellos with them. Clearly, she didn't want anyone else to hear what she said to us.

Mrs. Parks's coconut-scented perfume made my throat close up. I thought about Uncle RB standing in Jeb's office, how he'd later said there was a right time for these things. This was a woman whose husband— a man she'd loved since she was my age— was inside this hospital, in a room down the hall. Now wasn't the time, but if I wanted a real shot at Tara, one day I'd have to take on Mrs. Parks. Nothing terrified me more.

"Mrs. Parks, I really am sorry your family is going through this right now." I didn't wait for Mrs. Parks or Tara to respond.

Walking out of the hospital, I took a deep breath and tried to shake off seeing Mrs. Parks and the memory of all she'd said about me.

I was almost to my car, when Tara caught up with me. "You're just going to leave? Let her win?"

Exasperated, I leaned against the car. Tara put her hand on my arm.

"I'm leaving so you can be with your dad."

She pulled me to her. It was the first time I'd held her in over a year, but it felt natural. I didn't get as anxious as I had in the past.

We stood there for the longest time, arms around each other.

"I don't want to let go," I whispered.

"This feels so good," she said and turned her nose toward my neck.

I expected Mrs. Parks to call the police, have them come and pull me off Tara and lock me up for good.

Two women walked by and I pulled away. "I'll find a way to see you," I said. "A way your mom can't stop."

"How?"

"I'll figure it out. In the meantime, call or text if you need me." I kissed her cheek and she pulled me in for a tight hug. Our hips collided and the ache came back.

Mrs. Parks was not getting rid of me this time.

The whole drive back, my body felt a wreck over that last hug and the fire it had reignited in me, something I hadn't felt since the band storage room. I tried to find a way to be near Tara again. Every time I called Tara's cell I got her voicemail. Once I drove by her house and Mrs. Parks saw me. An hour later, Tara sent me a text asking me not to drive by again.

Life at Wiley was also getting more difficult. One afternoon in May, things finally erupted with Rebecca and Sammy. The three of us always ate lunch together in the corner of the cafeteria, and on most days Rebecca dominated the conversation. But on this particular day,

Sammy leaned toward me as soon as I sat down.

"Did you talk to Principal Webb?" he asked.

"No. He'll just ask me if I know who it is. If I tell him the truth, that it's his son, he won't believe me."

"Wait. What did Jason do?" Rebecca asked.

My eyes shot over to Jason Webb at the table next to us. If he heard his name, he didn't acknowledge it. He held court at his table, surrounded by his buddies, making lewd faces at a girl nearby. She attempted to enjoy her dessert, a Jell-O pudding, but Jason turned it into a sexual act.

Sammy motioned for Rebecca to keep her voice down.

"There's been some notes with the N word in my locker," I said.

Rebecca's eyes zeroed in on me. "Why the N word?"

"Because Jason overheard me asking Peyton out a while back," Sammy said.

I shook my head at Sammy, but it was too late. Rebecca pushed her chair away from the table, stood, and yelled, "He asked you out and you didn't tell me?"

Sammy and I both attempted to get her to sit down. She refused. Her eyes burning with anger at me.

"How long ago? How long have you made me look like a fool?"

"You're all fools," Jason yelled from the next table. "Now shut the hell up and sit down, nigger lover."

His friends laughed.

I stood. "What'd you say?"

Sammy got out of his chair, too. Rebecca's facial expression melted from anger to fear.

"You heard me."

I did hear him. Everyone at the nearby tables

heard. Jason didn't care who heard him. No one would say anything because he was the principal's kid.

"Apologize," I said.

"Don't get your panties in a wad. Do you even wear panties, Freakenstein?"

His friends almost fell out of their chairs, laughing.

"I said apologize."

Jason nodded over toward Sammy. "Does your boyfriend know the only reason you hang out with him is because your girlfriend doesn't go here anymore?"

At that, I jumped over to his table and slammed my fist, like it was Thor's hammer, straight into his face.

Blood poured out of Jason's nose. He tasted it before wiping his nose and looking at the blood on his hand.

"You should've apologized," I said.

"What for? Speaking the truth? Dyke."

He wanted to push my buttons, wanted me to punch him again. Fine by me. Right after he said the word, I punched him again and again.

He got up and kneed me in the stomach. With me bent over, he smashed his lunch tray across my head. Chairs screeched across the floor. Students yelled, "Fight! Fight!"

Rebecca took off running to find a teacher. Of course, there wasn't one around. Teachers were never available when you needed them.

Sammy leapt in front of me and shoved Jason. "You would be the type to hit a girl," he said.

"What girl? I don't see a girl," Jason said.

He shoved Sammy back, and Jason's friends grabbed him. It took three of them to hold Sammy back from Jason as he lunged for me again.

I ducked, and he fell into the table. I thought back to that day in the eighth grade bathroom, what he and Tara had been doing in there, and I kicked him hard in the gut. But I was no match for him really. Like when a little dog charges toward a bigger one, I'm sure everyone around us wondered what this scrawny stick was doing taking on a varsity wrestler.

He grabbed my shirt and tossed me back. For a few seconds I thought, that's it? He's just going to let me go? Fight over?

I didn't want the fight to be over so I looked at him and said, "You're just pissed because I got further with Tara Parks than you did."

Jason's mouth clamped shut and he nodded at his friends. Then, two of them grabbed my arms, allowing him to punch me square in the ribs not once...

"That's for ruining my lunch."

Not twice...

"That's for *pretending* to be a nigger lover."

Not three times...

"Because you're really a fucking—"

But four.

"Dyke."

His two friends let me go, and I collapsed. My face hit the hard, cold cafeteria floor. A couple seconds later, something cold and wet poured down on my head. Milk mixed with blood trickled into my mouth. Then, a squashed empty milk carton smacked my cheek.

Sammy kneeled nearby, asking if I was okay. In the distance I heard Rebecca's voice and then a teacher yelled, "Stop fighting right now!"

Too late, of course. Several people scattered away, more chairs screeched across the floor. A pain shot all the way up and down my body every time I inhaled. It felt like Jason had done enough damage to kill me. And the really scary part? For a moment, I hoped he had. He'd said what everyone in Wiley thought about me: Dyke. Then my mind darted from Tara to Sammy to Rebecca and back to Tara. They'd all be better off without me.

The way the teachers and my classmates seemed to be tiptoeing and whispering around me, it felt like they all thought I was a goner, too. Then I passed out. The next thing I remember was waking up, shocked to see Mom crying.

"Mom, what's wrong?"

She cried even harder.

A pain shot through my left side when I sat up. Everything that had happened came back to me – being wheeled into the hospital, barely able to breathe, one doctor examining me and saying to another, "one, two, three – three broken ribs." Shortly after, a needle pricked my arm and knocked me out until now.

"Why? Why do you have to fight?" Mom asked between sniffles and sobs. She took another tissue from the box by my bed. "Why can't you be like other girls?"

Uncle RB took her shoulders, pulling her back from me a bit. "That's enough. Peyton's in pain and needs to rest."

"Pain? What do you know about pain? You're a man," she said to him.

Uncle RB steered her toward the door.

"I cracked a couple ribs while in the Army. Peyton's got three broken ones, so I can only imagine how much worse—"

"You don't know pain," Mom said, looking at

both of us. "Ten hours in labor, that's pain. And for what? A daughter who acts like a monster." She waved her arms at me.

Uncle RB looked up at the ceiling, as if asking a God he was uncertain about for help. I glanced at the call button next to the bed, wondering if a nurse would bring me something strong enough to knock me out again. I had the broken ribs, but Mom was acting like the one who got beat up.

"Claudia, why don't you go home and get some rest now that you know everything's going to be fine here," Uncle RB said. Mom hated her first name. My uncle was the only one who dared use it. She much preferred her middle name, Caroline or Mrs. Honeycutt.

Her eyes darted from him to me. "No more fighting, you hear me? My daughter, fighting!"

She hung her head, shaking it slowly back and forth, as she walked out of the room.

Uncle RB pulled up a chair. He leaned forward, folding his arms on the edge of the bed. "Much as I hate to admit it, she's right. You shouldn't be fighting. You could've been hurt even worse."

I closed my eyes. "I wish I was."

"Don't you dare talk like that!"

I heard the chair scrape the floor and footsteps moving away from me. When I opened my eyes, he had his forehead pressed against the window.

Angry with myself for once again disappointing Uncle RB, I said, "I'm no good. All I do is corrupt people."

Uncle RB walked back over to me.

"Corrupt? Where'd you get an idea like that? Claudia say that about you?"

No, but another mom did. Uncle RB had

probably been at the hospital all day when he should've been at the music store. I was interrupting his life, but he didn't mind. He was the only one who seemed to care at all.

"Jason Webb say that to you? Is that why you were fighting?"

"It hurts to talk." Not a lie, but a convenient truth.

Uncle RB sat down, leaned back in the chair and then sat up. I couldn't tell if the chair made him uncomfortable or something else.

He looked up at me through his hair. He did that thing where he moved some bangs to one side and some to the other. He always did it before launching into something serious.

"When I got back from the Gulf War, I wanted to die. Part of me felt dead. I lost a couple buddies over there and didn't know why I was still alive when they weren't. I started drinking. My girlfriend dumped me. That's when I got drunk and drove my Mustang into Dairy Queen—"

"Mom told me about that."

"It made the front page of *The Wiley Post*," he said with a shy grin. His hair had fallen back over his eyes. This time he just shook his head. It never occurred to him to ask Ms. Matteo for a trim until it was long enough to get into his mouth. With his hair out of the way, you could see his honey-brown eyes – same as mine. I wanted my eyes to have the same effect on one girl, the way his had on most of the women in Wiley.

"A judge ordered me to get some help, so a buddy of mine told me about this doctor in Charlotte. I think she could help you."

I sat up even though it hurt. "What kind of doctor?"

Uncle RB shifted in his seat and looked at the hospital bed.

"You know, one of those doctors you talk to. A psychiatrist."

"A head-shrinker?" I asked. It hurt that he thought of me as some nut job.

He stood up and went back to the window. "I had the same reaction, but she really helped me."

I leaned back into the pillows and thought about it. Could this doctor help me feel normal? Whatever "normal" was. Everyone in Wiley thought I was a dyke. Maybe this doctor could help me sort it all out. Uncle RB had stopped crashing cars after the Dairy Queen incident. He'd joined a band, written some songs, toured the country. One of the songs he'd written had even been played on the radio and recorded by famous people. It's how he was able to buy the house on Lake Norman and the music store. His life had turned out okay.

"Just something to consider," he said.

"I'm gonna be suspended for the fight. Principal Webb might even expel me. Even if he lets me come back, things with Jason will only get worse. Sammy got involved because of me. It's best for him if I—"

"Ms. Matteo said Sammy won't be suspended because he was trying to stop the fight." Uncle RB put his hands in his pockets. After a long time, he said, "Kids can be so mean."

"If I'm expelled the only other option in Wiley is New Life. Or no school at all." I grinned at the thought of not having to go to school.

"Peyton, you have to go to school." Uncle RB chuckled. "Your mom would love you going to New

Life."

I nodded.

A worried look crossed Uncle RB's face like a storm cloud. There was no way Mom and I could afford New Life, but he could. He was still getting royalty checks from his hit song, not to mention Wiley Music was doing well. But it wasn't his responsibility to pay for me.

"If I have to go to New Life, how about we do a loan thing?" I asked. "I always have a little money left over after the bills. I can also do a paper route before school and wash cars on Sundays to pay you back."

He waved it off. "We'll work it out."

If not money, then what was he worried about? He sat back down and clasped his hands together. "You'd be in the same school again with Moxie."

He knew what Tara meant to me. That had to be why he looked so worried.

That night, long after visiting hours, the door to my room opened, but the lights stayed off. The sweet scent of Dunhills filled the sterile room.

"I'm sorry I couldn't get here sooner," she said.

As much as the smell of Dunhills comforted me, I felt guilty. She should be with her dad. "You shouldn't be here. Your mom—"

"Doesn't know I'm here. I used to sneak out when Dad was in here, too, before they moved him to Charlotte. I found out when the nurses changed shifts and what times they did rounds. I'd sneak back in and read to him."

"You gonna read me a bedtime story?" I asked, trying to get her to smile. She didn't.

Only the streetlight through the window lit the room, but it was enough to see the strange, empty look on her face. Not anger or worry, I'd never seen this expression before. She climbed into bed and wrapped her arms around me as best she could. It wasn't comfortable, but I wasn't about to tell her that. Mixed with the pain from her weight on my ribs was the pleasure of her being close, the ache and burn that always came when her hips were up against mine.

"What were you doing fighting Jason?" she asked.

"If anyone deserves the crap kicked out of him, it's Jason Webb."

She propped her chin up on my chest, "Heard you got expelled."

"Yeah. Uncle RB said he'd help pay for me to go to New Life."

She sat up. "Peyton, don't. You'll hate it."

"There's not another school in Wiley. Besides how bad can it be?" I asked and reached up to run my hand along her face. "You're there."

She shook her head at me.

"How's your dad doing?"

At the mention of Col. Parks, Tara's smile disappeared. She lay back down next to me. After a long time, she said, "Daddy died."

Even though it hurt, I held her close while she cried. Throbbing pain shot through my chest. The physical pain was actually a comfort, an outlet. I'd lost my only ally in her family, but I ached even more for Tara.

Chapter 8

Rebecca laughed at me waddling – there's no other way to describe it – into her mother's home office wearing dress shoes with a slight heel.

She sat behind the desk pretending to be the head of New Life Christian Academy. She wore one of her mother's business suits. The shoulder pads were so wide she could've tried out for the NFL. A fake pair of granny glasses kept sliding down her nose.

"We need to take this seriously," I said and sat down in the chair across from her, legs spread wide.

She laughed even harder. "You seriously need to learn how to sit in a skirt."

Rebecca motioned for me to stand up. She walked around the desk and demonstrated how a lady sits down in a chair when wearing a skirt, by smoothing the fabric covering the back of her thighs so it didn't bunch up or reveal too much. The timing had to be just right. It took five times before I did it without sitting on my hand.

She also demonstrated how girls cross their legs and switch them seamlessly. I tried it, and going too wide with the cross, split the skirt a little.

"Don't worry," she said. "We can stitch it up later."

Another skill I didn't have. "How do you know all this?" I asked.

She shrugged. "I just do."

Rebecca made me sit and cross my legs a dozen times. She had agreed to help me in exchange for all the times I'd come over to run lines with her for whatever school or community play she'd been cast in. She'd never admit it, but a part of her didn't want me at Wiley

High. She saw me as her main obstacle to Sammy.

She returned to the desk and pretended one of Mrs. David's files was my school application. She cleared her throat and pushed the granny glasses up her nose.

"They're not going to call you Peyton."

I stared down at my feet crammed into the dress shoes, my toes popping out of the top, trapped, unable to break free. And in the dress, I couldn't move or breathe.

"And you have to wear the same uniform every day. That's gonna get old. Oscar says variety is the spice of life."

Oscar Wilde was Rebecca's idol since theater had become her religion and her escape from the boredom of Wiley. I felt it unwise to point out that William Cowper had actually said the thing about variety being the spice of life. I only knew because the quote had been the subject of a recent question on *Jeopardy!*, another one of Mom's favorite shows. A contestant had thought it was Oscar Wilde, too.

Instead of correcting Rebecca, I picked at the scabs of my skinned up knees. Being in a dress again was absolute misery. I hated it now even more than back in eighth grade when I first met Tara. I tried to talk myself into it. Telling myself things like maybe being forced to wear a skirt would make me feel normal. Maybe my only problem was that I liked a girl. Maybe I was like Shelby and LouAnn and just needed to accept it.

"You can't wear any of your Led Zeppelin t-shirts. My neighbor used to go there. He got sent home for wearing a Cheerwine shirt."

Rebecca looked down at her mom's file, but struggled to get into character. Even though she had something to gain by me leaving Wiley, I could tell by the way she tried talking me out of it that she didn't think New Life was the best solution for me. Yes was the girl's favorite word. She preferred talking people into things, not vice versa.

"Why New Life? Why not homeschool?"

"Uncle RB won't let me." And I had to listen to Uncle RB, otherwise he might take away my car and job.

"At least you're not just going to New Life because of Tara," she said.

"No." I sat back in the chair, but my skirt rose, forcing me to sit up again. God almighty, how did girls put up with this shit every day? I felt so exposed.

"We need to practice or you won't have a prayer." She switched to a convincing old school marm tone. "So *Katharine* Honeycutt, tell the admissions committee about yourself."

Katharine. It was awful to hear now, even from Rebecca's mouth. I liked the name Peyton. I'd been Peyton for three years. How could I go back?

The first thing the admissions committee asked was why I'd been expelled from Wiley High.

"You've probably talked to Principal Webb so you know about the fight back in May."

The admissions committee nodded. We sat around a large, square wooden table. Everything about the room was old and wooden, including the admissions committee. The only bright spot was one floor to ceiling window. I paused and looked each member of the committee in the eye, saving the head of the school for last. She wore granny glasses like the ones Rebecca had on when we'd rehearsed. It gave me an odd confidence about the interview, after I suppressed my laughter.

"I got in the fight because the boy said some very

unChristian-like things. But it was wrong to fight with him. I realize that violence is not the answer."

The admissions committee turned to the head of the school, who studied my file.

"That one fight was the only time you got into trouble, correct?" she asked.

"Yes, ma'am."

She adjusted her glasses as if they could somehow help her find something about me that she didn't like. I had on a white and blue dress, Mom's idea to match the school's colors. My idea of hell.

Another admissions committee member took my file and read through it. "Your grades are pretty consistent," he said.

My grades weren't bad at all. Over the past year, I'd worked hard, trying to forget about straight-A Tara. My file was passed to a third member. She glanced at my letters of recommendation from Ms. Matteo and two Sunday school teachers who knew Uncle RB. I didn't ask Uncle RB how he knew them, but they had raved about me in their letters. Even Mom had done her part. During her interview with the board, she'd impressed them with her ability to rattle off Bible verses, thanks to all the hours she'd spent watching the Bible Television Network, her favorite channel now that some of her soaps had been cancelled.

Everyone looked to the head of the school. Even though she didn't know my mother and we attended the smallest Baptist church in town, I had one advantage over all other potential students: Uncle RB. Long before she became saved, sanctified, and filled with the Holy Ghost, the head of the school had let Uncle RB feel her up in the back of the Ford Mustang he'd later crash into the Dairy Queen.

I shifted my legs all ladylike and put my hands on the table. These people thought like Mrs. Parks did. I hoped that, like her, they would decide I needed this school, the Lord, all the help I could get. All these people thought alike.

The head of the school closed my file. "Why do you want to attend New Life?"

I smiled. Rebecca had made me rehearse this question twenty times. "It's a critical time in my life. I'm at the age where most people either reject the faith of their community or claim it forever as their own. I believe New Life can help me do the latter."

The head of the school's eyes dashed around the table. After she received a nod from everyone, she faced me. "Well, Katharine, it certainly sounds like you've given this a lot of thought."

Katharine. I'd have to get used to being called that again. I never got used to it the first time, but tried to push that thought out of my mind.

"Now it's our turn," she said. "But I think you'll be hearing from us very soon with good news."

I could hear Rebecca clapping, saying bravo. Of course, she'd congratulate herself, too.

To ease Uncle RB's mind, I'd agreed to drive an hour to Charlotte to see Dr. Nancy Wainwright, his old therapist, even though she was annoying. For one thing, she never let me change the subject, and she always called me out for trying. We'd already met three times and never seemed to accomplish anything. I didn't see why I needed to keep coming back. I'd gotten into New Life. Everything was going to be fine.

And her office depressed me. Everything – her

hair, desk, coffee table, even her business suit – was dark brown like a coffin.

"Peyton, you still haven't answered my question. You think you're going to get along with everyone at this new school?" Dr. Wainwright asked again.

"It's a Christian school. Do unto others. Jesus wouldn't look too kindly on one of his followers picking on me."

Dr. Wainwright didn't respond. She sat in her leather chair, waiting.

I could see why Uncle RB liked her. She was pretty, but not in a fake way. She wore a little eye shadow, mascara, and dark lipstick, just enough to accent her features. She didn't need much help.

She also wore fancy black-rimmed glasses. When she peered over them at me, I knew she wouldn't let me drop a subject. Her super power was that she could see right through me. The only other person who did that was Tara Parks.

She had a large presence, like Mrs. Parks, only Nancy Wainwright used her powers for good. Uncle RB called her a force, making me think of *Star Wars*. If there was such a thing as the force, then Dr. Wainwright had it. She could see the invisible bullshit streaming out of my mouth: The way I talked about Mom. How I liked doing things for her like running errands and mowing the lawn. The way I talked about Sammy, how he had a crush on me.

She was a woman and pretty and smart. I wanted her to like me. I wanted all girls to like me the way they naturally liked Uncle RB. Lying to her probably wouldn't help. I tried not to think about that.

I shifted in my seat, thankful I could wear jeans to the appointments. She encouraged me to wear whatever made me comfortable, so I always showed up in a t-shirt and jeans even though her office was fancy. Fancy Nancy was what I called her around Uncle RB.

I'd talked about Mom, how she'd always wanted a little girl, a daughter to be her best friend. How, growing up, Mom longed for a sister.

I also told her about Dad, how he and Mom would fight constantly over bills and him spending too much time and money at the pool hall. She asked how I felt about him leaving. I repeated what Uncle RB always said: A real man wouldn't leave.

Every time I told her something, Dr. Wainwright asked me how I felt about it. I hadn't said one word about Tara Parks for fear she would ask me how I felt, and I didn't want to answer that, but I'd run out of other things to talk about. Tara was all that mattered. Maybe Fancy Nancy could help me. Maybe she could tell me if I was like Shelby and LouAnn or not.

I looked at the clock. Fifteen more minutes. Now or never, Honeycutt.

"Tara goes to New Life."

Dr. Wainwright said nothing. She didn't even nod or take notes. She barely blinked. Why didn't she ask about Tara Parks?

"We were best friends when she went to Wiley. Her family was supposed to move to Germany, but her dad got sick so they stayed here. That's when Mrs. Parks sent Tara to New Life."

I waited for her to ask questions, but she didn't. This was the most I'd ever talked in our sessions. Fancy Nancy sat there like it was no big deal. Why wasn't she asking me stuff? Why did I have to do all the work? This was bullshit.

"Tara's mom, Mrs. Parks, she doesn't like me. If I can show her that I'm a good Christian, too, then maybe she'll let Tara and me be friends again."

"Why do you think Tara's mom doesn't like you?" she asked.

"I heard her tell Col. Parks."

"What did she say exactly?"

"She called me a freak and said I was corrupting her daughter."

Dr. Wainwright would surely ask about the "corrupting" part. I'd have to talk about the band storage room. I still thought about what happened in that room with Tara, but didn't know how to talk about it. I wasn't even sure I should.

Dr. Wainwright tapped her foot. Maybe she thought I was a freak, too. Maybe she couldn't help me and I wouldn't have to come back.

"Peyton, what do you think Tara's mom meant when she used the word freak?"

I shrugged. Why didn't she want to know more about Tara? I looked at the clock.

"She probably thinks I'm a dyke," I said.

I waited for Dr. Wainwright to nod in agreement, but she didn't. Her eyebrows flatlined to match her tight lips.

"Do you think you're a lesbian?" she asked.

No. I'm a freak. She didn't get it. What was the point of driving an hour to talk to someone who looked at me funny and had no answers. She didn't even know what normal was. All she ever did was ask questions.

"This is pointless."

Without even glancing over at her, I stood up and charged out of the office. Fancy Nancy couldn't help me. Maybe, hopefully, New Life could.

The morning of my first day at New Life found me grinding my teeth in the mirror. Mom stood right behind me with a huge smile on her face.

At New Life, girls wore navy blue skirts and white blouses. Boys wore navy pants, white shirts, and a tie. I'd prefer the pants; she'd prefer me in something more colorful. We were both pleased about me getting accepted into New Life, but actually having to wear the skirt put me in a bad mood.

That and Mom insisted I put a little make-up on my face. I felt like a fucking clown.

"No foundation," I said.

"I wear foundation." And she looked like a clown.

She hadn't been this happy since before Dad left, way before. I told myself I'd be happy once I got to New Life, once I saw Tara. New Life was a lot smaller than Wiley High School. The junior class only had twenty-seven students, so Tara and I would be in the same classes together all day long.

I slammed my eyes shut and let Mom apply eye shadow. It felt like grains of sand falling into my eyes and grinding down my soul. She added some blush and lipstick. I'd wipe it all off during the drive to school ten minutes later, but that ten minutes felt like an eternity times ten.

She moved behind me. We both looked in the mirror.

"You look so pretty," she said.

My cheeks were too bony for blush, especially the cheap pink kind Mom thought was so girly. And the Leopard Lush lipstick, Mom's favorite shade, actually glowed in the dark. I wanted to rip the flesh off my face.

"I think this school is what you've needed all along to really flourish. Those Christian boys are going to love you. I bet you have a boyfriend by Halloween."

Boyfriends. I'd still disappoint her in that department. But she was happy, at least for today. "I need to go. Don't wanna be late on the first day."

"You look so lovely. I should've taken a picture," Mom said from the porch. A neighbor walked down the drive with his trash and waved at Mom.

I shook my head, walking to my car fast as I could. The drive to New Life was three times longer than to Wiley High, just enough time to get all that make-up off.

"We'll take pictures when you come home," Mom said.

Almost out of earshot, I heard Mom tell the neighbor how today was my first day at New Life. Eleventh grade. Her voice was bright and weightless. The sound of hope.

When I walked into my first class, Tara wore the opposite expression of Mom's. She saw my dress and said nothing, not even hello. She went back to sketching in her notebook.

Roll was called. I responded to Katharine without protesting. Tara stopped sketching, tossed her pencil down and sank further into her chair. She glanced over.

I shrugged and mouthed, "What?"

She refused to look my way for the rest of the morning. All through English, I tried to figure out why she wasn't happy to see me. Uncle RB had said she would need friends most in the months to come as she continued to deal with the loss of her dad. That's what I wanted to be – her best friend, her closest friend.

The taste of Leopard Lush still on my lips made me hate New Life. Tara being distant made me despise the school even more.

After Bible class, she went to her locker. Everyone else's lockers were dull, no posters or pictures hanging in them. Tara had covered hers with posters of David Bowie.

I walked up to her, cool and calm, pretending not to be bothered by her ignoring me. "Thought you'd be a little happy to see me."

She shoved all of her books from our morning classes into her locker. "It's this place."

Our Bible teacher walked out of her classroom and stopped right next to us.

"Tara, didn't you read the student handbook?" the teacher asked.

Tara didn't respond.

"If you did you would know that images of any kind are not allowed in lockers. Please take those posters down before lunch."

The teacher moved on down the hall to inspect more lockers. Tara flipped off the teacher behind her back and dropped her backpack to the floor.

She pulled down the posters, taking great care not to rip them. All of them, including an old *Rolling Stone* cover, were in mint condition. They'd probably belonged to her dad.

I put my books on the floor and offered to help. She motioned to the one at the back of her locker. I leaned in and carefully pulled it off.

"You'll get suspended if you swear. Girls and boys can't hold hands," she said.

I remembered that day on the way to the cafeteria

when she'd wanted to hold my hand, and wondered if she still wanted to.

"And you can't get into a fight here like you did with Jason."

"I'm more of a lover than a fighter," I winked, wondering if New Life had a band storage room.

Ignoring my comment, Tara focused on peeling tape off the back of a poster. I concentrated on pulling the tape off, too, fearing her wrath if I caused even the smallest rip.

The poster I'd removed was long, with several pieces of tape, so I kneeled down. I wanted to sit on the floor, but the damn skirt made it too difficult.

David Bowie was wearing make-up in the poster. Did Tara find him handsome? I found it gross. I didn't want to wear make-up at all. Why would anyone wear it who didn't have to?

Tara kneeled down and pulled the last poster from near the bottom of her locker. In that one, Bowie was dressed in a man's suit, complete with jacket and tie. Why wouldn't he want to look like that in every picture? That's what I'd wear if I had a choice, but everyone else seemed to like me better when I dressed like a girl. Well, almost everyone. Tara had barely looked at me all morning. When she did, her face had a confused expression, like I was a puzzle she no longer had the patience to solve.

"Aren't you going to miss Rebecca and Sammy?" she asked.

"They're not my only friends." I glanced over at her. "I mean, we're friends, right?"

She pulled off the last piece of tape and paused before nodding.

I didn't have too much time to wonder about the

pause. It was almost time for gym class - the part of the day I dreaded most.

The girls' locker room was just one big area, no corners or small alleys of lockers to duck behind. At Wiley, I'd slip into a corner or bathroom stall to change. There was only one bathroom stall in New Life's locker room and the lock on it was broken. The showers were an open square space.

All the eleventh grade girls changed into their white and blue gym uniforms around me. I tried averting my eyes, but everywhere I looked there were boobs. Over the last two years, I'd noticed the expanding chests underneath girls' blouses, but seeing so many, up close, in 3D, was too much. Mine were little stubs. I didn't want what little I had. I tried to not even think about them, which was hard with everyone else's bouncing around me. The idea of mine growing any bigger was unbearable.

Tara got to gym late. She hurried in and introduced me to some of the girls. She had to pause, almost calling me Peyton. Her jaw tightened when she said "Katharine," like she hated it as much as I did.

Tara was by far the wildest of her classmates. The other girls thought Tara was overreacting about the new "no posters" rule. "Thou shalt have no other Gods before me," one classmate reminded her.

"I don't worship David Bowie," Tara said. "I just think he's an amazing musician and hot – still."

Everyone reacted to this, except me. One girl made gagging noises. Another mumbled "gross." The general consensus was Tara had weird taste and Bowie was no Channing Tatum.

Tara stood right next to me while undressing. She

was so casual about it, increasing my anxiety. She tossed her shirt into a locker and snapped off her bra while asking me something about Uncle RB's music store. I couldn't focus on what she was saying, too busy reminding myself not to look at her. I wanted her to hurry up and put on her gym shirt. She was my friend and friends didn't try to steal glances at the moles on each other's stomachs or long to watch each other tug a sports bra down over her chest.

Sometimes, in the locker room, I half expected the police to barge in and arrest me for being somewhere I didn't belong. Didn't the other girls know this? Why were they all undressing in front of me?

Trying to distract myself, I glanced around. On the other side, two girls were already in their gym clothes. They sat on a bench braiding each other's hair, and while the one girl braided, she whispered in her friend's ear. They both cracked up. They laughed so hard they fell into each other and gripped each other's arms.

While they continued to laugh, I glanced over at Tara and tried to picture us like those two. It was impossible to imagine. My hair wasn't long enough to braid. I wouldn't begin to know how to braid hers. My eyes went back to the two girls, one still with her hand on the other one's arm, trying to stop the flood of giggles. They were different than Tara and me. Not just sharing a joke, they also shared an innocence, a simplicity. They'd probably never made out for two weeks straight in a storage room.

Did Tara ever think about the storage room at Wiley?

"So can anyone rent out your uncle's recording studio?" Tara asked.

Her sports bra rested just above two of the three

moles that formed the semi-circle. I looked down at the floor, but on the way, my eyes took in her long legs, tan from summer. Girls were all around us, slamming lockers, bouncing basketballs across the locker room floor, their gym shoes squeaking, making it hard to hear.

"What?" I asked.

One of Tara's friends yelled that she'd see us out there and jumped across the bench, using my shoulder as leverage. Another girl bumped into me while she pulled up her shorts. I felt her bare leg on mine and wanted to scream.

"Your uncle's recording studio, can anyone rent it?"

"No," I said. "I mean, yes, of course."

She finally put on her damn shirt. I could breathe.

Tara motioned at the gym clothes still in my hand. "You gonna put those on?"

"Yeah. Go ahead. I'll catch up." I waited until everyone else was gone and then raced to change.

Walking out into the gym, I said a prayer. It felt like the right thing to do in that school:

Dear God, please help me not worry about changing in the locker room. Please help me not notice the other girls changing in the locker room. Please help me not notice their bodies, especially Tara's. Please, please help me be the best friend I can be to her and not notice things about her or think things about her that I shouldn't because we're friends and friends don't think those things about each other, right?

Before I could finish my prayer and say Amen, Tara threw a basketball right at me. It bounced off my chest and back in her direction. She laughed. Not the same laugh the two girls shared in the locker room, Tara's was more complicated.

How I'd missed that laugh, my favorite sound. So

hearty and infectious, the sound of a girl who didn't care if the whole world knew she was enjoying herself.

All the other girls stopped playing basketball and looked over. Their eyes wanted to know why Tara was having so much fun.

Chapter 9

On Saturday, while I helped a little boy and his mother pick out a mini drum kit, Tara marched into Wiley Music. She hadn't been in the store since she left Wiley High. I never got nervous with customers, even little kids, but Tara Parks being in the store made my whole body tremble. She created my own personal earthquake.

"Try it." I held out the plastic sticks for the boy, but he was too shy. He hid behind his mother's leg.

"He's not like this when he's alone in the kitchen with all my pots and pans," his mother said.

I liked it when little kids came into the store. I liked seeing which instruments made their eyes light up. And I liked that Tara was watching.

This little guy had gone right for the mini kit with the blue flame design. I took the plastic sticks and – careful not to break the little seat – played the kit, showing him all it could do. He squealed every time I hit the cymbal. After a couple of minutes, he overcame his shyness and wanted to try. I surrendered the mini-drum throne. He sat down and smacked away. His mother put her hands over her ears, so I showed her how the kit came with muffs and plastic cymbals. I even played the kit with the muffs on so she could hear the difference.

I told the little boy's mother to call the store if she had any problems with assembly and carried it to the car. When I got back, Tara had a huge grin on her face.

"What?" I asked, even though I knew why she smiled.

"You were really good with him."

I waved her off.

"You were. Why does that make you uncomfortable?" she asked.

"It doesn't." But her smiling at me, her being back in Wiley Music, did.

I went back to unboxing and displaying new bass guitars.

"Need more pink picks?" I asked.

"No. I use Fender Heavys now. Thicker sound."

She plucked the strings on a fretless bass. She sat on a nearby amp with it and played the bass line to Queen's "Another One Bites the Dust."

While playing, she asked, "So how much would it cost me to record my songs here?"

The following Friday evening, Tara showed up twenty minutes early for our first recording session, right before closing time. A Record World nametag was pinned to her blouse. She glared, thinking I was staring at her chest, until she looked down. "Oh," she said. She took off the nametag and shoved it in her backpack. A gig bag carrying her guitar was draped over one shoulder.

"Mom thinks I'm at Rebecca's and she knows not to call because it's the Sabbath, so we're good."

She had lied to her mother to record some songs. Or maybe she had lied because she was recording them with me.

"We'll get started soon," I said. "I just need to finish closing."

"Can I help?"

"No, I've got it."

I locked the door and switched the sign from "Open" to "Closed." I felt confident enough to make a decent recording for a customer, but I was hardly a professional engineer. Ms. Matteo and Uncle RB had quizzed me all week on how to read the levels, what every button on the console did, how to mix and master a recording. They knew I wasn't working with just any customer.

I walked around turning off amps and locking display cases. I adjusted the thermostat in the acoustic room, which held the most expensive guitars and violins. Uncle RB didn't like the room getting too hot. It could warp the fret boards and expand the wood.

"Where's your uncle?" she asked.

"He left early for a gig in Raleigh." Even if Uncle RB didn't have a gig, he would've made himself scarce that night so I could be alone with Tara.

"He gives you a lot of responsibility."

"I don't mind."

I shut off the lights in the main room and the store went dark. I was nervous to hear her songs. God, I prayed, please let her suck so I won't think so much of her.

I motioned for her to follow me to the back. I wanted to take her hand to guide her down the narrow stairs, but just told her to be careful and turned on the light in the basement.

The recording studio was broken up into two rooms of equal size, divided by glass and a large console. One room, the live room, contained microphones, amps, guitars, a drum kit, and a booth for vocals. The booth had a stool, mic, and music stand. In the other room, the control room, there was one swivel chair at the mixing board and lots of analog recording tape that Uncle RB had insisted on using. He was old school like that. Along the back wall was the comfiest couch he could find.

I'd nicknamed the studio Oz.

"Wow, this looks like a real recording studio," she said and gave the swivel chair a spin.

"It is."

"I mean, I haven't actually been in one. I've only seen them in movies and magazines." Tara stood over the console, looking at all the knobs, levers, buttons. I followed, putting my hands on the edge of the mixing board, hoping she'd ask questions.

Ms. Matteo had labeled everything with masking tape and a Sharpie in case I forgot something. She had a name for every knob and button, her own short hand, like another language, a secret language – one I knew.

"Do you know what all these buttons are for?" she asked.

Tara leaned over the console, her hand touching mine. Soft. Warm. Maybe I wasn't prepared for everything that could happen that night.

I moved my hand away and nodded. One thing I'd learned while watching Ms. Matteo and Uncle RB installing, testing, and using the equipment was that the possibilities in a recording studio were endless if someone knew what they were doing. That was my concern – did I know enough to create a magical recording experience for Tara? I ran my hand along the console. We had everything we needed right there. All I had to do was focus, which became increasingly hard with her standing so close.

She walked into the live room to explore. She tapped the high hat, strummed the acoustic guitar and peeked in the vocal booth.

I sat down at the console and pressed the button to turn on the mic. "I am the all-powerful Oz."

Tara jumped as my voice from the speaker filled the live room. Once she got over the shock, she laughed and put down her bags.

"Wanna record something?" I asked through the

mic.

"That's why I'm here."

"Okay, plug the guitar into that tweed amp to your right."

To calm my nerves, I'd set up the room earlier in the day while Uncle RB was still there to help. The Fender Deluxe amp Tara plugged her guitar into was already mic'd. I'd set up the vocal mic for her, too, and adjusted the stand to her height.

We were still almost the same height, but while her body grew curves and filled out, my body had grown leaner. I'd built some solid muscle with the weight training I'd been doing since those ice skating classes three years ago. We couldn't look more different. Even our hair was the opposite, hers long and full, mine chin-length, wavy, and always shoved behind my ears or under my UNC ball cap. Still, our bodies weren't as different as I wanted them to be.

With only one musician, there was no need to use the separate vocal booth. She'd play the guitar and sing at the same time, old-school style – the way Uncle RB still preferred to record.

"Whenever you're ready," I said through the mic in the control room.

Although I loved everything about the recording studio, the soundproofing was my favorite thing. It's like Tara and I were the only two people left on the planet. No phones, no TV, no one else.

To my surprise, she pulled a metal slide out of her pocket and put it on her left middle finger. We'd never worked with a slide in Jazz Band at Wiley High School. Where had she learned to play it?

"I'm not great on slide yet so don't make fun of

me if I mess up. I mean, that's what recording is for, yes? I don't have to get it right the first time," she said.

I pressed the button to talk again. "You do realize we're already recording."

She flipped me off with the slide and a smile.

I sat back in the chair and wondered if it was even possible for me to be Tara's best friend. Maybe I should shoot for being her third best friend. Maybe that would be easier. We'd only talk at school, asking about each other's weekend, but we'd never actually do anything together on weekends, never see each other outside of school. Maybe that would be enough, because being around her all day at school and recording together was too much. Even now I found myself thinking less about Tara, my friend, and more about the red bra strap sliding down her shoulder.

She leaned over the guitar. The next sound was this sledgehammer riff, the metal slide driving down the strings. Sitting there listening, I saw what Tara the guitarist could do. It's not that I didn't think she was capable, but it's one thing to think it, and another to actually see her do it – and do it looking so hot.

I was crazy for thinking I could be just her friend.

Tara stepped up to the mic and closed her eyes. Her voice, like her guitar playing, sounded as if it were coming from another version of her. She had a voice gripped by pain and loss, a voice that could not be ignored.

The verse lyrics were as wild and fast as the guitar, but at the chorus, the tempo slowed. Her voice and guitar got quiet. She closed her eyes again.

"She wants him to love himself," she sang.

I leaned forward. What? Who was she singing about?

"She wants him to love himself."

Her eyes opened right onto me.

I looked down at the mixing console, pretending to check levels. My hands got sweaty, and not from working the board. She went back to the main riff with the slide, and I almost slid out of my chair.

She sang another verse and chorus. Each time she repeated the slide guitar riff at the end, she hit the strings harder. Ms. Matteo had mentioned dynamics when she was teaching me about levels. She'd said a sign of an amateur musician was no dynamics in their songs - no soft to loud and vice versa. How did Tara already know this?

She finished playing and asked, "Well?"

It was amazing. *She* was amazing. Did I tell her that? No.

I pressed the button, leaned into the mic and said what Uncle RB always did after a good take. "Let's have a listen."

She came into the control room and sat on the couch while I played it back for her. The chorus got me the most. Who inspired her to write it? Thankfully, the low lights made the room too dim for her to see the goose bumps on my arms. Another thing I loved about the recording studio.

When the song ended, I rolled around in the chair and hit stop. "Wanna hear it again?"

"No. It's missing something."

I rolled the chair back around and faced her. She waited, wanting my help, but I couldn't get past what I'd just heard – her voice, the guitar, that chorus.

She wants him to love himself.

"It's a great song. The slide riff is really..." I searched, wanting to give her the right word.

"Seductive."

She blushed. "Over the summer, I took guitar lessons from this friend of my brother's."

My mind flashed to her taking guitar lessons one on one with some college-aged guy. My chest tightened, making it hard to breathe. Did he teach her other things?

"And the lyrics—"

"It's about my dad," she said.

I turned to face the console again and hoped the disappointment didn't show on my face.

Tara got quiet so I shifted in the chair to watch her out of the corner of my eye. She tossed her gum and stared down at the thin black carpet Ms. Matteo had insisted on for better acoustics. She played with her necklace, running the cross back and forth across the chain. After a couple of minutes, she moved to the edge of the couch and leaned toward me.

"You cannot repeat what I'm about to tell you," she said.

I turned to her, afraid of what she was going to say. Was her family moving again, now that her dad had passed away? She had less than two years left of high school. Her older brother still attended Appalachian State, less than a two-hour drive from Wiley.

"Remember how I had to lie about the Rolling Stones concert?" she asked.

I nodded.

"That's how my family deals with everything." She was crying.

Fighting the urge to move next to her, I sat completely still in the swivel chair.

"My dad didn't die of cancer." She choked the words through her tears.

I moved to the couch and put my hand around

her back the same way I would if Rebecca was upset, only Rebecca didn't relax into my chest and shoulder the way Tara did.

I tried to distract myself. Not from what Tara was telling me, but from how good it felt to hold her. I grabbed a tissue from an end table and offered it to her.

"Your mom, is she sick, too?" I asked.

"No. I don't think they've had sex since I was conceived. Mom blamed 'the gays' for corrupting him. Dad let her. He lived with it for years." She cried even harder to the point where her body shook. "They both pretended nothing was wrong. They chose to live that way. Dad died that way."

I pulled her back toward me on the couch and held her.

After several minutes she sat up and turned to face me. She pulled her knees to her chest like a shield, wiped her eyes and stared at the carpet.

"Sorry to dump all that on you," she said.

"You can always talk to me." I wiped a stray tear from her cheek.

"Okay, now you tell me a secret."

An alarm went off in my head telling me to stop, to stay there in that moment with Tara and talk to her, but my brain rolled over and hit snooze. "Drums."

"What?"

"It needs drums. Your song." There were so many things about her dad, about myself that I could've said, but I didn't.

"You're changing the subject," she said.

"Uncle RB's been showing me some more stuff on the drums. I think you'll be impressed." The challenge of hammering out a drum part for her song was less terrifying.

She looked at me suspiciously. I wasn't sure if it was because she didn't believe I could play drums better than when we were in band class or if she saw right through my desperate attempt to deflect the conversation.

Immediately I was off the couch and at the board, turning up the levels on the drum mics. I motioned for her to sit in the swivel chair but she stayed on the couch. The look on her face was that of a dissatisfied customer, like she'd asked for a sweet sounding guitar and I'd given her a knockoff complete with a fat-ass neck, high action strings, and horrible sounding pick-ups.

Finally, she pulled herself off the couch and plopped onto the swivel chair. She put her fingers right next to mine on the console. Focus on the drums Honeycutt, focus. As if she read my mind, she tapped her black polish fingernails against the console in perfect 4/4 time. She'd probably master the soundboard in a day. It had taken me weeks of asking questions. Hell, she could probably even come up with a drum part.

She stopped tapping. This time, her hand touched mine. We stayed like that for almost a full minute until I couldn't stand it any longer and pointed to the big white button.

"When I say ready, hit record first, then the playback button."

"Got it," she said, "The big white button."

Relieved to have some distance from her, I went into the live room, put on a pair of headphones and sat behind the drum kit. Uncle RB had a wider frame so I adjusted the throne and the drums closer. Even though we were in separate rooms I could still smell her passion fruit lip-gloss, making me think of those band storage room kissing sessions. My mouth watered and longed for the taste of her Doublemint tongue.

Tara's voice came through my headphones, "Any day now."

I pretended not to hear.

"I know you hear me. I watched you press this button every time you talked to me."

I continued to ignore her.

"You need a haircut," she whispered.

I scowled and the next sound was that laugh.

Finally, I picked up two drumsticks. "Ready." The red recording light came on and the guitar riff played.

I had her stop, rewind, and playback her song. I listened over and over until I came up with a heavy, driving drumbeat to match her riff.

On slow days in the store, Uncle RB had given me drum lessons. Even though guitar was his first love, drums were always what he ended up playing in most bands, because as he put it: Good, consistent, reliable drummers were hard to find and even harder to keep. I actually liked playing drums more than guitar. I liked using my arm and leg muscles to hold a steady beat. More of a workout than basketball, I always felt better, awake and in control after beating the drums for a couple hours. When Uncle RB left me in charge, sometimes I stayed for hours after closing up, just banging away in the dark. While playing the drums I was able to let my body go in a way it couldn't anywhere else. My body could do what it wanted, unlike when I was around Tara Parks.

Of course, I loved her eyes on my arms as I pounded along to her song, hitting harder than I ever had before – not only to show her my strength, but also to demonstrate that I was capable of banging out a primal pattern to go with her slide guitar. By the time I'd worked out and recorded the drumbeat, sweat was running down my back. I walked back into the control room and explained that typically, drums were recorded first or with the whole band in one room, playing together.

She didn't say anything. With her head tilted slightly, she looked at me in a way she never had before, like I was a movie she'd seen but never fully understood until that moment.

My arms ached from all the hitting. I adjusted the levels on the drums, guitar, and vocal as everything played back.

While perched in the chair, she watched my hands. Her silence worried me. She probably thought I sucked. I was no John Bonham, but I didn't sound bad. I was able to lock a kick drum groove right into the rhythm of Tara's slide riff. Part of it was the high quality mics Uncle RB had bought and how Ms. Matteo knew exactly where to place them on the kit.

The song ended, and I played it again. This time, with the drum volume down. Tara stood up, leaned in and put her hand over mine to move the drum volume up. While we listened she kept her hand over mine. She had a great ear. The drums sounded better. I'd been afraid the drums would overpower her voice, but they didn't. Not that it was easy for me to concentrate or even hear over the sound of my own heartbeat, pounding louder than Bonham's kick drum in my ears.

Tara left her hand on mine even though there was no adjusting left to do. The drums were at the perfect level, slicing through the guitar and vocals at just the right volume. The heat from her hand was warmer than the console. It reminded me of the band storage room again, her hands on my neck and back while we kissed. My stomach tightened.

Afraid of what would happen, I moved my hand away. Friends didn't let their hands touch for that long. She slumped back in the chair and blankly faced the mixing board.

Chapter 10

If I wrote lists like girls did, my list of things I'd rather be doing instead of attending New Life's parent-teacher open house would go on for ten thousand miles. Mom wanted to attend the open house, unlike my basketball games or anything else I did. She'd had the date marked on her Michael Jackson calendar for weeks. We were headed to my Bible classroom when Mom spotted Tara and Mrs. Parks. Mom didn't wait for me. She charged down the hallway like they were famous.

"Tara! My, you are so much taller than the last time I saw you. It's been way too long since you've been over to our place."

Tara looked past Mom at me. I shrugged apologetically, not wanting to make things with her mother more difficult.

"You're obviously Tara's mother, although you look more like her sister," Mom said.

Mrs. Parks smiled and looked up at the ceiling, like she'd heard that more than once. She probably had. Tara got her height, the dimple on her chin and the bright eyes from her father, but she got everything else, including the blonde locks, from her mother.

Mom waited awkwardly for Mrs. Parks to say something back.

Mrs. Parks stood still. She was impeccably dressed in a cream-colored suit and giant purse she held with both hands. My mother wore her best jeans, frayed at the bottom because they dragged the floor, and her favorite bright orange autumn sweater. Under the bad fluorescent hall lights, her hair was the color of urine because she'd left the dye on too long.

If only an earthquake would strike. I didn't know who I was more embarrassed for: Tara, Mom, Mrs. Parks or myself.

Mom finally broke the silence.

"I don't know if you know this, but Katharine just adores Tara."

I glared at my mother. Mrs. Parks's smile faded. She ran her hand through Tara's hair.

"Katharine? What happened to Peyton?" Mrs. Parks asked.

Tara moved away from her mother's hand and bowed her head. "Mom, please."

I tried looking at the floor, too, but my eyes climbed up Tara's knee-high black boots. Uncle RB said women in knee-high boots were his kryptonite. I'd never known exactly what he meant until that moment. All the prayers, all the trying to see Tara only as my friend – powerless against those black boots. I wanted to be back in the band storage room or in the recording studio. We'd be getting together soon to record another song. I reminded myself once again – friends don't think about those things. But those boots...

"I hope this school is a good influence," Mrs. Parks said.

She spoke to Mom, but studied me. Her lips were pressed together and her eyes scanned me, like a computer calculating one of those number two pencil standardized tests. She was looking for wrong answers. Even though I dressed exactly how I was supposed to at school and acted how everyone expected, she still looked for something wrong.

"Oh, it's already made a huge difference. New Life is teaching Katharine how to be a lady."

"I'm so glad to hear that. She needs it," Mrs. Parks said. "Now, if you'll excuse us."

She and Tara walked out of the school, neither looking back.

As soon as they were out of earshot, Mom turned on me. "Did you say or do something to upset Mrs. Parks?"

I shrugged.

"No wonder the rides to ice skating stopped."

"Ice skating stopped because Tara and I no longer liked going."

Mom's eyes burned right through me. I could see the dots connect in her mind.

We walked into my Bible classroom. Mom didn't head to the middle of the room to join the discussion with my teacher and the other parents. She explored the edges of the classroom, the blackboards filled with Bible verses. She did the same thing in the chemistry and geometry classrooms and didn't speak again until we were in my car.

While I drove us home, she pulled down the visor and checked her makeup in the mirror.

"Why didn't you tell me?" She pointed to a line in her foundation, visible just under her chin. "It looks like I'm wearing a mask."

"I didn't notice."

"Mrs. Parks is so pretty. Clearly that's where Tara gets her looks. You should get some beauty tips from her. I wonder what shampoo she uses."

"Pretty sure it's Pantene."

Mom wrote the name down on a notepad as though it were some expensive brand.

"I just want you to have things I didn't – pretty dresses, a nice boy to take you to school dances. Tara could be such a good influence. You don't see her getting into fights. I want you two to be close again."

I wanted to be close to Tara again, but not so she'd help me with boys. God help me, I wanted the storage room, the mole behind her left ear, the never-ending scent of Doublemint gum, and to slide off those black boots.

"If you fix things with Tara and Mrs. Parks, maybe we can all be friends."

She was quiet the rest of the drive. At the open house, she'd watched the other parents interact with one another like a puppy watches bigger dogs play together. She wanted to be a part of it, desperately, but made no effort.

Tara showed up for the recording session even earlier than usual and marched up to the counter, where I sat in front of Uncle RB's laptop paying Mom's gas, electric, and phone bills online. Usually, I paid them right when they came, but I'd been preoccupied lately, my thoughts on my new school, the secret about Col. Parks, and Tara, especially the last time we were in the recording studio.

"Why are you paying your mom's bills?"

All I could think about was being in the studio with her. "Why don't you go on downstairs and tune up."

I'd been going home after work and reading the Bible before bed. I kept hoping that something in the Bible would help me forget about those black boots and the passion fruit lip-gloss stains on her half-smoked Dunhill cigarettes. It didn't work. I could have amnesia and still remember minty-fresh Tara Parks.

She stood there while I shut down the computer.

I nodded toward the back.

"Everything's already set up. I'll be down soon as I close."

I walked by her and turned off all the amps and lights. She watched me for another minute before stomping off in those black boots to the back of the store.

After locking up, I went downstairs and pulled the swivel chair up to the mixing board without looking up at her.

"Ready when you are," I said into the microphone.

"All I did was ask you a question!"

There was no need to raise her voice, especially with an ultra-sensitive vocal mic. Losing my patience, I charged out of the control booth, pointing at her microphone.

"That is an original AKG C12 valve condenser microphone."

"English," she said.

"You don't have to yell. We're not in a bowling alley."

Her eyes got wide, and for a second, I thought she might cry. Instead, she slowly blew a large bubble, inching it toward the mic. When it almost touched, she brought it back into her mouth. I may have been the one behind the controls in the booth, but she was pushing my buttons.

"Can we just record the song?" I asked.

"No." A pout took over her face, not unlike that of Veruca Salt in *Charlie and the Chocolate Factory*. The pout would've been deliciously cute if I hadn't been so livid with her.

"Why not?"

"Because I want you to tell me why my asking

about paying your mother's bills put you in a bad mood."

Thinking about working with Tara had kept me on edge all day. Last time we recorded together, it had become increasingly hard to keep my thoughts on the songs. It wasn't this difficult being Rebecca's friend or Sammy's — especially now that he'd finally stopped asking me out. Making matters worse, the straps of her dark red bra were peeking out of her tank top. I'd seen it at point blank range in the gym locker room. Sometimes during class a strap escaped, usually after she'd just raised her hand to answer a question. The worst was thinking about her guitar teacher getting more than a glimpse of it in their private lessons. Those thoughts made me want to rip off my skin.

"It's no big deal. So I pay Mom's bills."

"You shouldn't be paying her bills. You're just a kid."

I grabbed my head. "No, I'm not."

"I just mean she should be taking care of you, not the other way around."

"She can't work. She has bad circulation, and I like paying bills. I like working here. It's the only time I feel..." Comfortable. It sounded so lame.

I didn't feel any more at home at New Life than I had at Wiley. The only time I didn't want to cut myself out of my own skin, the only time I felt okay was at the music store, where everyone called me Peyton and I could wear jeans and talk about music. Even if someone came in who sort of knew me from school, I never felt awkward because I could answer any questions about music or our inventory.

Tara relaxed her arms over the guitar and tilted

her head. Her eyes didn't leave me, like she was afraid I'd disappear. As if she knew sometimes I wanted to.

"I'm sorry I got angry with you about the bills. I shouldn't have," she said. "We're friends, right?"

I nodded. That was what I hoped for, prayed for.

"Well, friends ask questions and tell each other stuff. Don't you want to tell me things?"

I nodded, even though telling her things scared the hell out of me.

I walked back into the control booth and tried to focus on the recording session. Once again, I'd gotten myself into a mess – trying to be Tara's friend. If I wanted to be close to her I'd have to open up about things, things that I hadn't even been able to think about myself. I wanted to rip my head off, but instead I pushed "record" and then the mic button.

"Whenever you're ready," I said.

She still watched me, but with the glass between us, it felt more detached, like we were at the zoo. Me, the monkey inside the cage. Tara, just there for the day on a school field trip.

She started the song, like all the other ones, by turning her back. This song had a slow tempo with a sexy strum and a slight country vibe to it.

Tara turned around, stepped up to the mic, and closed her eyes.

"You're five years too late or five years too soon. Don't mean to hesitate, don't know if I still believe in you," she sang.

When she got to the chorus, she opened her eyes and looked right at me like the last recording session. This time I didn't assume the song was about me.

"Throw away the moonlight. Don't waste money on the jukebox. I've got needs you'll never meet and kisses bittersweet."

She sang a second verse then repeated the chorus and played through the chord progression two more times to fade out the song.

"That's it," she said. "It might need a third verse, but that's all I've got right now. What do you think?"

This time, I pressed the button and told her what I thought instead of just playing it back. "I think it's beautiful."

Tara let a nervous laugh escape. "I think you're biased."

We recorded just the rhythm guitar part next. Then, she tracked a backing vocal for the chorus. We even played around with a guitar solo near the end, but it didn't add anything to the song.

Ms. Matteo always said to put the song before ego, that the fastest way to kill a solo was to play too many notes and the quickest way to kill a song was to have too many things going on in it. After listening to the song a few times, we decided to scratch the backing vocal. The song didn't need it.

Tara came into the control room and sat on the couch. She pulled a bag of Skittles from her backpack and munched on them while we listened to the song a couple of times. After the second playback, she motioned for me to sit by her. I moved to the couch, but had a hard time sitting still. I ran my hands along my jeans and stretched my fingers. They were a little stiff from working the console. She offered me some Skittles, but I shook my head. They were too sweet for me.

"What do you think it needs?" she asked.

"We could add drums and bass, but I don't think it needs anything. I don't want to add something just because we can. Maybe we should hold off for a few minutes and listen to it again with fresh ears."

She sat back on the couch cross-legged. I noticed a copy of *Cosmopolitan* in her open backpack and grabbed it. She tried to get at it, but I turned away and opened it to the marked page.

"What Red Flags to Look for in a Man," I said, reading the title of the feature.

She tried to reach for it. "It's my mother's."

I stood up and read through the list, laughing. "Does he hold the door for you? Is he interested in what you have to say? Able to laugh at himself? Does he speak with authority? Does he complain about work? Is he a me person or a we person?"

She snatched the magazine back and shoved it in her bag. "You think lists are silly?"

I thought about the one I'd written in Jazz Band. The one that upset her. "I think they're a waste of time. And a list like that is impossible for any guy to live up to. Romeo, Rhett Butler, Mr. Darcy, hell, both those guys from *The Hunger Games* wouldn't stand a chance against that list."

Tara laughed. "Mr. Darcy? *The Hunger Games*?"

"What? I read."

Tara sat completely still and gave me a look like she was about to jump off a very tall building. "I know someone who stands a chance against that list."

My heart yanked up and down like a yo-yo. I was 50% certain she was talking about me. The other 50% said she couldn't be talking about me. My body wanted one thing while my mind prayed for another.

I glanced at the mini-fridge Uncle RB had insisted on installing. The moment begged for beer. Thankfully, he kept it stocked and wouldn't notice if a couple were missing.

I'd never seen her drink. "Wanna beer or wine cooler?"

"Beer's fine."

I opened two cans of Bud and handed her one. She tapped my can with hers and played with the beer tab until it popped off before flicking it into the trashcan.

I sat next to her on the couch and tried to relax. When I did, she turned toward me and moved her leg so that it touched mine. I told myself to get up, move to the swivel chair, but didn't.

"Next time we record, I'll try to swipe a bottle of wine from Mom's stash," she said.

I smirked. "So there'll be a next time?"

"Don't do that."

"Don't do what?"

"Other Peyton."

I stared at her.

She pointed at me with that magic wand index finger. "You just went from my Peyton to inauthentic Peyton."

Her Peyton. I took a long sip of beer.

"Inauthentic?"

"You're putting on an act, a front, not being yourself. Like all that Harlem Globetrotter shit on the basketball court. It's all for show."

I didn't want to tell her, but at the same time, couldn't stop myself. "For you."

"I don't want a show. I want the Peyton who held the door open for me on my first day at Wiley Middle School, the Peyton who hated wearing dresses, the one who doesn't care about what people think."

Did that Peyton even exist? That Peyton existed

for Tara. She saw me. She saw the Peyton I wanted to be, the Peyton I really was. No thought had ever made me more nervous and excited. Not knowing what to say, I finished my beer.

She chugged hers like she was in a hurry to get somewhere and tossed the empty can in the trash. "Have you been with a girl yet?"

Why did she want to know? I pretended to drink even though the can was empty. No way was I admitting I hadn't been with anyone. Still, I didn't want to lie to her so I kept my head bowed and stared at the floor.

She touched my arm. "You know there's nothing wrong with it, right?" I set my empty beer can on the floor and kicked it. "I mean, there's nothing wrong with you liking girls."

"I don't like girls." I still kept my head bowed, but watched her out of the corner of my eye.

She rolled her eyes. "Peyton—"

"I like *a* girl," I said and looked down. Was that authentic enough for her?

She took her hand away. After a few seconds, she turned away slightly and put her hands on her knees. Her eyes examined the console, focusing on the red recording light as if to make sure I'd turned it off.

She turned back toward me. "I want you to know that everything you feel is okay. I don't want you to lie about how you feel."

Her big blue eyes turned from caution yellow to green. Not able to keep my foot from flooring the pedal, I reached up and pulled her into me. I kissed her mouth, her apple cheeks, her eyelashes, the mole just behind her left ear. I slipped the hair tie from her hair.

In came a rush of her – hair all around me, vanilla, lavender, Skittles, passion fruit lip-gloss,

Dunhills. The scents created an intoxicating blend, and I had to have more. Her kisses were softer than the storage room kisses. Had she kissed someone else since then? Her guitar teacher? Those thoughts were chased away when she sat up and pulled off her shirt. In gym class, she took off her shirt because she had to. This time, she took it off for me.

What was she thinking? Why did she want to be with me? Was this a joke? I couldn't think anymore, some *thing* took over my body. I tried remembering comments I'd heard guys say about being with girls. I hadn't heard much because they got quiet whenever I walked into a classroom or near them in the hall. Except Sammy, he talked louder when I was around.

Finally, I got to run my hands over that red bra. How many times had I imagined it over the last few weeks? The material was almost as soft as her skin and hugged her chest tight.

Tara giggled. "It comes off."

Not only had I been running my hands over the bra, I'd been staring. My face lit on fire. "Sorry," I said.

"Don't apologize," she said before kissing me again.

Removing the bra took some work and some assistance. There were three hooks in the back. I made note for next time. If, when, there had to be a next time.

We were confined on the couch, which I loved because everywhere I touched and moved there was Tara. I rolled her over and tried to focus. I wanted to explore every inch of her. Moving to her waist, I slid her skirt down those long legs.

"Come up here." She tugged at my hair and shirt.

I kissed my way up one leg. Her hips tensed. I

had no idea what the hell I was doing, but I'd heard Sammy once brag to a friend – in front of me – that girls liked him because he knew how to ring their doorbell. I wasn't quite sure what that meant or where a girl's doorbell was located exactly, but this was my shot at ringing hers.

I took a deep breath and dove in. I felt the laugh first, her stomach and ribs trembling, trying to hold it in. Usually, I loved her unrestrained, contagious laughter. This time it horrified me. When I looked up, she was biting her lip.

"Come here," she said, attempting once again to pull me up.

I shook my head and dove back in, this time sliding my arms under her legs. One of Sammy's older friends had said finding a girl's sweet spot was the surest way of getting repeat action. Pleasing Tara in this way wasn't an option; it was mandatory.

I glanced up at her. "Just tell me when I'm getting warm."

"It's the same place as your—" she stopped herself.

Unlike me, she'd probably explored her body. At least she seemed to have an idea of where things were and what they could do. It made me wish I'd at least tried masturbation even though I loathed the idea of exploring anything on my body.

"Want me to give you directions?" she asked.

"Yeah. Like hot or cold."

"The game?" She laughed. "You don't have to—"

But I was already between her thighs again.

After a few seconds she whispered, "Cold."

I moved farther down.

"Colder."

Completely confused, I inched my way back up. "Warm. Warmer. Yes. Okay. Right. There. I mean, hot. Hot!"

Then she couldn't talk or forgot how. I got a little concerned, but kept at it. Her breathing got fast and deep. She moaned when my tongue moved in a circle so I kept that up. I loved listening to the beautiful sounds she made. Before too long, she went all kinds of crazy, pulling my hair, grabbing at my hands, yanking the pillows off the couch. The way Tara yelled my name the moment her hips bucked was the most beautiful sound I'd ever heard, even more than her laugh.

I made my way up her body and held her.

"This feels so right," she said between kisses. "Being with you feels right." She ran her hands down to my jeans and started unzipping them.

No. That was my one thought: No, please no, don't put your hand there. I reached down and pushed her hands away.

"It's okay," she whispered. "I want to." She tugged at my jeans. No. Don't touch me there. "I want you to be my first."

Her first – like there would be others, after me.

She went for my jeans again, and I shoved her hands away.

She sat up. The look on her face was harder to take in than the one after she'd read my list in Jazz Band.

Not able to stand it, I reached down on the floor and picked up her shirt. "We should get you home. It's getting late."

She yanked the shirt from my hands and wouldn't look at me while she got dressed. I told myself that her 'I want you to be my first' comment was the reason I'd pushed her away, but I couldn't let her explore and find what? Nothing.

"I can get myself home," she said and slammed the door.

Halfway under the couch, her dark red bra strap poked out. I picked it up, running my hand over it. She was just there on the couch with me, and now she wasn't.

Chapter 11

The morning after Tara stormed out of the recording studio, Uncle RB and I searched for pheasants in the hunting grounds a few miles past his lake house. But I hoped we wouldn't find any. I thought I'd like hunting. After all, I liked everything else Uncle RB liked. I loved shooting empty Cheerwine cans off tree stumps with a BB gun. I loved the feel of the gun in my hands, but the act of shooting and killing a bird just for sport seemed pointless. If my family needed food, I'd be out there every day. But to kill something, even a bird, for no reason other than just to do it?

"Are you trying to blow your head off?" Uncle RB asked.

He grabbed the shotgun out of my hand as we headed for the clearing.

I knew how to fire the gun, but my mind wasn't on hunting and I'd been pointing it up in my direction while we walked.

"Never point a gun at something unless you wouldn't mind it getting shot," he said.

"Sorry."

Uncle RB held up his hand, a signal for me to stop walking. He aimed the gun at a pheasant a few feet away. In my head I chanted, "Miss him, miss him, miss him."

He fired, and the pheasant flew away. "Damn. So close."

"That's okay, we'll get the next one"

We circled the edges of the clearing. I wanted to talk to Uncle RB about what almost happened the night before, but didn't even know how to begin.

"Do you and Ms. Matteo ever fight?"

Uncle RB lowered the gun. "Sure."

"What about?"

"She's not too crazy about me going hunting or owning guns, but mostly we fight about the lake house." Ms. Matteo wanted him to sell it and get a house in Wiley with her. Miles from town and with so few neighbors around, she found the lake house impractical and lonely. "Why?"

A pheasant landed a few feet behind Uncle RB. If I didn't keep talking, he'd turn around and see it. He'd have a clear shot.

"Tara got mad last night and stormed out of the studio, right in the middle of a session." In the middle of a *make-out* session, so it wasn't a lie.

Uncle RB ran his free hand through his hair. "What'd you do?"

"I didn't do anything." Again, not a lie, but not exactly the truth.

Uncle RB motioned toward the tree. He didn't even react when the pheasant flew off. He sat on the ground. I sat next to him and folded my arms around my legs.

He took a long sip of coffee from his thermos. "Moxie's a firecracker. You say or do something she doesn't like, it's gonna set her off."

I grabbed a stick and poked at the grass. "How can I make her understand something when I don't?" I hoped Uncle RB wouldn't ask me to explain what I meant.

He drank some more coffee before putting the thermos back in his pack. "You start by telling her that. Like Evie with the lake house. I can't explain why I'm not ready to give it up yet. I'm just not."

I watched an ant carry a dead worm four times

its size across the ground. I wanted to be strong enough to carry something four times my size.

Uncle RB tapped my shoulder and pointed to a pheasant across the clearing. He handed me the gun, and I pressed it against my shoulder.

My head was mixed up. I didn't want to shoot the bird, but I wanted to make Uncle RB proud. I blocked the "miss him" chant from my head and pulled the trigger, really trying to take down the bird, but he flew off. Hunting. One more thing I couldn't get right.

After an hour, we went back to my car empty-handed. Uncle RB whistled while he put the gun and ammo in my trunk. Maybe he liked the idea of hunting more than actually killing things, too. Maybe hunting, like the lake house, was his way of holding on to something – his manhood, youth, independence.

I tried to convince myself that I pushed Tara's hand away because I wasn't ready, like Uncle RB not selling the lake house. If I could've been with her the way I wanted to, the way I imagined it in my head, the way a boy like Jason could be with her, I wouldn't have pushed her away.

"Testosterone is a steroid hormone necessary for the production of sperm. It is made in the testes." Mrs. Parish displayed a detailed slide of the testes from her PowerPoint presentation. Half the class snickered, the other half tried not to. Two students weren't there because their parents refused to sign the permission slips. One parent had petitioned against New Life teaching the lecture to boys and girls together. On this, New Life stood firm: Teaching boys and girls together meant everyone received the same message, abstinence until marriage for both the man and the woman.

I think the real reason was because the student body and teaching staff were so small, they really didn't have the resources to break the eleventh grade up into two groups. Eleventh grade was late to learn sex education. Most of us knew by then, but two girls had dropped out recently to have babies so New Life made the rest of us suffer through the pointless class.

"Testosterone also influences the development of male secondary sex characteristics. These begin to appear at puberty. These characteristics include broad shoulders, deeper voice, increased muscle development, as well as hair on the face and the chest." Mrs. Parish paused, giving us time to take notes. My pencil slid around in my sweaty hand, making it difficult to write.

Until recently, biology had been my favorite subject. Unlike most of my classmates, I loved dissecting worms, starfish, and frogs. I liked seeing inside things. Because I didn't mind doing the part they found gross, all the girls wanted me as their partner. They put aside the stuff they didn't like about me and became super friendly on dissecting days.

Except Tara. Since that night at the studio, she'd avoided me in every class. As soon as the bell rang, she was off to the next one. When she wasn't in class, she hung out at the library, where talking wasn't allowed. She was the last one in the lunch line and the first one to leave the table. In the locker room before and after gym, she changed clothes between other girls. I didn't know what was worse, standing next to her when she got undressed or being across the room. I was aware of her every move either way.

In biology, Tara sat one row over and one seat behind me. While Mrs. Parish showed us slides of human body parts, I couldn't stop glancing back at her. She pretended not to notice. She sat arms crossed, face drawn in tight as a boxer's fist.

Mrs. Parish popped a cough drop in her mouth, Halls Mentho-Lyptus, so strong it stung my nostrils from three rows back. She sucked on them all the time, even though she rarely coughed. Ancient Mrs. Parish described the human reproductive system with far less enthusiasm than her upcoming retirement.

"The testes are located in a pouch called the scrotum."

Most of the class snickered. Mrs. Parish moved from a slide with a testes image to a side view of the male reproductive system and the giggles continued, along with whispering.

I couldn't get comfortable in my seat. I tried sitting up, but my knees knocked against the bottom of the desk. If I leaned back, my legs hit the back of the seat in front of me.

"A lower temperature than the average body temperature is required for the development of sperm. Located outside the body cavity, the scrotum is several degrees cooler, making it ideal for normal development."

Mrs. Parish had gone full throttle with all the radiators in the room. It was late January, but in that room, it felt like July. Sweat trickled down my spine. I shifted in my seat and struggled to get comfortable. I heard Tara sigh and caught a glimpse of her clamping her teeth down on the chain of her cross necklace. Her eyes were on me for the first time since that night in the recording studio.

"Testosterone can lead to balding or a receding

hairline later in life."

"Later?" One boy cracked up, pointing to the guy behind him with a huge forehead. Everyone laughed, even Tara.

Mrs. Parish moved on to the female reproductive system and fertilization. A slide showed one egg surrounded by several eager-looking sperm. I swear the sperm were grinning. "Sperm enter the vagina of the female's reproductive system when strong muscular contractions ejaculate semen from the male's penis during intercourse."

That's about the time I started feeling like the main course being spun round and round on a Lazy Susan.

"The second meiotic division is complete only if fertilization takes place. That's when the zygote is formed. Now, remember class, this only happens when a man and woman are married."

"My mom said the baby comes out deformed if the parents aren't married. Is that true?" the girl whose earthworm I'd dissected said sarcastically.

The whole class snickered.

Mrs. Parish paused, appearing to be deep in thought. "It is a possibility."

"Bullshit," Tara whispered.

I wanted to turn and nod in agreement, but what was the point? Every time Mrs. Parish mentioned marriage I felt a little more left behind, like a broken guitar even Uncle RB couldn't fix.

The sperm in the slide began to multiply and dance around in circles of light. They teased as if they were saying, "Ha, ha, you'll never know what it's like to share us with the girl you love."

Why was I there? Why was I even born?

I closed my eyes and shook my head, trying to block out the dancing sperm and Mrs. Parish's voice. Calm down, Honeycutt. Breathe. When I opened my eyes Mrs. Parish had turned off her PowerPoint presentation. She shoved a disc into the DVD player.

"Now class, the video you're about to watch is very graphic. It's a real woman giving birth. We show it here at New Life because we want you to see what a serious, life-changing event childbirth is. By watching this video, you will see why you must wait until you are married, because only a couple recognized by the Lord as husband and wife are truly prepared for such a task."

Mrs. Parish asked for a volunteer to get the lights.

A woman shrieked high-pitched screams like someone had stabbed her. Next came deep breathing and shouting about how much it hurt. Knees up, legs forced apart. The top of a baby's head draped in blood. A woman's hand clutching the side of the bed.

New Life's agenda wasn't lost on Tara. She crossed her arms, narrowed her eyes. I heard a growl from the back of her throat like a dog being teased too much.

I tried not to watch, but there was no escaping the sounds.

Finally, I surrendered and glanced up in time to see the baby's head coming out from between the mother's legs. Blood and what looked like slime made its way out of her, too. The woman was blonde and looked only about five years older than Tara. My lunch slowly climbed back up my throat. I had to tell myself, Not Tara! Not Tara!

"Gross!" yelled the girl whose starfish I'd dissected.

"Breathe!" the doctor commanded from the screen.

I tried, but I couldn't take a deep breath. As the mother pushed the baby through, I pressed my thighs and knees together. I didn't know a lot of things, but one thing was certain: A baby was never coming out of my body. I'd rather die.

As I struggled to breathe, the screen got blurry and for a minute I thought the DVD had finally worn out from all the times New Life had used it to scare students. I looked away, dizzy, but the blackboard, the clock, and the boy sitting in front of me were all filled with white polka dots.

A voice asked, "Are you all right?" A baby cried from far away. "Elevate her feet," a woman said. "I'll get the nurse." It took a moment to realize it was Mrs. Parish speaking.

Tara was the first person I saw. She yanked my legs up on the desk chair and kneeled down beside me. I reached for her cheek, smooth like the wood on her Stratocaster right after a good polish.

"What's wrong?" I asked.

"You fainted."

"I'm sorry."

Tara got a puzzled look on her face, like I was speaking Latin. "It's not *your* fault."

Yes, it was. Uncle RB never fainted. Thor never fainted.

"Maybe she's pregnant," said the same boy who made the balding joke.

Everyone burst into laughter, except Tara and me.

Tara moved away from my hand. Her cheeks looked like someone had set them on fire. No wonder.

Everyone was staring at us.

I tried to sit up.

Tara backed farther away from me. "You should stay down for a few minutes. You don't want to get up too soon and faint again."

She was too young to have lines on her forehead, but there they were, three of them, one for me and two for the way everyone looked at us.

"Please don't worry abou—"

"Just stay there. I'll go see what's taking Mrs. Parish so long."

Tara walked out of the room. I got the feeling she wanted to run.

I knew something was up when Rebecca called on Saturday wanting to meet during my dinner break. I assumed it was a reminder about *My Fair Lady*, her first time as the lead in a musical.

The dining area of Know Good was a small room with white candles on every table. Shelby and LouAnn had painted the bricks white. I guess it was to make the place more romantic or homey, but the white paint depressed me. Why mess up the natural brick color?

Rebecca waited at a table for two by the front window. Of course she would choose to sit there.

As soon as I got settled, she pounced like a puppy. "How are you?" Her tone suggested aliens had just returned my body to planet Earth.

"I'm fine. We got in a new shipment of amps. I've been unloading those all day."

"No, I mean—," Rebecca looked around, "the fainting." She whispered the last word. Not because she was shy but because she was embarrassed for me.

Great. Now I'd be known as the fainter. Tara had probably told her.

Shelby grabbed two menus and brought us a pitcher of water with lemon slices. Rebecca studied me while she recited the specials for the evening.

"I think we're gonna need some time to decide," I said.

When Shelby left, Rebecca reached across the table and put her hands on mine. "I'm worried about you."

"Why?" I slid my hands out from under hers.

She sat back in her chair and folded her arms in a huff. "I thought we were still friends."

"We are."

"Well, friends usually tell friends when they have sex."

The place was crowded, but no one sat too close to us, the only good thing about being in the front window. Rebecca had sex? With Sammy? I waited for details.

She waited, too, her way of building suspense. Such a showman, she waved her arms like she wanted me to ask questions. Finally, she dropped her arms back on the table. "Are you gonna tell me about you and Tara or not?"

I glanced around the room, trying to figure out what Rebecca was talking about. "Tell you what?"

She swatted me with the menu as Shelby returned. Rebecca ordered the chocolate chip pancakes because she could. Her favorite thing about Know Good was that breakfast was served anytime. I ordered the meatloaf with mashed potatoes.

When Shelby walked away, Rebecca took her red cloth napkin and unfolded it dramatically, like a matador flapping his cape. Next, she inspected each piece of silverware. Everything was spotless but she kept staring, probably more at her reflection than anything on the knife.

I surrendered. "What?"

"I'm trying to figure out which one of you is lying," she said. "It's not easy."

I unfolded my napkin and tried to pretend that we were not discussing the most important thing in the world. "What did she say?"

"Tara said you two had sex over a week ago on the couch in the recording studio and you haven't called or texted or emailed her since."

What? We'd had sex?

Shelby brought us a basket of yeast rolls, right out of the oven.

"Thanks," I said to Shelby, before stuffing half a roll in my mouth. I didn't like having this conversation, much less in public. Rebecca waited for me to say something, but all I could think about was how Tara thought we'd had sex and I hadn't called afterwards. Why did I have to call? She was the one who stormed out.

I reached for a second roll, but Rebecca took the basket away. I sat on my hands to keep them still. Rebecca was my friend. I should be able to talk to her about anything. I leaned across the table. "That wasn't sex. Sex is when a guy, you know..." I made a half-ass attempt at a gesture with my hands. "Enters a girl."

Rebecca surrendered the breadbasket. "Where'd you get that idea from? There are lots of different ways to have sex. I have it with myself just about every night."

I held my hands to my ears. Rebecca pleasuring

herself every night – didn't she realize images like that would stay in my head? No, in her mind she was talking to one of her girlfriends. That was the problem. She didn't get it. No one was ever going to get it.

"How do you think they do it?" Rebecca nodded toward the kitchen again. "You'd be screwed if that was the only way two people could have sex."

She laughed so hard at her own pun, she snorted.

Even though the fireplace was on the other side of the restaurant, I felt like a marshmallow being roasted on its flames. I struck the table. "I'm not like that."

Always up for a scene, Rebecca turned her head to see if anyone noticed, but in Wiley people pretended not to notice. Everyone kept on eating. I wondered what it felt like to be out on a date, having a nice meal and a normal conversation. What did normal even feel like?

"Look," Rebecca said. "I know it's not easy. My director last summer at theater camp grew up not too far from here and he's gay. He said coming out was difficult. And I know you've heard the nicknames." Rebecca nodded toward the kitchen at Shelby and LouAnn. She kept going, but my mind wanted to focus on what Tara had said about the night in the recording studio. That wasn't sex. We were just fooling around, like in the band storage room only we'd gone a little further. But it wasn't sex.

"I'll be honest. I was a little freaked out at first, but I talked to my theater camp director and Mom." Good Lord, who had Rebecca not talked to about me? "I'm okay with it now. I mean, I don't really get it and I'm kinda shocked that Tara's into it, too. No offense. I thought she liked boys as much as I do."

Tara liked boys. She liked them a lot. Jason Webb. David Bowie. Ryan Gosling.

"My director said you might deny it at first. He was in denial until he was almost thirty. Can you imagine? Your whole life is, like, over at thirty."

I tried to get a clear image of what I'd look like at thirty, but couldn't. Instead, an image of Uncle RB came to mind. Did everyone in Wiley think I was in denial? Did Tara think I was like her father?

Rebecca waved for me to take another yeast roll, but my appetite had vanished. Instead, she took one herself.

We sat in silence for a couple minutes.

"I'm not like that," I said.

Her head tilted and those monster brown eyes of hers narrowed in a way I'd never seen. Her mouth opened and closed. For the first time in the nine years I'd known her, Rebecca David didn't know what to say.

She reached over and wiped my cheek. I hadn't even realized I was crying. I pulled back from her hand.

"Damn fireplace." I placed my napkin on the table. "The smoke gets me every time I'm in here." My unused dishes and utensils would still need to be washed. I slid a twenty-dollar bill on the table, more than enough to cover my dinner.

"Wait. Peyton."

I walked toward the door. Shelby saw me and exchanged a worried look with LouAnn as they greeted some friends. They probably thought I was in denial, too. Maybe they'd work with Rebecca and hatch a plan to save me. It'd be nice if just one person understood. But how could they when I didn't have a fucking clue?

Chapter 12

On Monday morning, my feet couldn't move fast enough from the student parking lot to the library. Nervous as it made me, Tara and I needed to talk about what had happened in the recording studio. I needed to apologize for not calling or texting and try to explain that I didn't think it was sex. What did I have to lose? She was already pissed.

Lately, Tara had been getting to school early to study in the library. She said it was because her grandparents were there on an extended visit. She said she couldn't concentrate at home with her grandmother putzing around the kitchen every morning. She'd said this at the lunch table to someone else.

She wasn't in the library. No one was. When I approached the eleventh grade hall, I heard a God-awful scraping noise.

Rounding the corner, I saw the familiar tan and blue backpack and those black boots planted in front of her locker. Tara scraped a large piece of sandpaper over the words that had been written with a black Sharpie: TARA PARKS IS A DYKE.

"Who wrote it?"

Tara jumped at my voice. "Doesn't matter."

"Yes, it does."

She sneezed from the dust cloud of sandpaper.

I dropped my coat and backpack to the floor and offered to help. She surrendered the sandpaper. The handmade sign came off her locker slowly, but it burned a permanent place in my brain.

"I'm gonna find out who did this."

"Don't. Please just let it go. If we don't react, they'll stop. They'll have no reason to keep doing it."

"It's happened before?"

"Twice in the last week." Was that the real reason she'd been getting to school so early? "I just want it off my locker."

I went back to work, scrubbing so hard a layer of my skin came off. Soon, there wasn't a trace of the letters, but I kept going, furious.

"Don't take the paint off underneath. The goal is to avoid attention."

She sounded like her mom when she said that. I wondered if Mrs. Parks had always worried about Col. Parks attracting attention.

Tara put the sandpaper inside her backpack. She exchanged books in her backpack for others in her locker. My brain scanned through all of our classmates, wondering who would write that crap about Tara. I remembered the way they'd all watched us when I fainted, how I put my hand on Tara's cheek, how she'd backed away, embarrassed.

"Why are you here so early?" she asked.

I wanted to talk about the recording studio, but didn't know how to bring it up without help. I pulled a plastic grocery bag out of my backpack.

"You got me a present?" Her smile faded when she saw the dark red bra inside the bag.

I leaned against the locker next to hers. "I'm sorry."

"Unfuckingbelievable." She tossed the bag in her locker.

I stepped back. "I'm sorry I didn't get it back to you sooner. I'm sorry that I haven't said anything about that night, but I didn't—"

"Rebecca's the only reason you're talking to me

at all right now." She slammed her locker shut.

"Why are you more pissed at me than the jackass who's writing shit about you on your locker?"

"I don't care about the jackass who's writing shit about me." She walked in the direction of the library.

I grabbed her arm. "Tara—"

"Don't." She shoved my hand away and went into the library.

I'd hoped by returning her bra I could find a way to talk to her about how I was feeling. Instead she was more furious than ever.

My anger surged to an all-time high, too. I had to find and punish Sharpie Bitch. I stayed in the hallway until I had just enough time to get to first period. I lurked near Tara's locker between every period, staying there for as long as I could without being tardy to the next class. Our classmates walked by, but no one lingered.

As soon as the last bell rang, I pretended to clean my locker, but it was pointless. No one was coming while I stood there. The only place in the hall to hide was inside my locker, but the space wasn't big enough. Before leaving, I went into the girls' bathroom and cracked a window to have access super early in the morning, even before the entrance to the school was unlocked. By 6:30am the next morning, I'd crawled through the eleventh grade girls' bathroom window and waited. Every time I thought I heard a noise, I peeked out the door.

Fifteen minutes later, someone walked by the bathroom. I glanced out and saw the other blonde from our biology class armed with a Sharpie.

She was on the 'r' in Tara's name by the time I snatched the Sharpie out of her hand. Startled, she jumped.

"Yeah, that's right. You should be afraid," I said.

Sharpie Bitch faced me. "What are you going to do? Tell? Dyke."

I shoved her hard against the locker. The Sharpie fell to the floor. "You say one thing about Tara to anyone, you write one more thing, you even look at her wrong, and I will drag you out of this school by your hair and beat you in the face until you don't recognize yourself. Understand?"

She nodded. I'd pinned her so tightly against the locker, she couldn't react any other way. Beneath my hands, her body shook.

She looked up at me the way girls had looked at Jason Webb when he bullied them. Trying to defend Tara, I'd become the asshole.

I backed away and released her. She sprinted down the hall. She didn't pick up the Sharpie. She didn't look back. She ran to get away from me.

I sat on the floor by the lockers until Tara showed up. I stood and presented her with the Sharpie. "You don't have to worry about Sharpie Bitch anymore."

Tara's eyes grew as wide as two baseballs. "What did you do?"

She didn't want to know Sharpie Bitch's identity. She wanted to know what I had done, so I told her. "I was protecting you."

"I don't need protecting." She kicked her locker. "The rules are worse here. If you even give someone a threatening look, you'll get suspended."

"I don't care what happens to me."

She shook her head and her eyes filled up with tears. Once again, I'd screwed up.

"You've made it worse. Why couldn't you just let it go?"

I stood there long after she left, after the tardy bell, leaning next to her locker.

During Bible class, an office assistant came for Tara. She returned ten minutes later, her face empty. She didn't sketch in her notebook. She didn't fidget with the cross necklace. She sat there, lifeless.

Our Bible teacher droned on about how David was chosen by God. I leaned back in my too-small desk and wished that God had chosen me for some huge mission of death. I'd like to take on some giant monster. But no, God had made me the monster. That's what I was – a monster. Freakenstein. As long as I was around, bad things would happen. Tara's words "You've made it worse" repeated in my head like a chorus from one of her songs. She was right. Every time I was around her, even while attempting to make things better, I made them worse. Someone wrote the word dyke on her locker because of me. She had problems with her mom because of me. I tried to fix things by writing that list. I tried to stay out of her life. That didn't work. I was the one who needed to go.

After lunch, an office assistant came for me. Tara hadn't given me up; Sharpie Bitch did. The head of New Life had called Tara in because Sharpie Bitch said I'd gotten some crazy idea in my head that Sharpie Bitch and Tara didn't get along.

While I sat across from her desk, the head of the school put on her granny glasses and read through my thin file. I'd only been there a few months. There wasn't much in it.

A painting of Jesus hung over her shoulder. His head was turned upward, his eyes on heaven.

"You remember when I explained our probation policy?" she asked.

"Yes, ma'am." I wondered what Jesus thought of New Life's one-year probation policy.

"And I have your signature here on the form that states you read the student handbook where unacceptable behaviors are clearly listed."

She was worse than Fancy Nancy. Why couldn't she just get on with it?

"Threatening a fellow classmate is on the list."

Another list. I wanted to live in a world without any lists. I also wanted to point out that Sharpie Bitch was the first to do the damage, but it would only put more negative attention on Tara and what had been written on the locker in the first place.

She closed my file and clasped her hands firmly on top of it. "Tara Parks is one of our best students. Straight As, ranked second in the class. Her mother is a friend of mine from church. I know she would hate to see her daughter involved in any trouble."

"Tara didn't have anything to do with it."

"Because she's a good girl with a bright future ahead of her. She doesn't need any trouble from you." No wonder the head of school and Mrs. Parks were friends. They sounded just alike.

She pushed her granny glasses up the bridge of her nose and pulled out an expulsion form. She wrote the name Katharine Honeycutt on top and slid it across her desk. "Read and sign this. Then, you are to clean out your locker and leave school grounds immediately." She found my home number in my file and dialed it. Of course, Mom didn't pick up. *The Young and the Restless* was on.

"Your mom at work?" she asked.

"No. She might be out with friends or something." Not exactly a lie.

Mom had always said the characters on her soaps felt more like friends than any she'd ever had in real life. I didn't know how she was going to cope when all the shows got cancelled. She cared more about what happened to B-rated actors than what happened to me.

The head of New Life hung up the phone and watched as I pretended to read the form. I was a fool to think I could fit in at New Life, using the name Katharine again, wearing dresses. A fool to think I could beat Mrs. Parks and fit into Tara's world. Tara was better off without me around. No one would call her a dyke. She could find a boyfriend, one who could give her what she wanted and keep Mrs. Parks off her back.

I grabbed the pen, but paused before signing. "Tara's not in any trouble, right?"

"No. And with you gone, I doubt she ever will be."

I was done trying to make things fit. I signed the form Peyton Honeycutt and vowed to never use the name Katharine again.

I dumped everything from my locker into a recycling bin by the exit. I wasn't even that sad about getting kicked out. New Life was no life without Tara Parks. I'd failed as just friends, not able to be near her without wanting more. Wanting more only caused more trouble for both of us.

On my last trip to the recycling bin, my *Thor* comic hit the rim and fell to the floor. On her way back from the bathroom, Tara kneeled down to pick up the comic, but I beat her to it and tossed it in the bin.

She held a hall pass in her hand, a wooden cross. The seventh graders made them in shop class. She eyed my *Thor* comic in the recycling bin. "They kicked you out?"

I nodded.

"You don't seem upset." The Doublemint on her breath almost made my knees buckle.

I took a step back. "I'm sorry."

For loving her. For not loving her. Not able to say anything else, I walked out the door.

Mom had called Wiley Music before I even got there for my afternoon shift. She told Uncle RB to send me home right away. She always called the store, never saying what was wrong. With her, it was usually difficult to tell. She could be out of milk or in need of medical attention, but today I had a good idea that the problem was me.

She sat at the table, staring down at the ivy design on the placemat in front of her.

"Mom?"

I kneeled down beside her, but she wouldn't look at me, wouldn't even acknowledge I was in the room.

For the first time, I saw how she was growing old with the house she rarely left. Her cheeks were sinking. The little girl was also there, trapped inside the aging face, lonely and longing for a companion.

I felt her hands, her forehead. Her skin was frozen. I walked over to the thermostat.

"Don't. Heat's too expensive."

How the hell did she know? She didn't even look at the bills. I turned it up from 68 to 75.

"I'm turning it down as soon as you leave. What I need are a couple of those portable heaters to keep by my feet."

"Uncle RB says those take a lot of electricity."

"Well your uncle knows everything, doesn't he?" The words came out quiet and strained, like it hurt to talk.

A new phone bill waited on the counter, propped up against an empty candy jar where I couldn't miss it. It seemed like I'd just paid the last one.

"The head of New Life called," she said.

Old granny glasses must've kept calling until Mom's shows were done for the day.

"She said you're not a good fit for the school." Mom traced the placemat design with her index finger.

Finally, she turned toward me. Her eyes, mouth, and jaw were pulled in tight, an expression I'd last seen right before Dad walked out. "Just like your father," she said. "He wasn't a good fit, wasn't fit for anything."

I didn't know what to do. I was used to her crying, yelling, asking me to do stuff, not sitting at the table like she wanted to curl up and disappear. And she rarely mentioned Dad anymore.

"Don't worry, Momma. I'll figure it out."

She went back to tracing the placemat with her finger.

"You don't look like you're feeling well, Mom. Let me make you some soup. How about tomato soup and a grilled cheese sandwich with lots of butter – the way you like it?" I searched the cabinets and pulled out every tomato soup can. The expiration date on each one had lapsed by several months. "You need to eat this stuff before it expires, or it's a waste."

She kept tracing the placemat like it was a maze and her finger was lost inside.

Even the chicken soup had expired so I gave up

on the canned foods and closed the cabinet. Maybe a nice dinner at Shoney's would cheer her up.

"Mom, when was the last time you had something to eat?"

"There's no place in this town for someone who is different. God knows I have tried and tried to make you fit." She looked up, beyond the ceiling, closed her eyes and raised the back of one hand to her forehead.

"I think it's that uncle of yours. You're spending too much time with him." Her eyes focused on me leaning against the counter, shoulders squared. "You're even starting to look like him."

"What's wrong with that? Uncle RB is handsome. I want to look like him."

I crossed my arms and held them tight to my chest to keep my hands from shaking. I was saying things I'd never said out loud to her before.

"There's a lot wrong with it. It's not right. There are people who do very cruel things to anyone different. They'll hurt you, and they'll hurt me."

I walked over and rested my hand on her shoulder. "I won't let anyone hurt you, Mom."

She moved her shoulder away. "You're the one hurting me."

Shocked, I stepped back. "I do everything for you."

"You've never been a daughter to me."

If she'd pulled out a gun and shot me, it would've hurt less. I paid the bills, her bills. All those months of working extra hours, I could've been playing more basketball with Sammy or spending more time with Rebecca. I wore dresses and pretty things that I hated – for her. Never again. "Fine. You pay the bills and pick up the groceries and do all the other crap I do for you."

"How dare you take that tone with me? Get out of here. Get out of here and don't come back."

I didn't hesitate, I just walked out of the house, straight to my car and thought about Dad. She'd told him to get out, too. Maybe I was like him, not fit for anything. My cheeks still burned as I reversed down the driveway. The songs Tara and I had recorded together played through the stereo speakers, the volume turned up, but not loud enough.

I drove down Fisher Street, thinking about what Mom had said, how she'd rather have no daughter at all. Oh really? Well, there's a gun in my trunk. Why don't I just blow my brains out, Mom? How would you feel then?

"Fuck you," I said to a person honking as I rolled through a stop sign. I'd gotten there first.

"Here Comes the Wait," my favorite song of Tara's came on. I turned up the volume, almost as loud as it would go.

"I'd rather you kick the shit out of me than walk out that door," Tara sang.

A bicyclist came out of nowhere, almost scraping the side of my Mustang. When I dodged him, he had the audacity to flip me off. I slowed down and flipped him off with both hands.

"Asshole!" he yelled.

I sped off. He was probably on his way home to a mom, dad, sister, brother, and girlfriend who loved him.

Too warm inside the car, I rolled down the window. The wet air meant it would rain soon, maybe even snow. It only snowed in Wiley once a year. Tara loved the snow. She once told me that every time it snowed back in New York, she'd made a snow groom for herself and asked her brother to marry them.

"Because I would hit you back, but I'm not chasing down love anymore," Tara sang.

I'd go to the clearing where Uncle RB had taken me hunting, where the grass was so high a hunter would have to trip over a body to find it. Hell, a bear might find it first. That would be the best way. No body, no mess.

The railroad crossing was coming up. I'd always wanted to hit it fast, see how the Mustang would take it. I pressed the gas pedal, speeding up to fifty, fifty-five. I flew across the tracks like something out of that movie *Drive*. My mind flashed to Rebecca talking about how cute Ryan Gosling was in the movie and Tara agreeing. I sped up to sixty-five.

"I thought we were timeless, but you couldn't last one month." Tara sang with so much authority, so much certainty on this song.

Uncle RB would tell everyone it was an accident because that's what he'd want to believe. He'd recall our recent hunting trip, how many times he had to remind me to point the gun away from my head.

Ms. Matteo would win all of their arguments after my "accident." Uncle RB would stop hunting and get rid of all his guns. He'd sell the lake house just like she wanted.

"Here comes, here comes the wait," Tara sang.

When I turned onto Bringle Ferry Rd., the sun was setting like the last scene in one of those old western movies, where the cowboy rides off on his horse never to be seen again. Only no one saw me as the cowboy. Ryan Gosling would never play me in a movie.

A trucker approached from the opposite direction

and honked. I looked in the rearview, but didn't see any other vehicle on the road.

"Is everyone drunk?" I yelled.

"Here comes, here comes the wait."

The part in the chorus where Tara whispered was coming, so I reached over to turn the volume all the way up. The damn honking almost drowned out her voice.

I glanced back up. The truck swerved off the road to avoid hitting me. I slammed the brake pedal down to the floor and jerked the steering wheel in the opposite direction, but it was too late. My car headed right for the truck. I squeezed my eyes shut. Tara's voice was the last sound I heard.

"Here comes, here comes the wait."

Chapter 13

A bright, hazy light burned right in my face. Was it the sun? Around the light, voices whispered like they were speaking through layers of gauze.

"She's lucky to be alive," one said.

No feeling in my right arm. Was this death? Throbbing ache through my jaw. Stinging above my left eye. Not death.

I struggled to hear the voices as they went on about some girl. I fought my way back, like one of those dreams where you can't wake up. I wanted to be awake, to understand. I bit down on my tongue, but didn't feel any pain. However, every time I inhaled, I felt an ache down my throat and into my ribs.

"Thank God she was wearing a seatbelt."

They were talking about me. Uncle RB had always said he'd take back the Mustang if he ever caught me driving without a seatbelt.

I tried to focus on the big light above. It got brighter, but stayed fuzzy. Not able to stand it anymore, I closed my eyes.

The smells hit me next: a mix of rubbing alcohol and bleach along with the doctor's aftershave as he wrapped something cold and hard around my neck. The last time I'd smelled rubbing alcohol and bleach was while visiting Col. Parks in the hospital.

When I woke again, I heard the same things.

"You're lucky to be alive."

"Thank God you wore a seatbelt."

This time, the words came from Uncle RB and Ms. Matteo. They were right by my bedside but their voices sounded a football field away.

I tried to speak, but felt even weaker than the first

time I woke up. Ms. Matteo squeezed the arm that didn't ache. Uncle RB said, "Rest."

The next time I opened my eyes, Tara was sitting cross-legged on the only chair in the room. She sat frozen like a statue. She wore her winter coat, even though the room was warm. Her eyes didn't leave me.

I tried lifting my head, but it felt like a fifty-pound weight. I remembered Tara's dad, weak, in the hospital. Just before drifting off again, I told myself – Honeycutt, you can't die and leave her like her father did or like your dad left you.

I woke up to a nurse changing a bandage over my eye.

A doctor explained what had happened, like I hadn't been there. "It was pretty bad. You crashed into a semi and rolled over several times."

"The trucker?" My chin jammed into the brace around my neck every time I spoke.

"He's going to be okay."

Going to be? Shit.

The doctor listed my injuries: concussion, neck strain, multiple fractures to my ribs, lacerations, and a broken arm. He said some injuries take a while to show up, so there could be more, like nerve damage.

When the nurse had changed all my bandages, she asked if I was up for visitors. I nodded, figuring Mom waited to give me an earful.

A few seconds later, Uncle RB, Ms. Matteo, and Tara walked in. They all had raccoon eyes, like they hadn't slept in a year. Mom wasn't with them.

Uncle RB and Ms. Matteo came to my bedside while Tara stayed back, sitting in the chair, cross-legged like before. Ms. Matteo's eyes were red. Uncle RB had stubble and his hair was a mess.

"I'm sorry," I said.

"You got nothing to be sorry about. It was an accident," Uncle RB said. The pain I'd caused Uncle RB hurt worse than the injuries from the accident.

What sounded like a grunt came from Tara. Uncle RB must've thought so, too, because he glanced back.

Ms. Matteo held his hand. She put her other hand on my cast.

"Don't worry about the car," he said. "Once you're up and around, we'll get you another one."

His eyes got all watery, making me feel worse. I didn't deserve another car.

"We're just glad you're all right." His voice cracked.

Ms. Matteo squeezed his hand and said they should leave so my other visitors could come in.

"Yeah, better let Mom in," I said.

Uncle RB glanced at Ms. Matteo. "Your mom's at home," he said. "I've been calling, giving her updates."

When they walked out, I waited for Tara to get up or say something, but she didn't. She'd at least taken off her coat, half draped over the back of the chair.

Rebecca and Sammy came next. In her arms, Rebecca carried a stuffed bear on crutches, a flower arrangement, and a box of chocolates. She'd sampled some of the chocolates.

"There's a lot of yummy dark chocolate ones," she said.

When I didn't respond, she put them on the table by my bed.

"You don't look comfortable." She adjusted my pillows. She wanted to be the first to sign my cast.

Sammy signed it next. "You'll want to keep this cast when it comes off. Not sure about Rebecca's, but my signature will be worth something one day." He winked at Rebecca, and then offered the marker to Tara, but the blonde ice princess shook her head.

"I've got rehearsal, but later I'll smuggle dinner in from Know Good. How's that sound?" Rebecca asked.

It sounded great, but I didn't deserve the fuss. "Please don't go to the trouble."

"Save it," Sammy said. "You can't talk her out of anything."

Rebecca reached into the box for one more chocolate. "I want you out of the hospital in time to see me in *My Fair Lady*."

"But you getting better is most important," Sammy said.

"I suppose I can always act out the whole thing right here." Rebecca said, but her usual overly excited tone wasn't there. Sammy's voice had an edge to it, too. They were both worried about me even though I'd survived the wreck. And neither one of them brought it up, neither one said the word accident.

Sammy found the Tar Heels game on TV for me. He also caught me up on Wiley basketball. Tara had probably shared the news that I'd been kicked out of New Life. He and Rebecca stood close to each other, but I couldn't tell if things had progressed beyond friendship with them or not. Rebecca would be all over him if they had, so they were probably still just friends.

When they left, Tara didn't come over. She hadn't said one word the whole time. Her silence stood out even more after the outpouring of emotion from everyone else.

"I'm gonna be okay. You should go."

She had to clear her throat before speaking.

"Are you going to tell them?" she asked.

She got up and pulled *Thor* from her coat pocket. She tossed it on the bed. "That day we first talked in the eighth grade bathroom, you said I could have any comic except *Thor*."

"If you really want it that bad, take it." I reached down and offered it to her. I even managed a wink, trying to lighten things up. Her face was stiff, like a guitar string wound too tight.

"You never loan out this comic and you'd never get rid of it unless—"

"Tara, I just got banged up a bit. I'm going to be okay."

"Are you?" She leaned forward like someone had kicked her in the stomach. "Tell me that you running into that truck was an accident."

I leaned forward, too. Pain shot all through my body. "It was."

"You're lying."

"No, I'm not."

She spread her fingers across the foot of the bed and bowed her head, like a bull preparing to charge at me.

"The trucker you hit has three kids."

"The doctor said he's gonna be okay."

"You could've killed him."

"You think I would intentionally hurt someone else?"

"Those three kids could've lost their father."

Why was Tara being so mean? She reminded me of Mom, who cared more about Michael Jackson and her soaps than her own kid. Where was she? "It's like you don't give a shit about me," I said.

Her eyes filled up with tears. "If that's what you think, then you don't know me at all."

She took her coat and headed toward the door. I grabbed *Thor* with my good arm and threw it past her head.

"I could've died and you're mad at me?" Every word slammed my chin into the neck brace.

Tara stopped at the door and turned halfway. Those Windex eyes cut right through me. "Please get help before you hurt yourself or someone else again."

"I'm the one in the hospital. I'm the one hurt."

Livid, I looked for something else to throw. Tara watched the box of chocolates slam into the wall and the candy pieces scatter across the floor.

She left the room quickly, almost knocking Uncle RB over.

Her last words played over and over in my head. *Please get help before you hurt yourself or someone else again.* Why couldn't she be sweet and bring me gifts like everyone else?

Two days later I was cleared to go home. Tara hadn't come back and Mom never came. No matter how long Uncle RB and Ms. Matteo stayed, they couldn't fill the void in the room. Mom had meant what she'd said. She didn't want me home. Her words hurt worse than any injury from the car crash.

Uncle RB had already moved my things to the lake house. Clearly, Mom wanted no part in taking care of me even though I'd taken care of her for years.

Unfuckingbelievable.

Uncle RB pushed me through the hospital in a wheelchair. He stopped by a desk to sign the release forms. The lady took her time finding the forms, flirting with him. I wheeled the chair down the hall to the water fountain.

Three young kids ran into a nearby room, chanting "Daddy, Daddy!" I peeked in at their father, his left leg in a full cast, his neck in a brace. The trucker told his youngest son to get off his leg. I'd never forget his face. I'd seen it right before slamming on the brakes.

Later that evening, Uncle RB refused to let me help make dinner so I sat at the kitchen table, my neck still in the brace, my arm in a cast. He had steaks out on the grill and pasta for Mac-n-Cheese cooking on the stove.

"Sure you don't want me to go check on the steaks?" I asked.

"No. They need a couple more minutes."

Wanting to do something, I stood. "Let me just go — "

"No. You don't need to go check on the steaks. What you need to do is go back to Dr. Wainwright." He sounded tired. He'd been quiet during the car ride from the hospital. Maybe Tara had told Uncle RB.

"She can't help me," I yelled.

"Why not?" he yelled back.

I sat back down. He wiped his hands on a dishtowel and threw it on the counter. Tara hadn't told him her theory that day in the hospital. She didn't have to.

He rubbed the back of his neck. "We've got to figure out what to do about school."

"Evie said she'd help me study for the GED." Ms. Matteo had finally convinced me to start calling her Evie.

Uncle RB held his hands up in surrender.

"Okay." He turned off the burner and drained the pasta. He didn't say another word until after he mixed in the cheese sauce. "I just… there are some things I don't know how to help you with and you're like my own kid. If anything ever happened to you—" he stopped because his voice broke. I'd never seen him even close to crying. He swiped at a tear before heading outside to the grill.

I'd always known he cared about me, but hearing how he thought of me as his own kid made something inside me snap into place.

Uncle RB returned to the kitchen with the steaks, and I added Kraft cheese slices to the Mac-n-Cheese. We sat down to dinner, both of us quiet for a while.

"If you think it will help, okay," I said. "I'll go back to Fancy Nancy."

He smirked. "You're almost as stubborn as me."

Dr. Wainwright sat across from me in a white shirt, black vest, and black pants. She looked like Han Solo in that outfit, but something told me she wouldn't take it as a compliment.

It'd been three months since my accident. My neck brace and cast had been removed. I sighed, studying her office. Nothing had changed since my last appointment except the box of tissues, yellow this time. It made me wonder how many people cried in her office every week.

The office smelled like cinnamon. I glanced around and found the source – an orange coffee mug on her desk with a cinnamon stick popping out. Neil Young's "Cinnamon Girl" played in my head.

Dr. Wainwright had asked me to pay attention to what was on my mind between our sessions. Lately, most of my thoughts had been about studying for the

GED and wanting to take some business classes to help out more at Wiley Music.

One other thought nagged at me. "I've also been thinking about how no matter what I do, I disappoint people. That's why I was out on Bringle Ferry Road driving so fast when I had my accident. "

At the word accident, Tara's voice thundered through my head: You're lying.

Dr. Wainwright wasn't interested in the accident. She asked me who I thought I'd disappointed.

"Mom."

"When was the last time you talked to her?"

"Right before my accident. She told me to get out."

Fancy Nancy didn't respond. She sat completely motionless like a certain opinionated blonde. When something really bothered Tara Parks, she got completely still and quiet, like a stupid rock ballad right before it explodes into a cheesy guitar solo.

"I know what you're sitting there thinking," I said.

"You do?"

"You're thinking it wasn't an accident, but if I was gonna do something it wouldn't involve anyone else. I wouldn't slam my car into someone. I'd go somewhere with no one else around."

"Have you been thinking about suicide a lot lately?"

I rubbed the left side of my head. "What?"

"You just said you'd go where no one else was around. That tells me you've thought about suicide."

Suicide. Such an ugly word, especially when said out loud.

"People consider suicide when they think they have no other option." Dr. Wainwright leaned forward in her seat. "Peyton, do you feel like there are no other options?"

My head pounded, making it hard to think. "No. I just feel like all the other options suck."

"Tell me what you think your options are."

I'm sure it came out like one of Mom's grocery lists that I repeated in my head on the way to the store instead of taking the time to write down. "I could continue to wear dresses like Mom wants or be lesbian since everyone thinks that's what I am or move to a big city..."

Dr. Wainwright interrupted my thoughts. "Okay, how about this: If you could have any option, any kind of life, what would that be?"

I pictured myself wearing a suit and tie. An image of Tara flashed in my head.

My hands were clammy so I rubbed them along my jeans. I felt hot and dizzy like the day in biology class when we watched that horrible film of the woman giving birth. Why was it so hard to focus on what I wanted?

"Do you know what you want?" she asked.

"It doesn't matter. My mother—"

"Kicked you out. What if there was no one around, no one in your life you had to worry about disappointing? What if you could dress however you wanted, look however you wanted, do whatever you wanted? Who would that Peyton Honeycutt be?"

I thought of Uncle RB in a t-shirt over a long sleeve one, hovering in the repair shop, refusing to give up on some old electric guitar. I shrugged, not knowing why Uncle RB had come to mind.

"That's your homework. Next Thursday when you walk through that door, I want you to start showing me who that Peyton Honeycutt is."

Usually the idea of homework made me want to gag, but this assignment didn't sound so bad. Plus, unlike most homework, I already knew the answer.

The night before my next appointment with Dr. Wainwright, Ms. Matteo sat at the kitchen table of the lake house, quizzing me on the timeline for World War II while I scooped smoke bombs out of a frying pan and placed them onto aluminum foil. The two ingredients for smoke bombs, sugar and saltpeter, smelled like candy and were edible, but I wanted to set them off with Uncle RB later by the water. Fireworks were illegal in North Carolina, but this was a chemistry project, part of my studying for the GED, or so I claimed.

Ms. Matteo had been impressed by how fast I learned stuff, but history and science were my favorite subjects. While I was still healing from the accident, I had nothing else to do except study all the GED materials she brought over. I had memorized the periodic table and studied U.S. History up through World War II while hanging out on the pier or in Uncle RB's boat. Gazing out at Lake Norman while reciting chemistry formulas made me feel like I could do anything. If a group of people could turn fifty miles of dry land into a beautiful lake, what could I do?

As productive as I was studying for the GED, every time I thought of Dr. Wainwright's assignment, Mom came to mind. Up until now it had always been about pleasing Mom and other people.

"And when did the allies catch Hitler?" Ms.

Matteo asked with a serious face.

"They didn't. On April 29, 1945, he married Eva Braun. The next day, she took a cyanide capsule and he shot himself with a Walther PPK."

Finished with the smoke bombs, I put the frying pan in the sink to soak. I craved a break from studying history, the past. I wanted to focus on me and the present.

"Okay, let's move on to the War in the Pacific—"

"Ms. Matteo—"

"Evie." She reminded me again.

I turned to her. "Can you cut my hair? Like how you cut Uncle RB's."

It took her a full minute to respond. "Sure."

Five minutes later, I'd drenched my hair and spread newspaper all over the kitchen floor. She had the scissors ready and motioned for me to sit in a chair. She draped a towel over my shoulders and ran her hands through my hair to separate it into pieces for cutting. Her hands reminded me of afternoons in the band storage room when Tara ran her hands through my hair. Evie's fingers moved faster though. They were all business.

Pieces of my hair hit the newspaper, making tiny sounds. She wasn't even halfway done, but my head already felt a ton lighter. How did girls like Tara do it, all that hair on their head? We hadn't even talked since our fight at the hospital, but thoughts about Tara didn't stop. I thought of her every time I saw couples holding hands in the grocery store or kissing in the city park. No longer Not Tara, now all I saw was Not Us. Each couple having a romantic dinner in Know Good: Not Us. Every boyfriend who picked up a guitar and played something to impress his girlfriend in Wiley Music: Not Us.

I watched through the handheld mirror while

Evie focused on the back. The shorter she cut my hair, the better I felt.

"Did Uncle RB ever get rid of all his old clothes?"

"Don't get me started. He insists on keeping everything. He has three large Hefty bags full of shirts and ripped up jeans he hasn't worn since, I don't know, 1994? I love your uncle and how nostalgic he is, but enough."

"He just doesn't like giving things away to strangers, where he won't see them again. He'll give them to me if I ask."

"You don't want those old clothes."

"Yes, I do."

She pushed my head down. "Hold still."

Through the mirror, I saw a small smile on her face.

While Evie trimmed the last of the stray hairs, Uncle RB came home and poked his head in the kitchen. We had the exact same haircut. Finally, at seventeen, my hair matched my face and how I felt inside. I couldn't stop looking at my hair and smiling. For the first time, I liked who I saw in the mirror.

I jumped up and hugged Evie. "Thank you. I love it."

Evie and Uncle RB also smiled, but their smiles were nowhere near as big as mine. I sat back in the chair and stared into the mirror. Everything about me – the square chin, the thick eyebrows, even my broad shoulders and scrawny long arms – looked better with the haircut.

Evie put the scissors in the sink and took the towel off my shoulders. The air danced against the back of my neck.

"It does look good," Uncle RB said to Evie. "You could always get a job as a hairstylist."

"I still think expanding Wiley Music to a school is a better idea," I said.

Uncle RB and Evie didn't respond right away. She rinsed my hair off the scissors.

"Maybe it isn't such a bad idea," he said. "We could spend the summer converting my apartment above the store."

"And you'd live here full time?" she asked.

He grinned and she tried to hide her annoyance by helping me pick up all the newspapers off the floor, but I could tell she was frustrated by the way she balled the paper up and threw it in the trash.

The lake house was where Uncle RB and his buddies played poker and drank beer until 4am. All wood paneling, exposed brick, and deer heads, the lake house wasn't Evie's style at all. Plus, it was a forty-minute drive to Wiley Music.

"A school would be a ton of work," Evie said. "Not just teaching the classes, but administration, marketing."

"I can help," I said. "The only other thing I've got going on right now is studying."

"Listen to you. The only thing. It's a huge thing," Uncle RB said.

"We could change the name to Wiley Music Company because it's like a one-stop shop: store, school, studio, and repairs," I said.

Uncle RB rubbed his chin with the back of his hand, his way of pretending to mull something over before he said yes.

I checked myself out in the mirror again. With Uncle RB standing right there, I grinned at how much we looked alike. He smiled, too, and then ran his hand across my hair to mess up Evie's styling job just a little.

The way Dr. Wainwright studied my haircut made me nervous so I ran my fingers across the top to make sure it wasn't sticking up. The chair in her office was more uncomfortable than usual so I checked underneath to see if the stuffing was coming out. Maybe someone super heavy had sat in it.

"How does the haircut make you feel?" she asked.

I sighed. Why was she always asking how I felt? With as much as she charged, she should be answering my questions.

"The air feels good on the back of my neck." I ran my fingers through the back.

"That's how it feels externally. How do you feel on the inside?"

"I don't hate what I see in the mirror now."

She shifted in her seat and glanced at the clock, confirming my suspicion that she was getting sick of me and having to ask me so many questions. But I didn't know what I was supposed to say. She kept looking at me.

"I like that the haircut makes me look more like my uncle. Evie cut it like Uncle RB's." I sat up and wondered why the chair was so uncomfortable and if Dr. Wainwright found what I'd just said crazy. As usual her facial expression didn't change.

"You want to look more like your uncle?"

My turn to glance at the clock: We still had forty-five minutes left in our session.

"I know where you're heading with this." She sat

perfectly still and waited for me to continue. "You're going to say that I like my hair short because I'm the kind of girl who likes other girls."

"Not every lesbian likes to wear her hair short."

I shifted in my seat again. Lesbian. There's that word again. Maybe Dr. Wainwright was one. She didn't have a wedding ring or any pictures of a husband or boyfriend in her office. She had long dark hair. Maybe she was offended by everything I said. She probably dreaded her sessions with me, her least favorite client.

"I find it interesting that you see it as either you're lesbian or you're not, as if those are the only two things you can be. Either black or white."

That got my attention. I sat still.

"There are other possibilities. Have you heard of the term transgender?"

"Like Cher's kid?"

She nodded. "It means you feel your gender identity is the opposite of the one in which you were born. It has nothing to do with who you're attracted to, with sexual orientation."

Bells rang in my head, and my mouth went dry. I cleared my throat, but said nothing. No one else had ever mentioned transgender to me. Uncle RB had never mentioned it, and he'd met all types of people while touring the country with rock bands. Ms. Matteo grew up in St. Louis and went to school in Chicago. She'd never mentioned transgender. The word sounded complicated, confusing, and painful. So different from male or female, girl or boy. I didn't want to be different or complicated. I wanted simple, normal.

My body got hot, like someone had doused me with kerosene and lit a match. I glanced at the simple dark brown coffee mug on Dr. Wainwright's desk and the tears rushed out. I couldn't say yes, that sounds like me, because I didn't want it. I just wanted to be like Uncle RB and Sammy.

Dr. Wainwright pushed the box of tissues across the coffee table. I'd never used one and often vowed I never would. Feeling like a failure for giving in to the waterworks, I grabbed a tissue.

While I wiped my eyes, Dr. Wainwright went to her bookshelf. She handed me a thick book, titled *FTM: Female-to-Male Transsexuals in Society*.

"Take it home and read through it. It's full of interviews with people at various stages of their transition."

I was too nervous to open the book and look through it in front of her. I wanted to ask questions, but was afraid of what the answers would be, afraid of wanting something so foreign, so different. If Jason Webb and most of Wiley still thought being a dyke was wrong, what would they think of this?

Chapter 14

Dr. Wainwright didn't mention the FTM book for the next few sessions and neither did I. But I read every page in my room at the lake house. Uncle RB and Evie thought I was studying for the GED. I did study, but after a couple of hours, I pulled out the book and read about people born with girls' bodies, but who were boys.

One night, I was reading an interview about someone who was afraid of how his seven year-old son would react to him after his surgery when Uncle RB knocked on my door. I threw the book under my bed and grabbed a calculus book.

"Can I come in?" he asked.

Uncle RB walked in and pulled over a chair to sit by the bed. I looked and realized my calculus book was upside down. I flipped it quickly, hoping he wouldn't notice, but he did.

He sat back in the chair. "Maybe you should take a break from studying."

"No time for a break. The test's next week."

"Evie thinks you're more than ready." Uncle RB yanked up his sleeves and leaned forward. Had he come into my room while I was out mowing the yard and seen the FTM book? I wasn't ready to talk about it.

"I've decided to sell the lake house." He said it like he'd just gotten the idea, instead of something he'd been arguing over for months with Evie. "It's not practical anymore. The only thing it's close to is the highway." He went to my window and peeked out the blinds. "It's time for Evie and me to get a place of our own together."

Great. Dad was long gone. Mom had kicked me out. Now Uncle RB had found the FTM book and he wanted to get rid of me.

He stared out the window at the lake for a while before he came back to the chair. "Now don't worry. I'm not leaving you without a place to live. You'll stay with us."

Relieved that they didn't want to completely abandon me, I still didn't think sharing a new space with Uncle RB and Evie, their first place together, sounded like a great idea. They'd never admit it, but I was certain they'd prefer to move in just the two of them. Who wouldn't?

I had a different idea, one I'd been thinking about ever since Evie cut my hair.

"How much more money will I make managing the school?" I asked. The plan was for Evie to teach, Uncle RB to run the recording studio and repair shop, while I managed the store and school.

"Depends on how well it does."

Even through all those months of paying Mom's bills, I'd managed to save a little. "I could buy the lake house from you," I said, although, I had no idea how much a down payment would be. "You could come visit it whenever you wanted." I grinned.

He leaned back in the chair and crossed his arms. "I wouldn't feel right taking money from you. You need to save up for college and other things."

I glanced at the floor and wondered if Uncle RB had come across the FTM book. He wasn't one to snoop around, but maybe emptying the trash can in my room he'd found it by accident and read about some of the surgeries I might want down the road.

We hadn't discussed my haircut or my wearing his old clothes, but I'd caught Uncle RB studying me from across the store several times. He always seemed relieved when I left the store early on Thursdays for therapy. Even if he hadn't seen the book, he had to suspect something.

"I don't want you offering to buy this place on account of me."

"Are you kidding? I love it here. Other than the music store, it's the only place that's ever felt like home."

Uncle RB smiled at that and for a second I thought he might cry again. "Owning a house is a lot of responsibility. You'd be all the way out here by yourself."

My mind flashed to the car accident and what Tara had thought. Uncle RB had suspected the same thing. It's why he'd wanted me to go back to Dr. Wainwright. I'd been able to admit to her that I was driving recklessly that day and, even though I didn't intentionally smash into the truck, that I was having suicidal thoughts at the time. "I could get a dog."

He laughed, but shook his head. He wasn't letting me off that easy.

"You know I'm seeing Dr. Wainwright every week now."

He nodded and moved the hair out of his eyes.

"It's going well. You don't need to worry. I'm going to be okay."

Uncle RB leaned over, put his hand on my shoulder and squeezed. "I don't want you to just be okay, Peyton. I want you to be happy."

I looked down at the bed and thought about the book underneath it. A lot of the people interviewed in the book said it wasn't just how they dressed, but how they lived that had helped them. Owning the lake house, having my own place where I could live how I wanted would be a huge help.

"You think owning the lake house would make you happy?" he asked, as if he could hear my thoughts.

I nodded.

"Most kids your age want to go off to college, party, blow off classes. I should know better with you. You're not like most kids."

Once again, I got the sense that Uncle RB wanted me to say something, to share my thoughts with him, but I wasn't ready.

We were silent for a while. He picked up my calculus book and flipped through it. He pretended to be interested, but really he was stalling. That's when I realized his hesitation wasn't just about whether or not I was ready to live out there by myself. He was having a hard time letting go of the house.

He tossed the book back on the bed. "We could do a rent to own. You pay a certain amount every month that goes toward paying it off."

"You can do that?" I asked. "I mean, it wouldn't put you in a bind?"

He shook his head.

"I want it on paper, so it's official," I said. Uncle RB would end up telling me payments didn't matter or something. I wanted to buy the house. The rent to own was gracious enough.

He held out his hand and we shook on it. I made sure my grip was as firm as his. Even more than when Evie gave me the haircut, I felt like the person I wanted to be.

As manager of the new school, one of my duties was getting the word out. Uncle RB had an artist friend design a poster of kids rocking out on instruments. I spent my weekends in June putting them up all over Wiley.

I walked into Know Good with the poster, waving it at LouAnn and Shelby. They both gave thumbs up from the kitchen.

Turning toward the front window, I saw Tara. We hadn't seen each other since my accident four months ago, when she'd called me a liar. She sat at a table by the unlit fireplace with a slightly older guy who wore an Appalachian State t-shirt. They sat close. Tara laughed at a joke or funny story he told. Like me, he was skinny with dark hair.

"Put the poster anywhere, Peyton," LouAnn said from the kitchen. It was busy, lunchtime on a Sunday so no one paid attention to her yelling across the room except Tara. Her eyes found me.

Play it cool, Honeycutt, play it cool.

Despite the chant in my head, my hand shot up with a goofy wave. Tara's smile faded, and the guy stopped talking. He watched her walk over to me.

I watched her walk over, too, that deliberate, slow walk, hips moving from side to side. I didn't want to miss that walk, but I did.

"Nice haircut," she said. It took me a few seconds to realize she wasn't being sarcastic. She bit her lip while studying the poster in my hand. "Your music school idea comes to life. I think it's great, especially since the school district cut the music program."

I glanced over at the guy she was with. The more I looked at him, the more I could see myself, the way his legs were too long for the close seating at Know Good, the way his brown eyes followed Tara's every move. I thought about the things he had that I didn't. A sharp ache tore through my chest.

"You look good, like you've recovered."

"I'm sorry about the hospital," I said. "For throwing the chocolates."

"I was upset that day, too." Tara squeezed my arm, the one that hadn't been broken in the car accident. Still, I felt her squeeze all the way to my toes.

I nodded toward the guy in the Appalachian State t-shirt. "He your boyfriend?"

Her cheeks got all rosy. She let go of my arm. "You want to meet him? He's a drummer, like you."

Like me. He seemed to be a lot like me except for the important parts. "I should get this poster up."

We both stood there for a minute, not saying anything. An elderly couple came in, and Shelby showed them to a table.

Tara watched the couple. Even though the man had a cane and struggled with it, he still pulled the chair back from the table for his wife. A smile crept onto Tara's face. She looked back to me. "It's good to see you, Peyton," she said before returning to her boyfriend.

I put the poster in the front window on the other side of the restaurant from where Tara sat. Still, I could hear her laughing at something the boyfriend said. I always loved hearing that laugh, like a favorite old song, but it ached a little, too.

I thanked LouAnn for the fresh biscuits she insisted I take back to Wiley Music and got out of there. Leaving, I noticed the poster was just a little high on one side, but it'd have to do. Seeing Tara smiling at her boyfriend was better than seeing her upset, but I wasn't going back inside.

In late July, a month before the opening of Wiley Music School, Evie, Uncle RB, and I hosted an orientation. Our biggest classroom was packed with parents and potential students. They had a ton of questions for Uncle RB and Evie. My job: making sure the orientation ran smoothly by supplying plenty of chairs, cookies, and fruit punch.

Overall, I felt better about things. I'd enrolled in summer business courses at Wiley Technical College. Sessions were going well with Dr. Wainwright. She kept encouraging me to dress how I wanted, not just during my visits with her, but all the time, especially since I didn't have to deal with trying to fit in at school. At the store, it usually wasn't a problem. The customers were mainly interested in what I knew about the instruments or if they could get a deal on multiple packs of guitar strings. People sometimes stared a little too long, but I never felt unsafe.

Uncle RB and Evie never questioned how I dressed. Evie taught me how to put on a tie. She even helped me pick out a suit for the orientation. She'd sighed the whole time, wishing she could get Uncle RB to wear one.

The only nerve-wracking thing: Rebecca sat in the back of the room and watched me. She wouldn't stop looking at my suit. We hadn't spent much time together lately and soon she'd leave for her annual trip to Israel.

While a parent asked about the size of the classes, I made sure everyone had a copy of the class descriptions. Trying to avoid Rebecca's stare, I noticed a pretty, green-eyed girl a little older than me in the second row. She had auburn hair, which made her eyes look even wilder. She wore an Art Institute of Chicago t-shirt. I handed her a schedule, and she winked.

Evie answered one last question on the difference

between intermediate and advanced classes. Or it was supposed to be the last question, as the orientation was already running a half-hour longer than scheduled.

The green-eyed girl raised her hand.

"Okay, one more," Evie said.

"What class do *you* teach?" the green-eyed girl asked me. She giggled. So did the friend next to her.

My mouth went dry. They were making fun of me, the suit. Dr. Wainwright had said there'd be people who wouldn't know how to respond to me, especially in the beginning. She told me not to take it personally, but it was hard not to when they were laughing at me.

"Peyton's the school manager," Evie said.

The two girls whispered to each other while people gathered their things and chatted in clusters. After a couple minutes, everyone made their way downstairs to the store. Uncle RB and Evie had exited first to greet people on their way out.

I folded and stacked the metal chairs in the corner, trying to forget about those two girls laughing at me. Things were bad enough with Rebecca there.

The green-eyed girl came up and slipped a small sheet of paper in my hand. "I go back to Chicago for school at the end of August, so call me soon, Manager."

She and her friend headed for the door, but she turned back to look at me again before leaving. I went back to folding chairs, pretending that what had just happened was no big deal.

Rebecca came over and grabbed the slip of paper from my hand. Scribbled on the paper in red ink was a girl's name, Valerie, and a phone number.

"Call me soon, Manager," Rebecca said in a breathy, Marilyn Monroe voice. "Maybe you can manage me sometime." She laughed at her own joke.

When I didn't laugh, she handed back the girl's number. "She's obviously confused."

I shoved the paper in my pocket. "How so?"

Rebecca motioned at my suit. "You, trying to dress like a guy. She thinks you are one."

I slammed a chair on the stack in the corner and yelled, "I'm not trying to do anything."

Rebecca jumped back and her face crumbled. Before I could offer an apology, she left the room.

I sighed and followed. "Rebecca."

She stopped halfway, but didn't turn around.

"I'm sorry. I shouldn't have lost my temper like that."

She waited, needing more. She should've been the one who apologized. But whatever, it wasn't worth the trouble.

"Thank you for coming and supporting the school. I'm sorry we haven't spent a lot of time together lately. The GED studying had me really busy, but that's over now."

Her face unlocked. I'd said the secret code.

She came back up the stairs and hugged me. "I miss you," she said. "Let's hang out when I get back from Israel." She pushed me away, but held my shoulders. "And this new look of yours. I'm not saying I don't like it, but it's going to take some getting used to."

I wanted to say it's not a look, but that would bring up questions I wasn't ready to answer. She left after another hug. Whether she'd ever completely understand me or not, Rebecca loved me as much as she could love anyone other than herself.

A little over a week later Uncle RB stood at the front

counter on the phone while I unboxed new Zildjian cymbals, his favorite. He wanted one of each new cymbal displayed on a drum kit. I figured Uncle RB kept looking over to admire the new cymbals, but soon as he hung up, he came right over to me, wringing a dust rag in his hands.

"You still talk to Moxie?"

It had been so long since he'd used that nickname, it took me a few seconds to realize he was talking about Tara. A crash cymbal slid through my hands. Uncle RB caught it. He held the cymbal while I tightened it on the stand.

"Yeah. Just saw her last month at Know Good."

That wasn't what he meant. He wanted to know if we were still close, but I couldn't admit that we weren't. We didn't hang out or even talk on the phone anymore.

Uncle RB rubbed his hands over the rag. When he caught me staring at his hands, he shoved the rag in his back pocket. "The guy on the phone books Shadows in Charlotte, and Tara's band is opening for mine next Friday. That okay with you?"

Tara had a band and Uncle RB knew about it before I did.

"Peyton, is it okay? I know you and Moxie—"

"It's fine." I cut him off before he could say anything. Whatever he was going to say, however he was going to describe us, I didn't want to hear it.

Chapter 15

Usually, I loved coming home to the lake house and sitting out on the back deck after being at Wiley Music all day. The stillness of the lake was a nice contrast to customers attempting to play various instruments, many of them trying to show off when they could barely play. The worst was when a guy came in and tried to impress his friends or girlfriend by playing Hendrix or Van Halen. An impulse I understood but grew out of by fifteen. But that night, the way the moon bounced off the lake and the fireflies danced around made me lonely.

The night after Uncle RB told me about Tara's band opening for his, I couldn't sit still. Over a week had passed since the orientation, but Rebecca's words about Valerie being confused that I'm a guy still ran through my mind. Maybe she was right. Maybe Valerie was only interested in what she thought I was.

Something about living at the lake house by myself, miles away from Wiley, gave me confidence. More than anything else, I wanted to go check out Tara's band, but not alone. Pulling the scrap of paper out of my wallet, I walked into the kitchen and grabbed my cell phone.

"Hold on a sec," Valerie said over loud punk music. A couple seconds later, the music was gone. "Hello?"

"Hey. It's me. Peyton. From Wiley Music."

The longest pause in the history of the world followed. In truth, it was only about five seconds, but it felt like the longest pause in the history of the world.

"Usually, if someone doesn't call within a week, they're not going to call," she said.

I leaned against the counter and wondered how Uncle RB called girls. I should've asked him and planned it out instead of just picking up the phone. Had Rebecca been in town, she would've rehearsed with me after going into her theory again about how Valerie was confused.

"Wow. You're really bad at this," she said.

I hadn't said anything. "Bad at what?"

She laughed. "I'll make it easy for you. Yes."

What? I hadn't asked anything.

"Make that terrible. You're terrible at this. Yes, yes, I'll go out with you."

I went from leaning against the counter to sitting on the kitchen floor because my knees buckled. "I'm sorry. I've never done this before."

She laughed, but in a friendly way. "Obviously."

"I don't want to give you the wrong idea." I ran my fingers through my hair like Uncle RB. It always helped him say the right thing. Maybe it would help me.

"So you're not asking me out on a date?" she asked.

"No. I mean – yes, I am, but I'm not...I..." I couldn't say I'm not a boy, I'm a girl, because it wasn't the truth. One thing was true; I'd botched my first time asking a girl out.

"How far along are you in your transition?" she asked.

I pulled my knees up to my chest. Aside from Dr. Wainwright, no one had ever suggested I was anything other than a lesbian. I'd never mentioned it, not a word, to anyone. My first impulse was to hang up the phone and rip up her number.

"I don't mean to make you uncomfortable."

I didn't know what to say. She had made me uncomfortable. My fingers held the phone so tightly they cramped.

"My best friend at the Art Institute just had top surgery. He's so much happier without tits."

Hang up or talk, Honeycutt. Don't just sit there saying nothing, you idiot. A million questions about her friend flooded my head, but I didn't want to come across like a dumbass or self-absorbed.

"Is there anyone around here you can talk to about this stuff?" she asked.

"Yeah," I said and then stopped. I didn't want to tell her about Dr. Wainwright. "What do you study at the Art Institute?"

"Art," she said and laughed.

What a stupid question.

"Sorry. Couldn't resist. I'm a painter."

I thought about Uncle RB, how he talked to women in the store. I grinned like he would. "Who's your favorite painter? Besides yourself?"

At least I made her laugh. "Magritte," she said.

I knew nothing about art. I glanced at the computer down the hall, wondering how fast I could Google Magritte.

"He's a surrealist."

I ran to the computer and typed in "surrealist" while she talked.

"One of his most famous paintings is called the *Treachery of Images*. It's a pipe, but underneath he painted the words "this is not a pipe" in French because it's not a pipe. It's a painting of a pipe. He wanted to challenge preconditioned notions of reality."

She was faster than my internet connection so I gave up the online search. "Sounds like my kinda guy."

"So where are you taking me on this date?"

"My uncle's band is playing at Shadows in Charlotte next Friday. It's all ages."

"A Friday night in Charlotte as opposed to Wiley. I like how you think."

We picked a time and I wrote down her address. Hanging up the phone I was hopeful, even excited. The last time I'd invited a girl to a concert, she'd cancelled. I had a feeling this girl wouldn't pull out at the last minute.

Shadows didn't look like much on the outside, just some tinted windows with a small neon sign barely visible from I-85. On the inside, there were fancy lights and a motorcycle hanging from the dome ceiling. The most popular drink was the Aqua-Velva. It had a green glow stick inside, making it radiate light in the darkness of the club. Almost every woman over twenty-one had one. Most of the guys drank beer.

I bought a root beer for Valerie and a Cheerwine for myself. I eyed one of the couches in the back, but she wanted to stand near the front. A crowd had already formed around the stage so we made our way through it.

"What time does your uncle's band go on?" she asked.

"Later, there's some other band before his. A girl I used to go to school with is in it or something."

Valerie's eyes narrowed. It drove me batty how girls picked up on these things. I'd made a point to keep my voice low and steady when I mentioned Tara's band. I hadn't even mentioned Tara by name, but Valerie still knew.

Avoiding her suspicious gaze, I glanced down at

what I'd decided to wear: jeans and my favorite Led Zeppelin shirt. I'd thought about wearing a dress shirt and tie, but Evie had said it would be too much for Shadows. She was right.

First, we listened to some bozo attempt to play an acoustic guitar and sing a few songs. He only played for twenty minutes, but it felt like two hours. He didn't even play a decent acoustic like a Martin or Washburn. His guitar rattled and hummed at times it shouldn't. The strings were too tight, making the action too high. Even worse, through the mic we could hear his hands scrape the strings, my second least favorite sound on the planet next to flip-flops.

Bored with the music, I glanced around the room. That's when I noticed two guys staring at me. They were across the crowd on the other side and had to strain their necks to see me. They didn't look familiar. They wore their ball caps low and held beers. They weren't checking me out, more like they were trying to figure me out.

Valerie didn't notice the two guys. But she did notice that I was nursing my Cheerwine. I'd been hoping to avoid the whole bathroom situation, but with the drive to and from Charlotte, plus the long night of live music, it was impossible. I decided to get it over with while the boring acoustic guitarist played his set. Maybe the two guys would find someone else to stare at in the meantime.

The bathroom had always been something to dread. For years, girls did a double take when I walked into their bathroom. Now that I was finally dressing and looking how I felt, I'd started to use the men's room when the bathroom couldn't be avoided. I often waited until I got home, trying to obey the speed limit while I held it in, ready to burst. Many times, I pulled over to the side of the road.

The men's bathroom at Shadows had one stall. Thankfully, no one was using it so I didn't have any awkward wait. While in there, I thought about the bubble I lived in, working at Wiley Music, living at the lake house. Life didn't put me in this situation too much. I was lucky in that aspect. Even while taking classes that summer at Wiley Tech, no one had bothered me. I always sat at the back of the classroom. That was one good thing about college classes, getting to choose where we sat in class, unlike grade school or high school where seats were always assigned and usually alphabetical.

At Wiley Tech, I used the restroom by the instructor's offices, which were mostly empty at night. But there at Shadows, I was out of my bubble. Charlotte was a big city, full of different kinds of people, but some of those people wouldn't like me very much.

One of the guys who'd been staring at me out by the stage was in the bathroom when I came out of the stall. He looked at the stall I'd just walked out of and then at me. He didn't just do a passing glance. His eyes scanned my chest, hips, and legs.

I washed my hands and got out of there. Something about the way he looked at me, how he'd been in there when I'd walked out of the stall gave me the creeps. Maybe it was just coincidence, but it was hard to shake off. A couple minutes later, I noticed him back on the other side of the room. He still stared while whispering in his friend's ear.

Thankfully, it was time for Moxie. No longer just a nickname given to her by Uncle RB, Moxie was the name of Tara's band. Tara Parks rocking out on stage would take my mind off the weird vibes the two staring guys sent my way.

Of course, Ms. Rock Star didn't walk out with the rest of the band. I recognized the drummer right away from that Sunday afternoon at Know Good. He was also her boyfriend. How predictable. How cliché. How boring. How infuriating that it wasn't me.

Finally, Tara Parks walked on stage, Fender Strat slung over her shoulder like she was marching off to war. Several people in the crowd screamed. The audience leaned forward in anticipation. Valerie had one eye on me, so I stood completely still.

Tara plugged the cord into the Marshall amp and nodded to the drummer, but they didn't smile at each other. Maybe it was part of their rock star act. Maybe onstage they were all business. He counted them in, and the band broke into a blisteringly fast rock song.

Tara put one foot up on the monitor and ripped into a rapid riff like her life depended on it. The way she held the guitar tight to her hips, the way her black knee-high boot leaned into the monitor and the way her babydoll dress rode up, I didn't want to blink for fear of missing one millisecond. When I did take my eyes off her it was to glance around the room.

Tara's voice commanded the room's attention. All the boys and some of the girls around me, Valerie included, swooned. I couldn't believe it – my own date making eyes at Tara. Even the two guys who'd watched me earlier had turned their attention toward the stage.

Tara was the only female in the band, but onstage she was no girl. During the chorus, she swung the guitar behind her back. The mic stand brushed her inner thigh as she pulled it to her. I was jealous of that mic stand against her hip and the microphone inches from her mouth.

The height she got teased about in school made her a goddess on stage. The rest of the band wasn't on her level. The lazy bass player made the obvious choices. The lead guitarist played too many notes, but the weakest link by far was the drummer. He almost lost the beat every time she stepped up to the mic to sing.

In his defense, he probably got distracted. Every time he glanced up, there she was. Still, I wouldn't miss one beat if I were her drummer.

Everyone in the audience leaned toward Tara a little more each time she thrust her hips into the guitar. Drummer boy watched, too. He also had the knowledge of what she looked like underneath the dress. He probably helped her out of the knee-high boots after the show. Thinking about them together, my veins were like drum sticks beating against my skin. I wished I was an irresponsible twenty-one year old so I could get drunk.

By the second song, Tara opened her eyes and worked the crowd. That's when she saw me. She didn't smile. I hadn't seen or talked to her since that Sunday in Know Good. She had been happy to see me then. Had something changed?

She closed her eyes again for the rest of the song and most of the set. She barely addressed the audience, which made them want her more. Everyone in the room wanted her attention, wanted her. She didn't even make eye contact with her band. The drummer, guitarist, and bass player communicated with each other, but not with Tara.

The songs were good, but not nearly as good as the ones we'd recorded in the studio. These songs didn't have Tara's melodies. The lyrics didn't seem like her either until the last song. It was up-tempo and super catchy, but the lyrics were dark, a Tara Parks trademark.

During the chorus she repeated one haunting line, "My baby will never be." On the last chorus, she repeated the line seven times. On the eighth time, she sang, "My baby will never be my baby."

While the rest of the band continued to play the chorus, Tara waved her guitar right in front of her amp, creating tons of feedback. The audience went berserk. That's when I saw Uncle RB watching from the backstage area. Watching Tara, he had a huge grin on his face.

Tara didn't look back at the audience or up at her bandmates. She slammed the guitar into the amp repeatedly, causing even more distortion. The audience leaned even closer to the stage.

Tara unplugged her guitar and left the stage. Everyone in the audience screamed. The bass player and guitarist looked to Tara's boyfriend. He counted them to the end of the song. The crowd yelled long after they'd left the stage. Everyone wanted more Tara, but she didn't return for an encore.

After her bandmates cleared their equipment off the stage, Uncle RB's band came on to set up. They got some claps and screams in anticipation of their set.

Uncle RB stepped up to the mic. "No amps or instruments will be harmed during our set." The audience laughed at his joke. One woman screamed. He already had the audience and he hadn't even played one note. "Let's give it up for Moxie. What a fantastic set, huh?" The audience followed his lead, clapping and cheering some more.

Valerie returned from the bathroom and asked if I wanted another Cheerwine. Before I could answer, Tara made her way over from the backstage area. People in the crowd tried to talk to her, saying 'great show,' but she made a beeline for me. She had a backpack over her shoulder and carried a guitar case.

"Hey. Can I get a ride back to Wiley?" she asked.

Tara stood so close I could smell the vanilla in her hair. I expected to smell Dunhills, too, but didn't. I glanced over her shoulder toward the backstage area and wondered why her bandmates weren't driving her home. "Of course." My next thought was Valerie. Was it rude to give Tara a ride home on our date?

Valerie's eyes darted from me to Tara and back to me.

"Valerie, this is Tara," I said.

Valerie reached out her hand, and Tara shook it while studying me. "You were amazing," Valerie said. "A rock star."

Tara finally acknowledged her. "Tell my bandmates that. They're relocating to LA and replacing me with a guy. They want to be an all-boy band. But I get to keep the name since it's mine." She winked at me, an attempt to hide the fact that she was upset. Every time Tara Parks was super upset she tightened her jaw. She could never hide that from people who really knew her.

"What? They're crazy. You're the best thing about the band," Valerie said.

"You deserve better, a band where you write all the songs," I said. "That last one was by far the best."

Her eyes jumped from Valerie back to me. "The only reason they agreed to play it was because I threatened not to show up if they didn't."

I knew the last song had been hers. We were

silent for a long time. Tara and I looked at each other like we hadn't seen each other in years instead of a few weeks.

Valerie slipped her arm into mine. "Peyton and I are on our first date."

Like a bullet, Tara's eyes shot to Valerie's arm. "Really," she said.

"Yeah." Valerie squeezed my arm.

"I'm sorry. I didn't mean to intrude. Never mind the ride." Tara headed backstage.

I watched Tara make her way through the crowd like a running back. Valerie noticed me watching.

"Go tell her she can have a ride." She forced a smile.

"You sure?"

She nodded. I unwrapped Valerie's arm from mine and headed off in Tara's direction.

I wasn't as skilled as Tara was in pushing my way through the crowd. To make matters worse the two guys from earlier still watched me.

Uncle RB tuned a guitar by the stage. When I walked by, he tossed his bangs out of his eyes and winked.

Down the hall that went backstage, Tara's bandmates were loading out their equipment.

"We're not going back to Wiley tonight, but you're welcome to stay at the motel with us," Tara's drummer said to her as I walked out back.

They stood near the van while the bass player and guitarist loaded their gear. No one in the band looked happy even though they'd just played a solid set.

"Great show, guys. Need any help?" I asked the bass player and guitarist as they went back into the club for more equipment. The guitarist rolled his eyes in a way that said this wasn't the first time he'd gotten stuck loading more than his share of the band's gear. Tara and the drummer were too distracted to notice.

"You know I can't stay in Charlotte tonight. My appointment is at nine tomorrow morning," Tara said.

"I thought you took care of that already," he said.

Tara's fingers folded into a fist. "I thought you were going with me." She stormed off toward the back door. Her eyebrows shot up when she saw me.

"Everything okay?" I stupidly asked. Clearly, everything was not okay. I followed her back into the club. "Let me give you a ride," I yelled over the crowd. I grabbed the guitar case from her hand.

"I'm not interrupting your date."

"It's just a date." I tried to shrug it off, but she wasn't buying it.

"When did you start dating anyway?"

I could've told her that Valerie was going back to Chicago soon for school, but part of me enjoyed seeing Tara's jaw and lips clenched. I knew the tension in her face had way more to do with losing her band and whatever was going on between her and drummer boy, but she watched Valerie talk to people in the crowd.

"She's pretty," she said.

"She said the same thing about you. Come on, come back to Wiley with us after Uncle RB's set."

Tara eyed her guitar case. I'd wrapped my arms around it. She knew she wasn't getting it back without a fight.

More people who'd been in the audience during Moxie's set approached Tara and told her how great she was. At one point, while thanking them, she reached up for her cross necklace, but it wasn't there.

While Tara talked with her new fans, I walked back over to Valerie. I didn't want to leave her alone too long. I told her about Uncle RB's history as a musician, his hit song, his touring days. Valerie nodded and tried to be interested, but something had shifted. Her eyes kept moving over my shoulder to Tara as if her suspicions had been confirmed.

Meanwhile, I kept looking for the two creepy staring guys. Relieved that I could no longer find them in the crowd, I stopped thinking about them and told myself it was probably just in my head.

After Uncle RB's set, I carried Tara's guitar out to the trunk of my car, a Mustang similar to the one I had before my accident. Valerie stood nearby, catching up with Tumblr on her iPhone. A few feet behind me, Tara dragged her heavy ass guitar amp.

"I told you I'd be back for it," I said.

"I'm capable of lugging around my own amp, Peyton Honeycutt. I do it all the time."

"You wouldn't if we were in a band together."

"Even if we were in the same band, I'd still carry my own shit." She also insisted on putting it in the trunk. Tara gave her stuff a quick glance and stopped me before I closed the trunk. "Wait. My case. It's got all my pedals and cords in it. I must have left it inside."

The front entrance of the club was already locked so we would have to go in the back. I didn't want Tara walking behind there that late at night. "I'll get it," I said.

"It's a black metal case, about the size of a shoebox." Tara didn't protest my going alone. Maybe she thought her bandmates were still hanging around back there and she wanted to avoid them, but they were nowhere to be found. The only van still back there belonged to Uncle RB's band and they were pulling out.

As they drove by, he waved and yelled, "Drive safe."

Everyone except for the bartender was gone. The stage was clear, the dressing rooms empty and the sound guy long gone. The bartender nodded at me before taking the last crate of liquor downstairs.

I searched the dressing rooms, the stage area and the hall. Finally, I found her metal case tucked away underneath the stage.

As soon as I walked out the back entrance, someone shoved me hard. I fell against the building, and Tara's case hit the pavement.

Hitting the brick wall had taken the wind out of me. I had to lean over, hands on my knees to catch my breath. The nice dinner I'd shared with Valerie earlier that night threatened to make its way up my throat, but no way was I throwing up in front of these two. Winded as I was, I could still see the two guys from earlier. I hadn't been paranoid after all.

"My friend and I have a bet going. We're wondering if you could help us out," the guy in the green ball cap said. He was the one from the bathroom.

I could guess what that bet was. Trying to protect myself, I kneeled down, pretending to be more hurt than I was. Tara's metal case was almost within my reach.

The guy in the green hat continued. "See, I think you're a girl, but he says no way."

I reached for the handle and slammed the case into the guy's head. His green cap went flying.

Seconds later, the other one grabbed me from behind. He yanked my arms so hard and fast toward my back that Tara's case hit the ground again. He didn't just look stronger than me. He was stronger. They both were.

"I'm starting to think my friend's right. You're acting like you've got something to hide," the guy holding my arms said.

The other guy got up and put his green cap back on his head. His lip was busted. He came back over at me. "Let's see what you're hiding." He pulled at my Led Zeppelin t-shirt, and I kicked my foot up at him.

Pissed, he punched me in the stomach. The impact threw my head forward and my face took a punch while the other guy had me in a tight hold. Hard as I tried to break free, I couldn't.

While I was hunched over, the guy throwing the punches snatched the wallet from my back pocket.

"Take it," I said. I just wanted them to go. Tara and Valerie weren't that far away.

"We don't want your money," he said.

He tossed my wallet on the ground. My eye ached and blood rushed into it, but I could see he had my driver's license in his hand. He chuckled. "Katharine Anne Honeycutt." He motioned at his friend who still held my arms tight. "You owe me fifty bucks."

Before the winner of the bet could collect, a stream of pepper spray filled his eyes. The driver's license fell.

The guy holding my arms let go, and I hit the ground. Two seconds later, Tara filled his eyes with pepper spray. He and his friend stumbled off in the opposite direction, clutching their faces and banging into each other along the way.

I shoved my driver's license into my wallet and slowly got up. Blood continued to trickle down my face and into my mouth.

Tara came over and examined my face. "We need to get you to a hospital."

I couldn't stand the thought of another hospital visit, the questions from nurses and doctors. They'd want to know what happened. They'd want to call the police.

"No. I'm fine." I stepped back, wishing she wasn't there to see me like that and hadn't witnessed what had just happened.

Valerie rushed toward us, on her phone. "Yes, I'd like to report an attack. We're at," she took her head away from the phone. "What street are we on?"

I grabbed her phone and hung up.

"We need to report what happened," Valerie said.

I handed back her phone.

"Those guys should be arrested!"

No one said a word until we got back to the car. I opened the trunk.

Tara followed with her metal case. "Let me drive," she said.

I shook my head.

She grabbed some tissues from her backpack and held them up to my face. "How can you even see?"

"I'm okay. It looks worse than it is."

She gave me a look that told me she knew I was lying. She'd heard what those guys had said before she fired off the pepper spray, and she knew I was not okay.

I needed to thank her for coming to my rescue, but the idea, just the words in my head made me choke up. I didn't want what happened with those bastards to make me cry. "I wouldn't get behind the wheel if I wasn't okay. Driving will help keep my mind off of it."

She nodded slightly. I shut the trunk and she headed around the side of the car.

"Tara."

She turned back to me.

"Thanks," was all I could manage.

"Dad would be proud. He insisted I carry pepper spray everywhere."

"I mean it. Thanks."

"You'd do the same for me," she said.

While she got into the backseat, I thought about that. I would do the same for her, but I'd never have to. She'd never be in a situation where two guys would make a bet over her driver's license.

To say the hour drive back to Wiley was long and awkward would be a huge understatement. Valerie played DJ, going through my CDs, asking if I owned anything other than Led Zeppelin. After she'd gone through everything, she rubbed my arm and asked if I was okay.

I nodded.

She ran her hand through my hair. "You're not alone, you know that right? I mean, you're not the only one going through this. I can put you in touch with my friend in Chicago."

I didn't respond, still fuming over what had just happened. She went back to rubbing my arm. It felt odd, forced, because I could see the disappointment on her face. If she'd been disappointed in the date earlier, picking up on the vibe between Tara and me, she was even more disappointed in me for not calling the police.

Tara sat in the back, diagonal from me. Every time I glanced at her through the rearview, her eyes were either on Valerie's hand on my arm or staring out the side window at God knows what. She had this blank expression on her face that I'd never seen, not when she told me her father had died, not when she visited me in the hospital after my accident. Her face didn't look sad or happy or even tired. It had no expression.

Valerie's parents' house was right off the highway. She said I didn't have to walk her to the door, but I insisted. As we walked up to the house, I felt Tara's eyes burning into my back. She'd moved up to the front seat as soon as Valerie got out.

I held the screen door open for Valerie, wondering what to say. This was the part where I was supposed to tell her how much I enjoyed her company and our date until the end of the night. Apologize for how crazy things got. Maybe ask for a second date. If I wanted a second date. If she wanted a second date.

I glanced back at Tara in the car. She flipped the overhead visor down and pretended to check her hair.

Valerie stood there under the front porch light and inspected my face. "You're going to have a black eye for sure, but at least the bleeding's stopped." She had on a green tank top that brought out her eyes. Her hair burned in the light.

"Our date didn't exactly end as planned. Sorry."

"It's not your fault. I really wish you'd call the police."

I didn't respond.

Tara had turned my keys in the ignition so she could blast Led Zeppelin's "What Is and What Should Never Be." She turned it up even louder when Valerie and I glanced toward the car.

"Thanks for going out with me." Lame, but I was still blown away that she'd said yes.

She balanced on her tiptoes and kissed my cheek.

"I'd go out with you again, but I think you need to figure out things with her first."

I glanced over at Tara, who was occupying herself by going through my glove compartment.

I turned back to Valerie, but the door greeted my face. I deserved it. A girl wanted to go out with me and where did I take her? To see Tara Parks. Slick, Honeycutt, real slick. And then, the night had taken such an awful turn.

Under any other circumstance, I'd be excited to be alone with Tara, but I didn't want to talk about what had happened with those guys. I got in the car and headed toward her house.

"Take a left here," she said. "I'm staying at Rebecca's right now."

"Rebecca and Mrs. David are in Israel."

"Mom and I had a huge fight. She kicked me out. I called Rebecca. Her mom got on the phone and practically ordered me to stay at their house."

Tara had called Rebecca in Israel instead of me. That's how far apart we'd grown. Maybe she no longer thought I was someone she could call.

And what was so bad that Mrs. Parks would kick Tara out? I thought about how awful it was when my mom told me to get out. Mrs. Parks was probably worse. I had a million questions for Tara, but all possible answers terrified me. Maybe Tara wanted to move to LA with her boyfriend. Maybe the fight was over Tara's band.

Tara interrupted all the questions zipping around in my brain with one of her own. "Would you mind if I crashed with you tonight? I'm sick of being alone."

All of my random thoughts were quickly replaced with only one: Tara Parks was coming to my lake house. The lake house I'd wanted to bring her to in ninth grade when we ran away. "Sure," I said.

Thankfully, I'd cleaned just in case Valerie had wanted to come over. I'd known it was a long shot, but even the thought of having a girl over made me want to clean. Crazy the way life worked because now *the* girl was coming over. If only it were under different circumstances.

I would've been happy if I thought Tara wanted to be with me at my place. But I suspected she wanted to come over because she was worried about me after what had happened with those guys.

"So this is the infamous lake house," she said when we entered. "I'd started to think it didn't exist."

We exchanged a shy smile. She remembered how we'd once tried to run away to the lake house, too.

"Want a tour?"

"We should get you cleaned up first."

I shrugged her off and began the tour by pointing out the living room off the hall from where we stood. I thought she'd just want to peek into it, but she not only walked into the room, she went through things. She thoroughly examined the vinyl records, the stereo set up, the DVDs. She looked at books on the coffee table, the coasters, and the candles on the fireplace mantel.

"Uncle RB and Evie left behind a lot of stuff for me. Or rather, they left behind everything Evie didn't like."

That got her to laugh. Next I showed her the back deck. The evening had taken such a terrible turn, I hadn't noticed what a beautiful night it was. The cool air felt good on the cut above my eye. The full moon shined down on the still waters of Lake Norman. Tara stood at the edge of the deck and looked out over the water. Amazing how after all that had happened, her eyes were as calm and still as the lake.

I continued with the tour, showing her the basement. She spent the most time there because that's where I had a mini practice space set up. She strummed the acoustic Washburn and a beat-up Les Paul. She sat behind the drum kit and banged around for a couple minutes.

She stopped when she saw me watching her. "Sorry. You probably hate it when people bang on your drums."

"At least you can keep a beat."

"Thanks," she said, sarcastically.

She had to run her hands over everything, every guitar pedal and drum accessory I'd bought with my Wiley Music employee discount.

We went back upstairs, where I showed her the bathroom. She smiled at a Led Zeppelin tour poster in the hall.

The smile faded when I stopped at the guest room. She walked in and set her backpack on the bed while I grabbed sweatpants and a t-shirt for her to sleep in.

She took the clothes from me and looked closely at my face. "We really should clean you up."

"I can do it." Why were both Tara and Valerie so concerned with my face?

I could tell she wanted to talk, but I didn't. Not at that moment.

"Peyton—"

"You should get to bed. You've got an appointment early in the morning, right?"

Tara sighed. She didn't have a car. Mrs. Parks

had refused to buy her one, another attempt to try to keep Tara in line. I could loan her mine. No one had ever driven my car except me, not even Uncle RB.

"Want me to drive you?" I asked.

Instead of responding, she changed her clothes right there. I forced myself to look down at the rug by the bed. She tossed her boots and dress onto the rug.

"I'm afraid if you come, you'll hate me," she said.

When I spoke again, my voice cracked. "You can borrow my car."

My eyes climbed to hers. Thank God she had on my t-shirt and sweats. She sat on the bed against the headboard and pulled the covers all around her.

After a minute of us not saying anything, I sat on the edge of the bed. "Tara, what's going on? What's the appointment?"

"You've had a rough night. I don't want to add to it," she said. "I can manage on my own. I'll walk."

I thought back to the conversation by the van with her boyfriend, how she thought he should go with her to the appointment.

My baby will never be my baby.

The catchy chorus came back to me and how Tara didn't smell of Dunhills for the first time since she'd started smoking them. All of the signs were there. Only an idiot wouldn't see them.

I opened my mouth to ask, but didn't need to. Tara stared at the royal blue bedspread.

I leaned forward until she had to look at me. By the expression on her face, I could tell that she knew I'd figured it out.

"I'm going with you," I said, putting my hand on hers.

"You don't have to."

"I'm going with you. That's the end of it."

She didn't say another word. Her jaw, her whole body tightened and she moved her hand away. She didn't want to talk about what was happening in the morning. I didn't want to talk about what had happened that evening.

"I'm just down the hall if you need anything," I said and closed the door.

Walking to my room, the words "Tara's pregnant" kept repeating in my head. She'd rescued me from those two bastards while pregnant. She'd carried that heavy-ass amp while pregnant. She'd made an appointment to take care of the situation, but she'd also stopped smoking. Had she stopped smoking when she found out she was pregnant? Was the choice to make the appointment hers? Did Mrs. Parks know? Tara probably told her mother she didn't need her consent since she's eighteen. Mrs. Parks would have definitely kicked her out for that.

With Tara just down the hall and pregnant, sleeping was impossible. I put on my headphones and one of Uncle RB's vinyl records he'd left behind, Cream's *Disraeli Gears*. He said it was the kind of record that every time you play it, you hear something new.

The headphones were high quality, the most expensive ones we had at Wiley Music. Even with my employee discount, they were a hundred and fifty bucks. They picked up every sound in the recording, every little pop and nick in the vinyl. They blocked out most noises: lawnmowers, boats motoring by, airplanes overhead.

As great as the headphones were, they couldn't block out the noise in my head of those two guys laughing at my driver's license, laughing at "Katharine Anne Honeycutt." And the music couldn't block out the fact that Tara was pregnant. I couldn't focus or sit still.

The light in the guest room was off.

Needing to get those guys off my mind, I walked outside with Uncle RB's BB gun. I grabbed some Cheerwine cans out of the recycling bin and lined them up. While loading the gun, I thought about how long it had been since I'd done any type of target practice. We'd been so busy getting the music school off the ground, Uncle RB and I had skipped hunting on weekends.

I squinted at the cans and imagined they were the two guys from earlier. My sides ached when I lifted the gun. Uncle RB's voice entered my head reminding me to keep the gun steady. I lowered the gun to take a deep breath and pull myself together.

An arm came right at the BB gun causing my hand to jerk. My finger snapped the trigger.

A sharp pain ripped across my thigh. I dropped the gun.

"What in the hell are you doing?" Tara yelled.

"What in the hell are you doing?" I yelled back.

"Stopping you from doing something stupid."

"I just need to shoot at things right now." I motioned to the Cheerwine cans on the tree stumps. She hadn't taken the time to realize that it was target practice.

Tara noticed the blood coming through my jeans. "Jesus, you're bleeding."

My thigh throbbed. I limped over to the car. Everything moved like slow motion.

She followed me, eyeing my limp. She kneeled down for a closer look.

"It's fine," I said.

"It's not fine. I shot you." She put her hands on

my leg. The way the jeans were ripped, I could tell the BB just nicked me, but Tara's eyes teared up like I was dying.

"Technically, I shot myself. Although contrary to popular belief, that wasn't my goal."

She kneeled down to get a closer look at where the BB ripped my jeans. "You wouldn't talk to me about what happened tonight. What was I supposed to think?"

She stood up and reached for my belt. I swatted at her hands. I hated her thinking I was some weak, suicidal coward.

"You're not supposed to think anything. I'm fine." I yanked my leg away. "Besides, do you think I'd let you to go to your appointment alone tomorrow?"

"Peyton, we need to see how bad it is."

I hobbled into the house. "It's just a BB nick."

She followed me to the bathroom. I tried to close the door, but she pushed it open and reached for my belt again. I grabbed her hands, but this time she wasn't having it. She pushed my hands away.

"Whatever your issue is, get over it," she said.

She pulled my jeans down. Her eyes followed the blood to the wound. She didn't even notice the briefs I wore or the hair on my legs, thick from months of no longer shaving.

"Tell me you have a first aid kit," she said.

I motioned under the sink. Uncle RB had given me a nice one as a housewarming gift.

Tara pulled it out along with some towels. She waved them at me. "These clean?"

I nodded, too afraid to talk, too afraid my voice would break in half with my jeans around my ankles in front of her.

She kneeled down and wiped the blood off my

leg and away from the wound. The BB had grazed the side of my thigh. She turned on the water in the shower and reached for my T-shirt, but I leaned away from her and gripped the edge of the sink.

"We need to wash the wound. Your leg's too long for the sink."

"Doesn't mean I have to take my shirt off."

"You could be dying and you're worried about being naked in front of me?"

Yep. Being naked in front of Tara Parks was way more terrifying than death. "It's just a nick."

With blood still running down my leg, she didn't waste any more time arguing. She helped me in without taking my shirt off.

Both of us got soaked while rinsing the wound. Tara pulled her hair back in a ponytail and took off the shirt I'd loaned her. She had no problem with it. The black bra she wore was one I'd never seen. I wondered how many times the boyfriend had seen it. The thought hurt worse than the BB grazing my leg.

She turned off the water and applied pressure to my thigh with a clean towel. She kept an eye on her watch, telling me if the bleeding didn't stop within five minutes, she was calling 911.

When the bleeding did stop, she took the towel away and stepped out of the shower. "It needs to air dry, then we'll put on Neosporin and a bandage. We still need to keep an eye on it. Anything odd looking and we're going to the hospital."

I wanted to ask how she knew exactly what to do, but it was probably from her dad. I was afraid mentioning him would upset her, so I just said, "Thanks."

She didn't want me putting any pressure on my leg so I leaned on her on the way to my room. She sat me on the bed and ran a finger over the goose bumps on my arm. For once, the goose bumps weren't from her. My shirt and what was underneath it were soaked and ice cold.

While Tara went through my dresser looking for clothes, I thought about Dr. Wainwright, how she'd said I needed to open up to people. Before I lost my nerve, I pulled off my shirt.

Tara heard the shirt hit the floor and glanced at me through the mirror. I'd recently started binding my chest with an elastic bandage to hide what little breasts I had. Dr. Wainwright had told me to do what made me feel comfortable. I'd read about binding in the book she'd given me. It sounded painful and it was uncomfortable at first, but it felt good to look in the mirror and see nothing there.

Tara didn't flinch when she saw the binding. She pulled sweatpants and a thermal top out of the dresser and placed them next to me on the bed.

My heart took a nosedive when she left the room. I knew it. I knew she'd be freaked out.

My arms trembled while unwrapping the wet binding. The tremble turned into full on convulsing and I couldn't breathe. I'd pulled off my shirt showing her who I was, and unable to handle it, she'd left the room.

Not a minute later, she returned with the Neosporin, gauze, and tape from the first aid kit.

She rushed to the bed and kneeled next to me as I gasped for air. "Is it your leg? If you're in pain, we should go to the emergency —"

"It's not my damn leg." I couldn't even finish unwrapping the binding.

"Here, let me." She took off the rest of the elastic around my chest and draped it across the nightstand so it could dry.

I tried wiping the tears away, but they kept coming. "You're freaked out."

"What? No." Tara sat beside me on the bed. She held my face. My tears ran into her fingers. She looked at me for a long time. "I think you're handsome."

Hearing her say that word, a sob erupted from deep inside my throat. The tears wouldn't stop.

"We have to dress the wound," she said. Her warm fingers spread a thick layer of Neosporin across my thigh. Her touch was so soft, but I felt it all over my body.

She slid back on the bed until she was against the frame and pulled me to her. She wrapped her arms and legs around me, comforted me, her fingers running through my hair and down my back until I fell asleep.

Chapter 16

The next morning, Tara sat in my bed reading the FTM book. She was somewhere in the middle of it, so engrossed that she didn't notice when I sat up next to her. In her lap was what I used as a bookmark, Dr. Wainwright's business card.

She didn't flinch at my seeing her reading it. "Hope you don't mind."

"No." I wanted to share everything with her, even that book. Especially that book, but I still wasn't sure how to talk about it. She put Dr. Wainwright's card back. "We should check on your wound."

She pulled the covers off and gently removed the tape around the gauze. After inspecting it, she left the room to wash her hands and returned to apply more Neosporin.

"Are you going to this appointment because you want to or because your boyfriend wants you to?" I asked while she covered the wound with fresh gauze.

"He's not my boyfriend anymore." She ran her fingers over the tape to secure the gauze.

She left the room again to wash her hands. I opened the blinds. The bird feeder that Uncle RB had left behind was empty. I'd promised him I'd keep birdseed in it. Birds were hopping around it, looking for something and flying away disappointed.

After throwing on jeans and a T-shirt, I found Tara in the bathroom. She was cleaning up all my blood from the night before. My eyes fell to her stomach and my mind jumped to how she got pregnant, the boyfriend, unprotected sex.

I thought about Uncle RB and how Evie wanted a family. He never said no, but it was obvious the whole thing made him nervous by how he changed the subject whenever it came up. Still, if Evie got pregnant he'd be right by her side. He still seethed every time Dad's name came up. I did, too. Cowards leave.

"What kind of jackass moves to Los Angeles when his girlfriend's pregnant?"

She turned off the water and sat on the edge of the bathtub. "We broke up before I found out. He offered to go dutch on the abortion."

Asshole. She deserved better, way better.

"What do you want?" I asked.

"This isn't your problem to fix." Upset, she left the room.

I wanted it to be my problem. Dr. Wainwright's voice came into my head saying I needed to communicate my feelings more.

Tara had plopped down on the couch in the living room, head bowed.

I sat on the coffee table across from her. "The night in the recording studio, the night when we—"

"Didn't have sex?" She smirked. Damn Rebecca. Tara leaned her head back against the couch and aimed those Carolina blues right at me.

"If I could've... If I had been able to be with you like your boyfriend, like I wanted, I don't know if I would've been able to stop."

Tara lifted her head. The look on her face was not disbelief, but surprise.

Hard as it was, I kept going. "What I'm trying to say is, I wanted you, I wanted to be with you that way. If I could've, this might have been our problem, and I wouldn't be moving to Los fucking Angeles. We'd be sitting here trying to figure it out together."

She sat there for a long time, just looking at me. I wanted to kiss her, but before I got up the nerve she sat up and checked the time on her phone.

"We should get going," she said.

I took her hand. "Afterwards, will you come back here and stay with me?"

I didn't like the idea of her being alone in Rebecca's house after what she was about to go through. For once, Tara Parks didn't argue.

We pulled into the parking lot of the clinic. Tara sat still in the passenger seat. Even after I turned off the car and opened my door, she didn't move.

"You don't have to come in. You can wait here."

"I'm going in with you." No way in hell was she doing this alone.

Tara still didn't budge. "You wanted to know if this is what I want."

"It's none of my business."

"It is what I want. I was afraid to tell you. I was afraid you'd hate me."

"I could never hate you." I turned toward her. "But if you wanted to keep the baby, I'd help with everything. You both could live with me at the lake house. We'd turn one of the rooms into a nursery. We could do it. We'd manage."

Tara tilted her head and attempted a smile. "Peyton, it can't be something we'd manage. It'd have to be something we both wanted and right now it's not."

Maybe she'd never want that kind of life with me. Or if she did later on, we wouldn't be able to have it. I couldn't let that get to me right now.

I walked around the car, opened the door for her and held out my hand. "Everything's gonna be okay."

She nodded and took my hand.

Later that afternoon, on my way back from picking up Tara's things at Rebecca's, I stopped by Food Lion. I studied all the cereal options, not knowing what Tara preferred. She used to eat Frosted Flakes, but that was in eighth grade. She was sleeping back at the lake house so calling her wasn't an option. I decided on Corn Flakes and Frosted Flakes before moving to the snack aisle.

There between Little Debbie and Sara Lee hovered my mother. Of course, I'd see her while sporting a black eye.

She pushed a shopping cart that had almost nothing in it, just basic items like milk, bread, and eggs. She held a Sara Lee pound cake in her hand and stared at the box. Part of me wanted to back up and go down another aisle, but this was my mother and we were going to run into each other. More than anything, it was a shock to see her out of the house – in a dress and make-up, doing her own shopping.

"Mom."

Her eyes stayed on the Sara Lee box.

I took a step closer. "Mom."

She pointed toward the slogan on the box *Nobody doesn't like Sara Lee*. "All my life, I thought they were saying 'Nobody does it like Sara Lee.' I had it wrong all these years."

She looked over at me and scrunched up her face. She hadn't seen me since before my car accident. She was used to the jeans, t-shirt, and work boots, but not the bruise on my eye or the short hair. She didn't hide the fact that she hated it.

"I don't even recognize you anymore."

"It's still me. Peyton."

"Still getting into fights." She shook her head. "I got a job working at the flower shop near your old school."

"That's great." I resisted asking which old school, worried it would set her off.

She dropped the pound cake in her cart, pulled out her shopping list and marked pound cake off of it. She pushed her cart on down the aisle toward the chips.

I followed. "Can I give you a ride home?"

"No, thanks. I like the walk." She never used to like to walk, but I took it as a good sign. She picked up two bags of chips that were on sale. "How's Tara?"

"She's at the lake house."

"Tell her I said hello and to keep you out of trouble, Peyton."

She'd moved on to another aisle while I stood there, unable to move and unable to suppress the smile on my face. It was the first time my mother had called me Peyton.

The following Friday after work, I came home to find Tara downstairs playing guitar. She sang the song she'd played that night at Shadows, "My baby will never be my baby." I recognized it right away. The melody of the chorus had stayed with me.

She stopped playing when I came downstairs. "Sorry."

"For what? It sounded great." I sat behind my drum kit.

"That night. What happened at Shadows – I didn't want the song to remind you."

"What are you going to do? Never play that song? Play it again."

An hour later, I still couldn't find the right drum

part. While playing it over and over, Tara watched me struggle. She stared at my arms flailing around and I worried she didn't think I was as good as him - LA drummer. More than anything, I wanted to write a good drum part, but this song was kicking my ass. It went from the verse to the chorus and back so fast. I kept at it over and over, asking her to play the song again and again.

Finally, Tara had enough. "I can't play this song anymore."

She turned off the amp and put down her guitar. That's when I realized the song was only cathartic for her to a point.

"I'm sorry. I wanted to nail the perfect drum part."

"You don't have to get it tonight. It doesn't make you less of a drummer. The fact that it's hard and you won't give up until you get it – that's what makes you a great musician."

I grinned and sat back on the throne, letting the sticks drop to the floor. She thought I was a great musician.

She went into the kitchen for a snack while I jumped in the shower. Later, I came into my room to find her waiting in my bed. Every other night that week, she'd slept in the guest room. She smiled at my pajamas – men's pajamas, the kind that matched top and bottom, a gift from Uncle RB and Evie.

Tara motioned for me to join her. I thought my legs would disintegrate walking to the bed. We'd spent that week watching movies, reading, sleeping, recovering from what had been a traumatic weekend for both of us. That's what Dr. Wainwright had called it during my session that week with her: a traumatic weekend. She'd said at least Tara and I had each other, but that made me nervous because there were some things Tara and I hadn't talked about yet and things we hadn't done.

I sat on the edge of the bed, facing her.

She grinned. "You don't have to be shy with me."

I stared at the green blanket covering the bed.

She leaned forward and put her arms around my neck. She brought her face so close to mine that I had to look at her. "You do realize I've wanted to be with you since eighth grade?"

"Me, too. I mean I've wanted to be with you since eighth grade. I kept thinking it would go away."

She laughed.

I took a deep breath and kissed her. Everything was still there, the passion fruit lip-gloss, the Doublemint flavor, the electric wave going all the way to my toes.

We kissed for several minutes before she tugged at my shirt. I let her take it off as well as my pants. She ran her fingers over the binding on my chest like it was part of my skin. I could feel her soft touch, the heat from her fingers through it and it made me kiss her harder. After a few minutes, my whole body convulsed.

She pulled back. "Are you cold?"

Embarrassed, I shook my head. "It's my first time being with anyone like this." I motioned to my mostly naked chest and legs. The only things I had on were my briefs and the bandage on my leg.

"It's not just anyone," she said. "It's me."

"I know. That's why I'm nervous."

"I guess we should make this fair." She took off her shirt and pants and turned off the light. We got under the covers, her right on top of me.

"You okay?" she asked.

"Yeah" was all I could manage. With her skin touching mine in so many places, I thought my body would explode.

She laughed, and we went back to kissing.

The next morning, an urgent knock at the front door made us both jump out of bed.

"Uncle RB didn't mention anything about stopping by," I said.

Tara took off down the hall since the window in my room faced the lake. I followed her to the kitchen.

"It's my mother," she said.

I looked over her shoulder, out the kitchen window. Mrs. Parks's SUV couldn't even fit all the way in the driveway behind my car. It stuck out into the dirt road.

We both ran back to my bedroom and grabbed at clothes.

"Want me to tell her to leave?" I asked.

"No. I need to deal with her."

Tara looked in the mirror. The t-shirt and jeans of mine that she'd thrown on were both snug. She ran her hands through her wild, morning hair and tried to calm it.

"Sexy," I said.

"Behave."

Tara left the room. I threw the sheets across the bed and cringed at my reflection in the mirror. The bruise had faded, but the cut was still there above the eye, slowly healing.

Just before opening the front door, Tara took a deep breath. I stood right behind her.

"Had a feeling I'd find you here," Mrs. Parks said. She didn't wait to be invited inside. Her eyes darted from Tara to the hall. She walked past us and glanced into the living room, paying close attention to the stuffing poking out of one side of the couch. She turned back to face her daughter.

Standing so close to Tara, I heard her breaths get shorter.

Mrs. Parks walked farther down the hall and glanced into the pristine guest bedroom before stopping at mine. She shook her head at my messy room.

"Get your things. You're coming with me," Mrs. Parks said to Tara.

"No, I'm not."

"I talked to your grandparents. They're willing to let you stay there and have the baby. I've already found an adoption agency near them. It's the best option."

"You're wasting your time, Mother."

Mrs. Parks ignored Tara and instead acknowledged my presence for the first time. "Your uncle lets you stay here? Alone?"

"It's my house now," I said. "And Tara's welcome to stay."

"I bet she is." Mrs. Parks walked back from the hallway, passing us again. As she walked by me, she stared at the cut on my face.

She stopped at the front door and motioned for Tara. "Let's go."

"No," Tara said.

"I will not have my daughter walking around Wiley, pregnant and unmarried."

"I'm not pregnant."

Mrs. Parks looked as if Tara had just pulled out a gun and shot her. She shook her head. "Look at you."

She leaned toward Tara. "You've ruined yourself. What man is going to want you now?"

I thought about what Uncle RB had said about there being a right time to make a stand.

"I do."

Both Mrs. Parks and Tara turned to me. They were completely silent, the only sound a distant motorboat out on the lake.

Mrs. Parks's eyes weren't usually as big as Tara's, but they matched at that moment.

I looked right at Mrs. Parks. Standing in my own house, next to Tara gave me a strength I'd never known. "I'm the man who loves your daughter, Mrs. Parks."

Steady as my voice was, my knees rattled together like two drumsticks.

"This is ridiculous," Mrs. Parks said. She turned to Tara. "You're coming with me."

"No. I'm not." Tara grabbed my hand.

Mrs. Parks stared at her hand in mine. Tara was eighteen so her mother couldn't make her leave. Even if she could force Tara to do something, it would attract the kind of attention Mrs. Parks loathed. She shook her head at us, but didn't say another word. On her way out of the driveway, she took out my mailbox.

Tara still held my hand. She closed the door with her foot. "We've got a lot to talk about." She played with my hand while I wondered how to begin. It wasn't going to be easy for us. The road ahead, the constant stares from strangers, deciding to have surgeries or not, it was a lot to ask of Tara.

Even in that moment Tara waited, giving me time to figure out what I needed to say. She'd been waiting since the moment we'd met. I wrapped my fingers tightly around hers.

I took a deep breath. My chest felt like it would collapse. "Do you think… could you be with… could you love a boy like me?"

She tilted her head and looked at me with those soft, Carolina blues. "Peyton, I already do."

Resources

National Center for Transgender Equality
1325 Massachusetts Avenue NW, Suite 700
Washington, DC 20005
202.903.0112
transequality.org

Transgender Law Center
1629 Telegraph Avenue, Suite 400
Oakland, CA 94612
415.865.0176
transgenderlawcenter.org

Lambda Legal
120 Wall Street, 19th Floor
New York, NY 10005-3919
212.809.8585
lambdalegal.org

Chicago Women's Health Center
1025 W. Sunnyside, Suite 201
Chicago, IL 60640
773.935.6126
chicagowomenshealthcenter.org

Boston Alliance of Gay Lesbian Bisexual Transgender Youth
PO Box 960814
Boston, MA 02196-0814
617.227.4313
bagly.org

FTMInternational
601 Van Ness Avenue, Suite E327
San Francisco, CA 94102-3200
877.267.1440
ftmi.org

Acknowledgements

First and foremost, Natalie Baumgardner, for never giving up and never giving in and for responding, "Of course, you can write a novel," when I first decided to write this.

The book you have in your hands wouldn't be what it is without the amazing support of Kelly Ford, Robert Guinsler, Sarah Pruski, and everyone at 215 Ink: Andrew DelQuadro, Michael Perkins, Will Perkins, Mark Schmidt, Taylor Scott, and Mark Bertolini.

A Boy Like Me was revised during Grub Street's inaugural year-long Novel Incubator program. A huge thank you to everyone at Grub Street, especially Lisa Borders and Michelle Hoover. I also want to thank my fellow incubees, the aforementioned Kelly Ford, Belle Brett, Amber Elias, Jack Ferris, Marc Foster, E.B. Moore, Emily Ross, R.J. Taylor, and Rob Wilstein. You not only made A Boy Like Me a better book, but you made me a better writer and gave me a community.

Thank you to Jamie Chambliss, E.C. Shelburne, and Yun Soo Vermeule for your feedback and encouragement during the early stages of this novel and for believing in it from the beginning.

And finally to the following for the inspiration and support along the way: Carolyn Bankowski, John Boveri, Jillian Butler and Provocateur, Anne Calcagno, Summer Chance, Steph Edwards, Tana Ford, Tate Fox, Shayna Goldstein, Vicky James, Aim Larrabee, Tina Lee, Jeff McComsey, Louise Miller, Katherine Mingle, Alex Myers, Georgianna Torres Reyes, Charlotte Robinson, Sarah Sayers, Wendy Schneider, Alicia Torres, Jorge Vega, Sherry Wood, Rowena Yow, John Yuskaitis, and Margaret Zamos-Monteith.

Jennie Wood is the creator and writer of *Flutter*, a graphic novel series. *Flutter, Volume One: Hell Can Wait*, the first graphic novel in the series, is available on 215 Ink. *The Advocate* calls *Flutter* one of the best LGBT graphic novels of 2013. She is also a contributor to the award-winning, *New York Times* best-selling comic anthology, *FUBAR: Empire of the Rising Dead* and *FUBAR: American History Z*. Born and raised in North Carolina, Jennie currently lives in Boston, Massachusetts, with her girlfriend. She writes non-fiction features for infoplease.com and teaches at Grub Street, Boston's independent writing center.

Learn more about Jennie's work at jenniewood.com.

Author photo by Michael Benabib, courtesy of Kobo Writing Life